CALICO CANYON

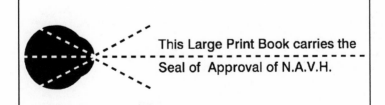

This Large Print Book carries the
Seal of Approval of N.A.V.H.

LASSOED IN TEXAS, BOOK TWO

CALICO CANYON

MARY CONNEALY

THORNDIKE PRESS
A part of Gale, Cengage Learning

Detroit • New York • San Francisco • New Haven, Conn • Waterville, Maine • London

GALE
CENGAGE Learning

Thorndike Press® Large Print Christian Historical Fiction.
The text of this Large Print edition is unabridged.
Other aspects of the book may vary from the original edition.
Set in 16 pt. Plantin.
Printed on permanent paper.

LIBRARY OF CONGRESS CATALOGING-IN-PUBLICATION DATA

Connealy, Mary.
    Calico Canyon / by Mary Connealy.
        p. cm. — (Lassoed in Texas #2)
    ISBN-13: 978-1-4104-2233-0 (alk. paper)
    ISBN-10: 1-4104-2233-X (alk. paper)
    1. Large type books. I. Title.
PS3603.O544C35 2010
813'.6—dc22   2009038132

Published in 2010 by arrangement with Barbour Publishing, Inc.

Printed in Mexico
1 2 3 4 5 6 7 14 13 12 11 10

Calico Canyon is dedicated to Marybelle Connealy,
one of my best friends in the world and
the mother of seven sons,
including my husband, Ivan. She and
Tom raised seven good men:
Larry, Tim, Del, Keith, Max, Ivan, and
Sean.
I don't think her sons spent as much
time under the table
during mealtime as the Reeveses did,
but Marybelle
can tell enough hilarious "little boy"
stories
to fill twenty books.

*It is of the L*ORD*'s mercies that we are not consumed,*
because his compassions fail not.
They are new every morning: great is thy faithfulness.

LAMENTATIONS 3:22–23

ONE

Mosqueros, Texas, 1867

The Five Horsemen of the Apocalypse rode in.

Late as usual.

Grace Calhoun was annoyed with their tardiness at the same time she wished they'd never come back from the noon recess.

They shoved their way into their desks, yelling and wrestling as if they were in a hurry. No doubt they were. They couldn't begin tormenting her until they sat down, now, could they?

Grace Calhoun clenched her jaw to stop herself from nagging. Early in the school year, she'd realized that her scolding amused them and, worse yet, inspired them. To think she'd begged their father to send his boys to school.

Her gaze locked on Mark Reeves. She knew that look. The glint in his eyes told

her he was planning . . . something . . . awful.

Grace shuddered. Seven girls and fifteen
boys in her school. Most were already working like industrious little angels.

Most.

The noise died down. Grace stood in front
of the room and cleared her throat to buy
time until her voice wouldn't shake. Normally she could handle them — or at least
survive their antics. But she hadn't eaten
today and it didn't look as though she'd eat
soon.

"Sally, will you please open your book to
page ten and read aloud for the class?"

"Yes, Miss Calhoun." With a sweet smile,
six-year-old Sally McClellen, her Texas ac-
cent so strong Grace smiled, stood beside
her desk and lifted the first grade reader.

Grace's heart swelled as the little girl read
without hesitation, her blue eyes focused on
the pages, her white-blond hair pulled back
in a tidy braid. Most of her students were
coming along well.

Most.

Grace folded her skeletal hands together
with a prayer of thankfulness for the good
and a prayer for courage for the bad. She
added prayers for her little sisters, left
behind in Chicago, supported with her

meager teacher's salary.

A high-pitched squeak disrupted her prayerful search for peace. A quick glance caught only a too-innocent expression on Ike Reeves's face.

Mark's older brother Ike stared at the slate in front of him. Ike studying was as likely as Grace roping a longhorn bull, dragging him in here, and expecting the creature to start parsing sentences. There was no doubt about it. The Reeves boys were up to something.

She noticed a set of narrow shoulders quivering beside Mark. Luke Reeves, the youngest of the triplets — Mark, Luke, and John. All three crammed in one front-row desk built to hold two children. The number of students was growing faster than the number of desks.

She'd separated them, scolded, added extra pages to their assignments. She'd kept them in from recess and she'd kept them after school.

And, of course, she'd turned tattletale and complained to their father, repeatedly, to absolutely no avail. She'd survived the spring term with the Reeves twins, barely. The triplets weren't school age yet then. After the fall work was done, they came. All five of them. Like a plague of locusts, only with less charm.

The triplets were miniature versions of their older twin brothers, Abraham and Isaac. Their white-blond hair was as unruly as their behavior. They dressed in the next thing to rags. They were none too clean, and Grace had seen them gather for lunch around what seemed to be a bucket full of meat.

They had one tin bucket, and Abe, the oldest, would hand out what looked like cold beefsteak as the others sat beside him, apparently starved half to death, and eat with their bare hands until the bucket was empty.

Why didn't their father just strap a feed bag on their heads? What was that man thinking to feed his sons like this?

Easy question. Their father wasn't thinking at all.

He was as out of control as his sons. How many times had Grace talked to Daniel Reeves? The man had the intelligence of the average fence post, the personality of a wounded warthog, and the stubbornness of a flea-bitten mule. Grace silently apologized to all the animals she'd just insulted.

Grace noticed Sally standing awkwardly beside her desk, obviously finished.

"Well done, Sally." Grace could only hope

she told the truth. The youngest of the three McClellen girls could have been waltzing for all Grace knew.

"Thank you, Miss Calhoun." Sally handed the book across the aisle to John Reeves.

The five-year-old stood and began reading, but every few words he had to stop. John was a good reader, so it wasn't the words tripping him up. Grace suspected he couldn't control his breathing for wanting to laugh.

The rowdy Reeves boys were showing her up as a failure. She needed this job, and to keep it she had to find a way to manage these little monsters.

She'd never spanked a student in her life. *Can I do it? God, should I do it?*

Agitated nearly to tears, Grace went to her chair and sat down.

"Aahhh!" She jumped to her feet.

All five Reeves boys erupted in laughter.

Grace turned around and saw the tack they'd put on her chair. Resisting the urge to rub her backside, she whirled to face the room.

Most of the boys were howling with laughter. Most of the girls looked annoyed on her behalf. Sally had a stubborn expression of loyalty on her face that would have warmed Grace's heart if she hadn't been pushed most of the way to madness.

Grace had been handling little girls all her life, but she knew nothing about boys.

Well, she was going to find out if a spanking would work. Slamming her fist onto her desk, she shouted, "I warned you boys, *no more pranks.* Abraham, Isaac, Mark, Luke, John, you get up here. You're going to be punished for this."

"We didn't do it!" The boys chorused their denials at the top of their lungs. She'd expected as much, but this time she wasn't going to let a lack of solid evidence sway her. She knew good and well who'd done this.

Driven by rage, Grace turned to get her ruler. Sick with the feeling of failure but not knowing what else to do, she jerked open the drawer in her teacher's desk.

A snake struck out at her. Screaming, Grace jumped back, tripped over her chair, and fell head over heels.

With a startled cry, Grace landed hard on her backside. She barely registered an alarming ripping sound as she bumped her head against the wall hard enough to see stars. Her skirt fell over her head, and her feet — held up by her chair — waved in the air. She shoved desperately at the flying gingham to cover herself decently. When her vision cleared, she looked up to see the snake, dangling down out of the drawer, drop onto her foot.

It disappeared under her skirt, and she felt it slither up her leg. Her scream could have peeled the whitewash off the wall.

Grace leapt to her feet. The chair got knocked aside, smashing into the wall. She stomped her leg, shrieking, the snake twisting and climbing past her knee. She felt it wriggling around her leg, climbing higher. She whacked at her skirt and danced around trying to shake the reptile loose.

The laughter grew louder. A glance told her all the children were out of the desks and running up and down the aisle.

One of the McClellen girls raced straight for her. Beth McClellen dashed to her side and dropped to her knees in front of Grace. The nine-year-old pushed Grace's skirt up and grabbed the snake.

Backing away before Grace accidentally kicked her, Beth said, "It's just a garter snake, ma'am. It won't hurt you none."

Heaving whimpers escaped with every panting breath. Grace's heart pounded until it seemed likely to escape her chest and run off on its own. Fighting for control of herself, she got the horrible noises she was making under control then smoothed her hair with unsteady hands. She stared at the little snake, twined around Beth's arm.

Beth's worried eyes were locked on Grace. The child wasn't sparing the snake a single glance. Because, of course, Beth and every other child in this room knew it was harmless. Grace knew it, too. But that didn't mean she wanted the slithery thing crawling up her leg!

"Th—ank—" Grace couldn't speak. She breathed like a winded horse, sides heaving, hands sunk in her hair. The laughing boys drowned out her words anyway.

Beth turned to the window, eased the wooden shutters open, and lowered the snake gently to the ground. The action gave Grace another few seconds to gather her scattered wits.

Trying again, she said, "Thank you, B-Beth. I'm not — not a-afraid of snakes."

The laughter grew louder. Mark Reeves fell out of his desk holding his stomach as his body shook with hilarity. The rest of the boys laughed harder.

Swallowing hard, Grace tried again to compose herself. "I was just startled. Thank you for helping me." Taking a step toward Beth, Grace rested one trembling hand on the young girl's arm. "Thank you very much, Beth."

Beth gave a tiny nod of her blond head, as if to encourage her and extend her deepest sympathy.

Grace turned to the rioting classroom — and her skirt fell off.

With a cry of alarm, Grace grabbed at her skirt.

The boys in the class started to whoop with laughter. Mark kicked his older brother Ike. Ike dived out of his chair onto Mark. They knocked the heavy two-seater student desk out of line. Every time they bumped into some other boy, their victim would jump into the fray.

Pulling her skirt back into place, she turned a blind eye to the chaos to deal with her clothes. Only now did she see that the tissue-thin fabric was shredded. A huge hole gaped halfway down the front. It was the only skirt she owned.

Beth, a natural caretaker, noticed and grabbed Grace's apron off a hook near the back wall.

Mandy McClellen rushed up along with Sally and all the other girls. Mandy spoke low so the rioting boys couldn't overhear. "This is your only dress, isn't it, Miss Calhoun?"

Grace nodded, fighting not to cry as the girls adjusted the apron strings around her

17

waist to hold up her skirt. She'd patch it back together somehow, although she had no needle and thread, no money to buy them, and no idea how to use them.

Grace looked up to see the older Reeves boys making for the back of the schoolroom.

"Hold it right there." Mandy used a voice Grace envied.

The boys froze. They pivoted and looked at Mandy, as blond as her sisters and a close match in coloring to the Reeves, but obviously blessed with extraordinary power she could draw on when necessary. After the boys' initial surprise — and possibly fear — Grace saw the calculating expression come back over their faces.

"Every one of you," Mandy growled to frighten a hungry panther, "get back in your seats right now." She planted her hands on her hips and stared.

The whole classroom full of boys stared back. They hesitated, then at last, with sullen anger, caved before a will stronger than their own. Under Mandy's burning gaze, they returned to their seats. Grace's heart wilted as she tried to figure out how Mandy did it.

When the boys were finally settled, the eleven-year-old turned to Grace, her brow furrowed with worry. "I'm right sorry, Miss

Calhoun," she whispered, "but you have to figure out how to manage 'em yourself. I can't do it for you."

Grace nodded. The child spoke the complete and utter truth.

The girls fussed over Grace, setting her chair upright and returning to her desk a book that had been knocked to the floor.

"Miss Calhoun?" Beth patted Grace's arm.

"Yes?"

"Can I give you some advice?"

The little girl had pulled a snake out from under Grace's skirt. Grace would deny her nothing. "Of course."

"I think it's close enough to day's end that you ought to let everyone go home. You're too upset to handle this now. Come Monday morning you'll be calmer and not do something you'll regret."

"Or start something you can't finish," Sally added.

Grace knew the girls were right. Her temper boiled too near the surface. She was on the verge of a screaming fit and a bout of tears.

My dress! God, what am I going to do about it?

These boys! Dear, dear Lord God, what am I going to do about them?

She tried to listen for the still, small voice of God that had taken her through the darkest days of her life during her childhood in Chicago. He seemed to abandon her today. The good Lord had to know one of His children had never needed an answer more. But if God sent an answer, her fury drowned it out. She'd been putting off a showdown with these boys all term. It was time to deal with the problem once and for all.

Sally slipped her little hand into Grace's. "Boys are naughty."

Grace shared a look with Sally and had to force herself not to nod. Seven sweet little girls stood in a circle around her. Grace wanted to hug them all and then go after the boys with a broom, at least five of them. The other ten weren't so badly behaved. Except when inspired by the Reeves.

God had made boys and girls. He'd planned it. They were *supposed* to be this way. But how could a teacher stuff book learning in their heads when they wouldn't sit still or stop talking or quit wrestling?

Digging deep for composure, Grace said, "You girls return to your seats, please. And thank you for your help."

Beth shook her head frantically, obviously sensing Grace wasn't going to take her advice.

"It's all right, Beth. I've put this off too long as it is. And thank you again."

Beth's feet dragged as she followed her sisters and the other girls to her seat.

Grace waited as the room returned to relative quiet, except for the usual giggling and squirming of the Reeves boys.

Glancing between her chair seat and her open desk drawer, Grace was worried she might develop a nervous tic. She sat down but left the drawer open. An almost insane calm took over her body. "School is dismissed except for Abraham, Isaac, Mark, Luke, and John Reeves."

Forehead furrowed over her blond brows, Beth shook her head and gave a little "don't do it" wave.

Grace could tell by the way the sun shone in the west window that it was only a few minutes early for dismissal. Good. That gave her time to settle with these boys, and then she'd have it out with their father. Things were going to change around here!

The rest of the students, stealing frequent glances between her and the blond holy terrors in her midst, gathered up their coats and lunch pails and left the schoolhouse in almost total silence.

And that left Grace.

Alone.

With the Five Horsemen of the Apocalypse.

TWO

Grace felt as if she were watching the second coming and hadn't repented.

Matching mutinous expressions settled on the Reeves' faces.

She said a prayer.

How do I reach them, Lord? Give me wisdom and patience.

Patience. She hunted through her mind for scripture about patience and remembered the long, cold years with Parrish. *"But in all things approving ourselves as the ministers of God, in much patience, in afflictions, in necessities, in distresses."*

That last part surely described her now. The Reeveses were an affliction. Getting through to them was a necessity. And her torn skirt alone qualified as sufficient distress, before she counted hunger and worry and a bruised backside. She needed to face all of that with patience.

She was fiercely determined to approve

herself as a minister of God and bear whatever needed to be borne in order to reach these boys.

Exhausted, short of food, cold every night, and now wearing a ruined dress when she had none to replace it, Grace folded her hands in front of her.

With a sigh she felt all the way to her toes, she faced Mark. The ringleader. If she couldn't control him, she couldn't control any of them.

Her jaw clenched so her anger would not erupt in a tirade. "What do you think is the appropriate punishment for your actions today?"

Mark didn't even bother to feign an innocent expression. His look was far more reminiscent of "Try and punish me, teacher lady."

"We didn't do nothin', Miss Calhoun," he said. "I wonder who put that snake in your desk. That was a right mean thing to do."

A red-hot flash of temper nearly shocked Grace. She was surprised she was capable of this much rage. They always denied it. They didn't try to fake honesty. Instead, with smug disregard for any punishment she might mete out, they lied straight to her face.

"So on top of hurting me and disrupting

class, you're also a liar — is that right, Mark? You can look me right in the eye and break a commandment?" Her voice rose with every word.

God, please give me patience. Please, I need a miracle to handle these boys.

Narrowing his eyes as if he didn't like being called a sinner, Mark didn't answer. He didn't mind *being* a sinner. *Just don't dare call him one.*

"You always blame us for everything, Miss Calhoun." Ike hitched up his brown, coarsely woven pants with two thumbs. The pants were short, dirty, and ragged as if he'd put them on new three years ago and never taken them off since. Red flannel under-drawers showed between his ankles and his scuffed brown boots.

"That's not very nice." John crossed his arms as if he were the injured party.

Grace clenched her hands together on the desk in front of her, picturing them wrapped around somebody's neck. She didn't care to imagine attacking children, so she settled for strangling their father. Clasping her hands as if she could physically hold her temper inside, she knew Beth was right. She should get these boys out of here and deal with them when she calmed down.

She pictured that snake striking at her

from the desk and almost jumped. In that bitter cold room above the diner where the school had located her, she knew nightmares would plague her sleep tonight. No, she'd let this go on for too long. She wasn't going to back down this time. She couldn't and retain any self-respect.

She studied the little wolf pack. Mark, the oldest of the five-year-old triplets, had an inexhaustible supply of ideas. Abe, the oldest of the ten-year-old twins, picked the ideas he liked, and his approval brought the rest of the boys along. Ike always dug in and saw things through to the end. Ike had a way with animals, and he'd probably found the snake.

John did the hard work. Grace would bet John had done the actual sneaking around to put the snake in her desk and the tack on her chair. Luke was the cleanup man. Being youngest had made him tough. If they ever got in trouble as a result of their antics, Luke was the one who got revenge.

The other students left Luke alone. Grace gave him a nervous glance now, and that flared her temper more. She was actually afraid of a five-year-old.

"I go back to my original question. What would you do if you were the teacher and a student did this to you?"

"Miss Calhoun, whatever punishment you're gonna give us, you'd better hurry up." Luke's cool, level eyes sent a chill up Grace's spine. "Pa doesn't like us to keep him waiting."

"So you think you deserve punishment, Luke?" Grace thought about the ruler in her drawer. She shuddered remembering the snake that had popped out. She glanced at the drawer, still wide open. Nothing was stopping her from getting that ruler now.

She prayed silently, hating that she might need to resort to swatting their little hands. Surely there was a better way to handle them. The worst of it was she'd always known it wouldn't work. Besides her natural loathing for anyone who would hurt a child, she knew from watching these boys that they weren't overly worried about pain. The way they shoved each other around, a whack or two with the ruler wouldn't even get their attention.

But swatting them wasn't supposed to *hurt* them — she'd never wield a ruler with that much force. It was supposed to shame them into being better.

"I think you're gonna hit us whether we did anything to you or not." Luke stood, all four feet of him. "I think you're mean and you're plannin' to do whatever you want, so

27

why waste time talkin' about it? You might as well get it over with."

The boys, all slim and wiry, stood. Luke walked to the front of the classroom, and the others followed.

Grace fought down the impulse to back away from him. She saw Luke's calculating eyes and knew the boy was up to something. Did he have a plan? Were they all in on it? Grace couldn't believe how paranoid she'd become. The boy was five for heaven's sake.

Luke stepped up on the platform that raised Grace's desk about six inches above the students'. He stood in front of her, his eyes insolent, daring her to punish him. "What's the matter, Miss Calhoun?" He sounded too polite. That wasn't like him.

Could they have more in store for her? Was there a rat in her coat pocket?

Luke gave her a wide-eyed, innocent look. "You know me and my brothers never done this to you. You just hate us and pick on us every chance you get."

"It's just the opposite, Luke. You boys hate *me* and pick on *me* every chance you get." Grace sounded like a five-year-old herself. She'd given them countless chances to change their ways, but patience hadn't worked. Firmness hadn't worked. She'd let this go on too long.

Shoving herself out of her chair, she grabbed the ruler out of the snake drawer. Facing Luke, she raised the ruler and hesitated. She'd never hit a child before — not as a teacher and not as a young girl who bore all the weight of raising her little sisters.

"I'll take the punishment for all my brothers, ma'am." Luke squared his shoulders. "We didn't do it, but I can see you're bent on blaming us. So have at it. Give me five times the whacking and be done with it."

"You did, too, do it, and not just you." She looked out at the boys, lined up behind tough little Luke.

Mark looked at her with self-satisfied amusement. All the other boys' expressions mirrored Mark's.

"I'm going to punish all of you." She raised the ruler again, staring at Luke, so fearless. It infuriated her that not even the threat of a lash on the hand with her ruler could make him back down. "Hold out your hand, Luke."

He extended his hand.

She looked into his eyes and knew she'd never be able to swing this stupid ruler.

Luke hissed at her, "Do it."

Whispering so his brothers didn't hear her, she said, "I can't."

"Why not?"

"Because I don't want to hit you."

Luke leaned closer, as eager to keep what they said between the two of them as she was for some reason. "We really did it, ma'am. I'm confessing clear as day. Have at it." He reached his hand a little closer as if worried she'd miss. He actually seemed to *want* her to hit him.

What was the little urchin up to? She almost smiled at him.

Her hand raised the ruler, planning to wave it at all of them and throw them out.

"Get away from my son, Miss Calhoun."

Grace jumped back. She bumped into her chair, and for a second she thought she'd end up on the floor again.

Daniel Reeves stood in the window to her right. The one Beth had lowered the snake through. How long had he been standing there?

She looked at Luke and saw the satisfied expression under his feigned innocence. He'd known his father was standing there. Every word he'd spoken had been planned to put her in the worst light for his father's benefit. All the boys had known their father watched.

"You boys get your things. Clay Mc-Clellen's here for the girls. Catch a ride with him to the gap then walk on home. Miss

Calhoun and I are going to settle this once and for all, and it could take awhile."

Daniel left the window. The boys ran, vanishing out the front door with as much noise and shoving as they could manage. The last of them disappeared just as Daniel came in.

Grace felt her cheeks heating up. But why was she embarrassed? These boys deserved a few sound whacks with the ruler. She'd done nothing wrong. The fact that she'd been planning to back down was almost worse than doing it.

And all of it — *all of it* — was this man's fault. This was the one she should be using the ruler on.

She stepped off her platform and practically charged. He came forward just as fast. They met in the middle of the room.

Grace barely came to his chin, and the second they faced each other, Grace wished she'd waited up front for him so he wouldn't tower over her.

But she was here, under his nose, and she was furious. Furious beat tall any day of the week. She was glad he'd shown up. This man was the problem. She'd asked him several times to speak to his sons about their behavior. His boys could do no wrong in his sight.

Grace realized she still clutched the ruler. She slapped it against the desk beside her, wishing she could use it to slap some sense into Daniel Reeves.

"You planning on using that on me, Miss Calhoun? Or aren't you so brave when you're facing an adult?"

"We have discussed your boys' behavior until I'm sick of hearing myself talk, Mr. Reeves."

"Well, I'm with you on that, ma'am. I'm sick of hearing you talk, too."

"You have to do something about them or I will. I can have them expelled from school."

"You think the school board will take your side over mine?" Daniel's blue eyes burned into her skin. They sparked with anger as he leaned over her. "I'd think a little woman who can't control a few bright, active boys wouldn't want the school board looking too close at her."

"Your boys *are* bright and active." He was trying to use his size to intimidate her, but Grace refused to back up when Daniel leaned close. In fact, she took a step forward. "Unfortunately, they use all their *intelligence* to think up pranks to disrupt the school, and they are most *active* when they're thinking of ways to harass me. Have you even *tried* talking with them?"

"Save your speeches for the school board." Daniel's nose almost touched hers. He wasn't yelling, but he spoke in his usual too-loud voice right into her face. "I saw Parson Roscoe and Zeb Morris just a few minutes ago. If we can hunt up Phillip at the general store, we'll have the whole board to hand. Then we'll see what they have to say about you picking on my boys."

"Lead the way." Grace extended her hand toward the front door. "This is long over-due."

"Oh no, *Miss Calhoun.*"

Grace heard her name said with such mockery she almost regretted insisting every parent — every person — in Mosqueros call her by it. But weren't teachers supposed to demand propriety?

"You're the one who's always such a stickler for manners. I insist, ladies first." Daniel crossed his arms, practically blocking the aisle, stubborn as a mule.

Grace fumed, looking at the narrow space he expected her to squeeze through. The man was a bully. She shoved at him as she squeezed past.

She got clear of the confounded man and stormed toward the back of the schoolroom.

She'd just made it to the door when her skirt fell off.

THREE

Grace had been sitting in her chair sobbing ever since the school board fired her. The straight-backed chair pressed mercilessly into her back. Tears that just would not stop had been flowing for an hour.

Opting for peace over justice, the school board had seen to it that Daniel didn't fare well either. His boys had been expelled.

They'd listened to both sides and made their pronouncement — hurried along by the freezing weather and a cow Zeb Morris had back home calving out of season. The ruling came with almost no discussion.

Grace had been too stunned to continue fighting. Penniless, hungry, and, come morning, homeless, losing her job seemed tantamount to a death sentence. Turning from that crowd of men, she'd run to her room like a coward.

Now, an hour later, amazed that there was enough water in her body to form tears,

Grace lifted her hand to wipe her eyes. Her hand shook until she couldn't bear to see it. She closed her eyes and let her long tangles of dark blond hair stick on her soppy face.

She'd come here by choice, wanting the West to be uncivilized, wanting to be far removed from her trouble with Parrish. But never had she imagined anyone or anything as uncivilized as Daniel Reeves and his sons.

Sitting in her one-room attic home was the loneliest moment in her incredibly lonely life. She felt as if she were shrinking away to nothing, hiding here from the fate that surely awaited a jobless, penniless woman in the unforgiving West.

She'd had such dreams. She'd planned to help children and protect them in ways she'd never been protected. She'd planned to make enough money that, once she was sure Parrish had been left far behind, she could send for her ragtag family in Chicago and have a real home at last.

Instead, she'd failed everybody who'd ever been foolish enough to trust her.

When she'd arrived home, she'd cast her ruined dress into a heap on the floor and pulled on her nightgown. Grateful in her misery that there was no mirror in the room to reflect her emaciated body, she held herself tight in the tissue-thin, dark blue flannel gown.

"What am I going to do, Lord?" She bowed her head. She heard the words slip past her clenched jaw. It hurt to move her lips. They were chapped from the salt of her tears and the bitter cold in the attic.

The room was heated only by what crept up from the general store downstairs, and the store banked the fire at night. She had her own potbellied stove, but it cost money to buy firewood or took energy to hike out and cut it herself, energy she just didn't have.

What did it matter anyway? She could freeze to death tonight or she could starve to death next week. Grace wept, not so much for her own failure as for the way she'd failed Hannah and the other children.

All her promises rang hollow now. She couldn't even take care of herself, let alone care for someone else.

Perhaps she shouldn't have sent Hannah every penny she had to spare each payday. If she'd set a few dollars aside for a time of trouble, she could have moved on and started teaching somewhere else. But she'd never dreamed of such trouble as Daniel Reeves. Holding nothing back for herself, she'd barely kept enough to eat.

She wept, ashamed of her weakness. But

what did it matter? There was no one to be disgusted by her. No one this side of Chicago cared if she lived or died. There was no way out. She'd finally hit bottom, plunged to the very deepest pit.

Her door slammed open.

The *bang* jerked her head up.

Everything that was wrong about her destroyed life suddenly meant nothing.

Parrish, with his stooped frame, hawklike nose, and cruel eyes, stepped into the room with a satisfied laugh. "Ah, Grace, have you missed your dear daddy?"

With a scream, Grace leaped from the chair. Parrish's eyes narrowed, and he rushed at her. Without making a conscious choice, Grace chose the only other exit.

Parrish tore at her nightgown. Fingernails clawed her skin as she threw herself out the second-story window. The jagged glass slit her as she crashed through. It rained around her, slashing her skin. The ground rushed at her. The icy December wind seemed to cut her skin as surely as the glass. She instinctively twisted to keep from landing headfirst.

"You won't get away from me." Parrish's roaring threats faded as she plummeted earthward.

The frozen ground hit like a fist. Glass

stabbed and sliced.

"You owe me, and I'm here to make you pay!" The ugly voice overhead stung her into moving.

She scrambled to her feet, pain in every movement. The soft flesh on her hands and knees ripped on the sharp edges of frozen ruts. She was driven to survive, even when, minutes ago, she'd been ready to give up.

She darted around the corner into the alley between the general store and the diner. She tripped, falling, imbedding rock and dirt in her bleeding skin. She staggered to her feet, pressing her back against the wall. She glanced around the side of the building and up.

The broken window no longer framed her nightmare come to life. There was no sadistic, menacing man to be seen. The only way down was the back stairs.

She ran toward the front of the building, mindless of the pain in her feet, only conscious of the need to flee. She darted out of the alley in the frigid Texas night.

Mosqueros was closing down for the evening. The door banged open in the back of the store. Parrish, coming.

She saw a wagon. She scrambled in and ducked under the tarp tossed over it. She crushed her body between wooden crates, scraping new wounds in her flesh. She dragged her bare feet under the cover and stopped dead.

He'd be on Mosqueros's main street by now. He'd know there was only one place she could be. He'd pull back the tarp and put his hands on her. And then he'd make her pay for every bit of her defiance.

The wagon tilted. She heard whistling, incongruous in her terrified mind. Was Parrish climbing aboard the wagon?

A shout and the rattle of leather and chains came from the driver's seat. The wagon lurched forward with a creak of old wood.

She gathered herself to jump out of the wagon and run again. Forever running and hiding, for years, across a continent. Even in this remote Texas town, there was no place he couldn't find her. She lived like a frightened animal.

"Hold there," Parrish shouted from the walk beside the wagon.

That voice, that threatening, brutal voice. How many times had he lashed her with it? How many others had he treated the same? She'd lost count, but the faces of the others haunted her.

Grace didn't dare move. Once she was discovered, any man would hand her over.

40

How well she'd learned that lesson.

"Whoa," the driver said, breaking off his whistling.

Grace's stomach clenched. She knew that voice. The man who'd ruined her life in Mosqueros, just as Parrish had ruined it everywhere else. The driver had seen to her firing and left her cold and hungry in a darkened room. It was the voice of a man she hated only slightly less than Parrish. Now she needed him to survive.

She didn't count on it. Daniel Reeves would probably hand her over with pleasure.

"I need to —" Parrish's voice halted.

Grace waited, trying to control her gasping breath that blew out white in the bitter cold. One move, one twitch of a muscle, and the coarse gray tarp would be thrown back.

"Need somethin', mister?" Daniel Reeves talked too loud, as usual.

"Forget it. Never mind." Footsteps clomped away on the wooden sidewalk.

"Hmm, what wazzat about?" Daniel Reeves asked under his breath.

But Grace heard him. He was mere inches away from her. She could have reached her arm out of the tarp and tapped him on the back.

There was a slap of reins on the horses'

backs. The whistling resumed and the wagon began rolling, swaying side to side.

Why had Parrish left? He had to know it was at least possible she'd hidden under this tarp. It wasn't like him to quit hunting.

He didn't want a witness.

The minute the idea came to her, she knew it was right. He was still out there. Watching. He had an instinct for the hunt. How many times had he proven that to Grace?

But he'd never minded witnesses before. He'd delighted in dragging her home, screaming and crying. He'd gloated and laughed about it to anyone who watched. That could mean only one thing. He wasn't here to drag her home. Not this time.

He was here to kill her.

He would want no witnesses to tie them together when she turned up dead.

After enough time had passed to put the town behind them, the cold broke into her terror. Inch by inch so no movement or sound would draw Daniel's attention to her, Grace curled in on herself. She pulled her knees to her chest, wrapped her arms around them, and bowed her head until she lay in a tight ball among the boxes and gunnysacks. Stiff as a corpse, she hugged herself. There had never been anyone else to do it.

The cold invaded her hiding place until her bare toes went numb. As the wagon rumbled over the rough trail and Daniel whistled his mindless tune, Grace lost the feeling in her body. She fought the need to shiver as her legs, then her arms and torso, grew chilled until there was no feeling left. But she was only distantly aware of that and the bruising of the wagon box and the sliding supplies.

She closed her eyes and let the tears start flowing again. She let the cold, cruel world beat on her to its heart's content. She remembered Jesus' lament as He hung on the cross: *"My God, my God, why hast thou forsaken me?"*

Why *wouldn't* God forsake her? Everyone else had.

She was surprised how much she regretted dying. Life hadn't held much pleasure for her. Clinging to it seemed at odds with the miserable existence she led.

She felt the cold wrap around her like icy hands, deepening her exhaustion, pulling her under to sleep. She didn't expect to wake.

She didn't fight it. She decided to let Parrish win.

Parrish had taught her long ago that she deserved it.

FOUR

Daniel Reeves let the winter weather cool his temper on his long drive home. The team clambered up the steep stretch of trail that twisted through the narrow mouth of his canyon home. The wind whistled through the walls of the canyon towering over his head.

The trail was so narrow in places he was tempted to suck in his gut as his sure-footed team slipped through the gap. One razor-thin switchback went almost straight sideways and straight up at the same time. A few flakes of snow drifted down on him, and he hated to think of scaling this path if it was slick.

Just as well the boys don't have to go to school anymore. Waste of time anyway. Most schooling was nonsense. Still, it burned something fierce to be told to stay away. He sucked in frigid air and shook off his anger.

Pay attention to the trail — watch the team.

These are the things a rancher needed to know, not a bunch of book learning.

The snow gusted into his face as he wound around another tight switchback. A wonder they'd found this place. The boys playing around their campsite had come up with it. As far as Daniel could tell, no man had ever stepped foot in this fertile valley before he'd claimed it.

Snow sifted down from his hat, and a breeze sent it whooshing down his neck. Shivering, he thanked God it didn't snow much here.

At least that's what he'd been told. He hadn't lived through a Texas winter yet.

Good thing. If the snow came down here like it had in Kansas, this gap would close up tight and stay sealed until spring.

After he'd gone a couple of hundred yards feeling so closed in the sensation almost smothered him, the canyon opened out and he caught his breath with delight. It was full darkness, but the moon glowed in the sky through gaps in the high, skittering clouds, lighting up the gentle snow flurries.

Daniel could see the wide-open spaces of the 6R Ranch. Belly-deep grass, cured lush on the stem, waved in the bitter wind as if it waved hello. Trees covered the steep edges of the canyon that disappeared out of sight.

Cattle, fat with spring babies, lowed softly as he passed by them. They were all as tame as dogs from being overfed and gentled by his boys.

Home. He loved it. He loved his brand — the 6R, chosen for the six Reeves men. He'd left grief behind and begun life anew. Finally, his life was in perfect order.

A single dark thought intruded. That awful, prissy Miss Calhoun. Well, he'd gotten even today in town, but the boys still weren't welcome back. He scowled at the thought of that fussy old maid.

He shook off his temper. Miss Calhoun was gone. Spring would come soon enough, and the board had said his boys could have another chance then. Daniel was tempted not to bother. He decided he *would* reenroll them, at least for a while, just so no priggish female could take credit for stopping his boys from learning.

Satisfied to know a good teacher might take the place of Miss Calhoun, he turned his thoughts back to his idyllic life at the 6R.

He always thought of God's promises when he looked at his canyon. *"Blessed are they that mourn: for they shall be comforted."* God had indeed comforted him. It had taken time for Daniel to accept that comfort, but he'd found it in his isolated canyon with his sons.

When he was within shouting distance of the cave, he yelled, "Boys, get out here and grab a box."

Daniel hollered to be heard over the commotion that came from inside the house. It sounded as though his boys were having a fine old time. He laughed as they tumbled out of their little house, all trying to shove through the door at the same time.

"I can hear the lot of you, through stone walls, from over a mile away. It's a wonder it didn't scare the team." Daniel pulled back on the reins, but the well-trained horses knew their job and stopped without much effort from him. He set the brake.

"What'd ya get, Pa?" Ten-year-old Abraham beat his brothers to the wagon, dragging his coat on as he came, none too worried about the wicked cold.

Isaac dashed out one step behind him. The twins always moved as a team. Abe fastest and first, but Ike sticking to the end and finishing whatever Abe started.

"Did ya get plenty of taters?" Ike swung himself up on the back of the wagon beside his brother.

"An' apples, Pa." Mark, the firstborn of his five-year-old triplets, stormed after his brothers, with his two mirror images just behind.

"You said you'd try 'n' get some winter apples," John shouted.

"We heard at school Mr. Badje had extras in his cellar, 'member, Pa?" Luke came out, his blond hair a replica of his four brothers'.

The cave door stood open in the teeth of the December night.

Abe threw the tarp back.

"Get that door, Luke," Daniel yelled.

"Did'ja get us a ma?" Abe asked.

"Luke, last one out gets that door closed. I'm gonna be chopping wood all winter if —" Daniel stopped. He turned to Abe. "What?"

Adam shoved the door open, glad to be out of the wind. He wouldn't be out of it for long.

Snow blew in with him. Clay looked up from his rocking chair where he sat grinning at Sally on his lap. Sophie turned from where she laid plates on the table, her stomach so huge Adam was surprised she didn't tip over forward every time she tried to move.

Mandy stirred something that smelled wonderful in the pot hanging over the fire.

Beth sat close by the fire, reading aloud to the whole family.

It was a perfect picture. One Adam had long wished for himself. He was nearing forty now, and a wife and family had never happened for him. But he'd helped Sophie have this idyllic life, and he was content.

He was also going to wreck things. "The teacher's missing."

They all turned to him and became alert. His urgency must have shown loud and clear.

"I was in town when the cry went up. Someone saw her window broken and went up to check. She's gone. Her door stood open, but from snags of fabric on the broken glass and tracks in the alley under the window, it looks like she fell or jumped out her window. They've got search parties out in every direction. I told them I'd fetch the hands."

Clay set Sally on her feet and rushed for his hat. "Don't hold dinner." He left on Adam's heels.

Adam noticed Sophie didn't try to come. She'd settled into leaving men's work to Clay and the hands . . . mostly. Being pregnant had slowed her down a mite, too.

Adam swung up on his horse. "It could have been hours ago. No one's seen her since she got fired."

Clay, striding to the barn to grab up his horse, stopped short and turned. "She got fired? What happened?"

"Daniel Reeves and his boys is what happened. Miss Calhoun and Daniel had another one of their squabbles and got the school board involved. They kicked up so much fuss the school board washed their hands of both of them. Fired her and kicked his boys out of school."

Clay got moving again. "Where'd she go? The train didn't come through tonight. Did she take her horse?"

Adam rode alongside him. "She doesn't have a horse."

Clay glanced back. "She used to."

"She came into the area on a horse, but the blacksmith said she'd sold it to him months ago. He got the idea she needed the money."

"You're sure she's not visiting one of the students?"

"We've searched every building in town, even the barns. Guess she was pretty upset after she got fired. Went to her room crying. When word got out she'd been fired and was missing, folks felt bad about it, so they've all pitched in to hunt, near tore the town apart. She's not there." Adam pulled his collar up to his ears against the cold. "No one's ever seen her with anything but her one coat and one pair of shoes, and she left them behind."

Clay wheeled and stared at Adam. "She went out her window and fell two stories then disappeared without shoes or a coat? In this weather? What's going on?"

Adam shook his head. "I've got no answers for you, Clay. I told 'em in town we'd cover the land between Sawyer Canyon and the plateau. She can't have gotten farther than that."

Clay jabbed a finger at the bunkhouse. "Go rouse the men. If she's not on a train, not on a horse, and not in town, she's in trouble."

"Bad trouble." Adam kicked his horse toward the bunkhouse. Luther and Buff were already outside in their buffalo-skin coats. The other men emerged. They couldn't know what had happened, but they'd lived long enough in a harsh land to sense danger and be ready.

"A ma." John shouted from the cave door. "We've been thinking it's a good idea 'n' all."

"You have?" Daniel remembered them saying such a thing, but he'd paid no attention. He wasn't taking a chance on another woman dying on him.

" 'Cept'n I don't know where she's gonna sleep," Luke added. "We could put the table outside at night I reckon."

Daniel looked where his son was staring. Ike was beside Abe, and Daniel couldn't see anything. Mark, Luke, and John clambered up into the wagon box and surrounded the supplies. They were all staring at something Daniel couldn't see.

"Not Miss Calhoun," Mark howled. "Take her back and get someone else, Pa. She's a grouch."

Daniel swung around on the seat and dropped into the back end of his wagon. With all six Reeves men in it, there was no room for supplies, let alone . . .

"A woman." Daniel couldn't believe his eyes. Then the shock passed and he realized she was asleep. Or dead. He bent down and swooped her into his arms. She weighed barely more than one of the triplets.

She didn't move, didn't even react when he touched her. "Something's wrong, boys." Her skin was white, and she was as cold as ice in his arms. He couldn't tell if she was breathing. "She's freezing. Let's get her inside."

"We don't want Miss Calhoun for a ma."

53

John stomped until he shook the wagon. Daniel jumped to the ground with the little wisp of a woman in his arms and headed for the house. He saw the door standing wide open. Any heat in the little cave was long gone.

"Take her back, Pa!" Luke yelled from where he was kneeling on top of the supplies in the wagon. "Get a better ma 'n her."

Daniel strode toward the cave, trying to sort out all he needed to do to help her. "I don't have time to explain any of this to you boys." No time — and no explanation if he had all the time in the world.

"Miss Calhoun may be dying. We're going to need lots of firewood to warm her up. All of you boys scatter and get some rounded up." Daniel glanced behind him at his boys, all wearing "stubborn" like it was a winter coat. He roared, "And I mean now!"

Daniel went into the house and, with Miss Calhoun held easily in one arm, closed the heavy, dragging door he'd fashioned into the mouth of this little cave. He hurried over to the stove and knelt beside it. After a moment's hesitation, he lowered her to the chilly floor.

"This won't do," he said to himself. "She can't get warm on the cold ground." He was suddenly irritated with himself for not getting a cabin built last summer. The boys were never inside, summer or winter, and the cave was an adventure for all of them. And heaven knew it was a cheap way to live, no room for furniture or bric-a-brac and no woman to nag him for such foolishness. Still, a warm, tight house right now might mean the difference between life and death for Miss Calhoun.

He went to the bedding wadded in a heap in the corner. The furs all but carpeted the floor when they rolled them out at night. He caught up all the blankets, went back to her side, and, gently lifting her, awkwardly spread the blankets on the floor for her to lie on.

The door flew open while he knelt there, holding Miss Calhoun in his arms.

Abe came in with an armload of wood.

"Abe, close that door. We'll never get ahead of the cold with it standing open."

Before Abe could obey — on the off chance he was going to — Ike came in loaded down with sticks. The other boys were right on his heels.

"We need to get this cave warmed up. Gather more wood, enough to keep the fire blazing hot all night. Then get back in here with it fast and keep that door closed." Daniel, a little surprised that they minded him, watched them dash out, shutting the door behind them.

Daniel settled the motionless woman on the blankets. He laid his hand on her chest and, with a sigh of relief, felt a heartbeat.

Daniel stuffed the stove full of wood and heard the reassuring crackle as the new kindling caught from the old. He picked up the teacher's limp white hand and noticed how fine-boned it was. She was so thin it was like holding bone draped with skin. He meant to rub some feeling back into her, but she seemed so fragile, he was afraid he'd hurt her. Instead of rubbing, he just held her hand between both of his, trying to share some of his warmth.

Lying here, silent and defenseless, Grace Calhoun, who had always seemed like an old bat who lived for the soul purpose of terrorizing children, now looked very young. Why, she was little more than a child herself. He hadn't thought of it for a while, but he remembered now that his first impression was that she was a pretty little thing.

Then she'd opened her mouth.

Daniel thought of how painfully proper she had been when they'd met. More than proper, she was snooty as all get-out and so prissy he'd decided she lived to keep her grammar perfect and her hands clean.

He'd let her enthusiasm for schooling sway him into sending the boys. Then the trouble began. Soon enough he'd pegged her for an old maid, made of pure gristle and spite. Although, truth to tell, he'd never given her much thought beyond avoiding her at all costs.

Careful to be gentle, he rubbed her hand between his to get some circulation into her fingers and saw blood. With a gasp he turned her hand over. Her hand was scraped raw.

"What happened to you?"

For the first time he really looked at her for injuries. Her other hand had bled, too, although the bleeding had stopped. He noticed the dark blue dress she was wearing. It was flannel and thin as paper. It was torn at her knees, and he could see that she had scraped herself there, too.

Dear God, what has this woman been through tonight? Don't let her die on me, Father.

The flannel had dried to her knee in one spot. Carefully, he pulled the fabric out of the wound. She'd been in his wagon since Mosqueros. There was no other possible time she could have slipped in. He'd just loaded the wagon and thrown the tarp over the supplies, then gone back inside the general store to pay for his order. He'd only been inside a couple of minutes. She must have climbed in then.

Daniel looked at her still features. Her lips were tinged with blue, her skin as fragile as a china plate Margaret had treasured right up until the day Ike had smashed it into a thousand pieces. He remembered how his wife had cried over that stupid plate. Of course, women cried over almost everything.

Grace's naturally fair skin seemed almost translucent from the cold. He spoke to her, even though she was beyond hearing him. "I've figured out *when* you got in my wagon, Miss Calhoun. That only leaves *why.*"

He realized that as soon as she was awake and able to move, he'd have to drive all the way back into town. Honestly, this woman seemed as though she'd been born for the sole purpose of pestering him.

The boys charged back in. Luke was last, and he carefully shut the door. Juggling his armload of sticks in his chubby, five-year-old arms proved to be a bit too much. He dropped half his load.

"Clumsy." Mark shoved Luke. "Be quiet. The teacher's here." Daniel noticed Mark said it at the top of his lungs.

"She's not the teacher." Luke shoved

back. Mark stumbled into Ike, who dropped his bundle of wood with a clatter.

Luke clapped Daniel on the back. "Sally McClellen told me today on the ride home that Pa got her fired right after school."

"Good for you, Pa." Abe stuffed more wood into the potbellied stove. "They're gonna hafta hunt up a new teacher. A nice one this time, I hope."

"Sally said we got kicked out of school, too," Luke added.

Pandemonium broke out. The boys shrieked with joy until Daniel half expected the stone roof over their heads to raise from all the ruckus.

The jubilation wore itself out while Daniel worked on getting circulation back into Miss Calhoun's fragile hand.

Out of the corner of his eye, Daniel noticed Ike collide with Mark and then blame Mark for the crash.

"Mark, you little —" The two of them stumbled into the table and shoved it until it hit Daniel in the back. The table, the stove, two benches, and the boys, and the house was full. There was no room for a wrestling match.

"You guys, cut it out." Daniel pushed the corner of the table out of his shoulder blades. He saw that the stack of wood behind his back had grown most of the way to his chest.

By golly, those boys can work!

"That's enough wood for now. You guys go get the rest of the supplies. Stow everything in the barn. Ike, you unhitch the team and rub 'em down. Abe, grain them for the night, hang up the harness, then all of you get back in here before you freeze. It's already past your bedtime."

Abe scowled. "Dad, we don't want to do all that."

Daniel ignored his son's complaining. He'd heard it all before. "And make sure you close the barn gate tight. If those horses get out again, you're all going to start sleeping in the barn and I'll bring the horses in here to bunk down."

Grumbling and shoving each other, the boys filed out. Ike saw to closing the door.

Daniel turned back to Miss Calhoun. He touched her face and saw that the fire had begun to warm her just a little. She still lay motionless, but she was breathing steadily under the deerskin blanket.

In the dim lantern light, Daniel leaned close enough to see an ugly scrape along one side of Miss Calhoun's face. A bruise bloomed on her forehead, and he saw several shallow slits. Inspecting carefully, he saw a sliver of glass in one cut and carefully extracted it.

With a dart of fear, Daniel wondered for the first time if she'd really climbed into his wagon. Or had she been knocked unconscious and put in the wagon by someone else? He thought of that stranger who'd hailed him when he'd climbed onto the wagon. He'd wanted something, but what? Grace?

Daniel reached for the pail of water he always kept hot on the stove. He took two rags to protect his hands from the searing tin and lowered the pail to the floor beside him.

He bathed Miss Calhoun's hands in the warm water. He washed her knees, mindful of how improper it was to see any more of her legs than necessary. Daniel finished quickly then covered her legs all the way to her toes.

He rubbed her arms and stoked the fire, planning to keep a prayer vigil into the night.

A long time later, the boys trooped back in, pink-cheeked and rowdy from working in the sharp cold of the night. They argued and shoved and fought over what blankets were left. But there was no harm in their rowdiness, just horseplay.

The boys saw to their own supper, and as they ate, Daniel could see their heavy eyelids. Even with the excitement of having the teacher in their house, he knew he'd won.

"A ma hadn't oughta take all the blankets, had she, Pa?" Luke asked, worried.

"She's s'posed to take care'a *us,* Pa," Mark whined. "Not us take care'a *her.*"

Daniel didn't answer. He had his hands full controlling the urge to flinch every time the boys called this little fussbudget "Ma." What a nightmare that'd be if it were true.

The boys were exhausted. Good. That was his daily goal. Let them play hard enough and work hard enough to get them to sleep at night. They eventually settled in, piled up together like a litter of puppies, probably warmer that way than if they'd have been wrapped in a blanket.

"Boys, before you go to sleep, say a prayer for Miss Calhoun to be okay. She looks bad hurt to me and half dead from the cold. We need God looking out for her special tonight."

"We don't mind praying for her," Mark said, the spokesman for the group. "We don't want her to die 'r nothin', but we don't want her to be our ma. We talked it over, 'n' we say take her back and get another'un."

Daniel didn't bother to tell his boys, yet again, that he hadn't brought the confounded woman home to be their ma. There wasn't enough stupid in the world for him to do a thing like that.

"Well then, pray she gets well so she can get outta here. She's not going anywhere as long as she's asleep like this."

The boys all sprang to their knees and prayed with a fervor that would have humbled a fire-and-brimstone preacher at a revival meeting.

The boys finished praying and lay down, covering the floor until there was barely room for Daniel to kneel by Miss Calhoun. He was stuck — pinned in here, in the dim light of the cold night, next to the rudest woman he'd ever known. The woman who had gotten his sons kicked out of school. He'd gotten her fired from her job in return.

Here they were, she without a job and he without an education for his boys; he trying to save her life and she doing her best to thwart him, as she did in everything else.

It suited him to pray, too, because he wanted her well. He wanted her out of here. He never wanted to lay eyes on this bothersome woman again as long as he lived.

Then she began to shiver.

FIVE

The wind cut like knives through his long black duster as Sid Parrish stared at the cave. His horse, a poorly trained nag the blacksmith rented out, jerked on the reins, fighting the bit.

"I owe you, girl," he said into the frigid Texas night. Parrish wanted to hurt Grace until the wanting ate a hole in his gut. He wasn't a man who forgot a wrong done him.

But he'd seen all those kids come pouring out of the cave. And he'd seen the savvy eyes of the man who had unwittingly helped her escape. He'd have a fight on his hands if he stormed in and took her by force.

He'd be a fool to try it, and Parrish was nobody's fool. But he was tempted. His trigger finger itched, and his hand caressed the gun on his hip. He wanted to see her eyes and hear her cry out with the pain he planned to inflict. He wanted to hurt her long and slow before he killed her. He'd been too easy on her before, and it had brought him low.

The horse skittered and snorted. Parrish had rarely ridden a horse in Chicago, and he'd never carried a gun. He'd used his mind to survive there. Now he had to learn some new tricks. And the tricks of the West included horses and firearms.

He brought his hand down with brutal power on the horse's flank and pretended it was that miserable little girl who thought she'd gotten the best of him. His arm hurt before his fury was spent, and he wished for a whip and spurs to work out his rage. The blacksmith had refused to give him either, saying the horse handled fine without them.

His lips curled in cruel satisfaction as he remembered Grace's terror when he entered her room. He'd almost had her. He'd touched her for just a split second before she slipped away. His fingers still felt the warmth of her flesh, vibrating with pure horror. Knowing she threw herself out of a window to escape him satisfied his hunger to punish her. He would live on that small feast for now. But it was only temporary until he could crush her thoroughly. He was going to take her and break her. No sniveling little *girl* got the best of Sid Parrish.

He turned his horse away from the cave

and headed back to Mosqueros. He was no hand for roughing it in the wilderness, and Mosqueros was a small enough town that he'd be remembered. He'd come into town on a mule skinner's wagon. The supply wagon was headed on west and had only stopped to leave a few orders at the Mosqueros general store. Parrish had slipped out into the hills around the town without talking to anyone. The townsfolk might ask questions if he turned up around the same time Grace disappeared. Parrish would pick his time and be back.

It was the longest night of Daniel's life. And he'd lived through birthing pains that produced triplets and killed his wife.

Miss Calhoun shook as if a cougar had its teeth sunk into her and wanted to snap her spine. Except a cougar would have been quick. This went on for hours. The tremors came and stayed. Miss Calhoun was never conscious through any of it. Daniel's boys slept, even when she sobbed aloud and cried out that she would perish.

Daniel pulled her into his arms and held her, trying to keep her from harming herself as the quaking went on and on. She was painfully thin, hardly an armful for him. He wondered at the sharp edges of her bones as he tried to rub circulation into her limbs. She had no cushion of warming fat to help.

After a time, the violent shivering eased and she seemed to collapse into total unconsciousness. A few moments passed; then the trembling began again. Miss Calhoun wept.

Daniel held her and prayed for her and murmured into her hair. "You'll be all right. I won't leave you. Hang on. Hang on." As he spoke to her, he sent petitions to God. However much he'd been at sixes and sevens with the snooty little teacher, he now wished frantically that she'd be all right.

And she did — hang on, that is. Her arms escaped the blankets, and she gripped him around his neck with all the strength of her convulsing arms. "Perish. No, not perish. Not again."

"You're not going to perish." Daniel kept up the comforting hum of his voice, hoping he could reach her. "You're okay. I'll keep you safe and warm. You'll make it."

The quivering she couldn't control, he knew. But he tried to ease the fear he heard in every gasp and sob. What was she so afraid of?

Miss Calhoun relaxed as the shivering passed. She lay still longer this time and made more natural movements. A pale pink flush darkened her cheeks and gave Daniel hope.

He stretched out fully alongside her. There really wasn't any other place for him in the crowded cave home. The blankets were firmly between them, but still Daniel felt an odd reaction to being this near a woman. Well, not odd exactly. Just long forgotten. He hadn't spent much time close to a woman. And, a few moments of weakness aside, that included his wife.

He tried to put a few inches between them. She clung to him, flowing toward him like warm liquid. He stayed because he had no choice, but he thought of Miss Calhoun's cruelty to his sons to keep himself from enjoying her slender arms.

And when that wasn't enough, he thought of his wife nearly dying with his twins.

And when that wasn't enough, he thought of his own stupidity to let Margaret convince him that more children were needed to make their lives complete.

And when that wasn't enough and he decided he had to get away from her, she started shaking again.

He held her through this one. Only a monster would let her face this bitter, soul-deep cold alone. And it would be an even greater evil to let her talk of perishing without trying to console her. He murmured comfort and shared his prayers with her and held on. This time the shivering didn't go on as long, and when it stopped, she seemed to drop into a true sleep.

Once he believed it, he let her go and stood away from her. He looked around the tiny cave. Why hadn't he built something? There was wood aplenty to build a log cabin in any size he chose. The work would be good for the boys.

Definitely next summer — before any more freezing-cold women happened by.

He saw her toes peeking out of the blanket and stooped to check her feet, worrying about frostbite. They had warmed considerably, and he could pinch her nails and see, in the dim stove light, that there was pink beneath them. He wrapped her again quickly.

While he crouched there, her eyes flickered open. Her eyes seemed to pick up the flickering light. They were dark golden, like her hair. Although the room was dark, the red-hot, potbellied stove cast enough light for him to see she was coherent.

"Where am I?" She sounded sluggish. Her words were slurred, and her lips barely moved.

Daniel leaned closer, trying to hear the

bare whisper of her words. Not sure what she'd said, he knew what must be going through her head. "Miss Calhoun, it's Daniel Reeves. I found you in my wagon nearly frozen to death. You're at my cabin. We'll keep you warm and get you back to town as soon as you're well enough —"

"No, not town." She gripped his arm until she cut off his circulation, as well as his thinking.

"I can't go back. I'll . . . I can't. I'll . . ." Her voice faded; her grip hardened.

Daniel leaned until his ear nearly rested against her lips. He was sure she said the word "perish."

He pulled back to reassure her that he wouldn't let her perish. Her eyes sparkled. He'd forgotten how pretty she was — because he hadn't been able to see past the meanness. But the sparkle was a flash of desperation. She was beseeching him. Her nails dug into the flannel of his shirtsleeve.

Whether she knew what she was saying or not, her fear was real. Daniel knew something terrible had happened to Miss Calhoun in town to drive her out into the night in this fragile dress.

"I promise I'll protect you, Grace." He spoke her forbidden name.

She always demanded the utmost propriety. He knew that, because she'd told him. And told him and told him. Until she had, he'd never heard the word "propriety," not to mention the word "utmost." Now, with her too afraid and hurt and cold to complain, he was surprised to find out he missed her prim manners and sharp tongue. A little.

"I won't let you perish." Vowing straight from his heart, he could do no less for this frightened woman. He patted her clinging hand, hoping she was rational enough to understand him.

"Thank you." She released her death grip on his arm, and her hand went to his cheek. She caressed his stubbly whiskers for a moment. He couldn't think when last he'd shaved. He usually cleaned up for church, so it was at least once a week.

Daniel whispered into the dark of the cave, " 'Yea, though I walk through the valley of the shadow of death, I will fear no evil: for thou art with me.' "

"Yes," she breathed. "God is with me. And you. You're with me, too. Thank you, Daniel. God bless you." Her eyes fell shut. Tears slipped over her lower lashes, and she moved her palm away from his face. Her scraped and battered hand fluttered to the floor like the last leaf of autumn. She relaxed into real sleep — at last.

Six

Grace woke up in a rat hole. And the king of rats was leaning over her.

"How are you, Grace?" The rodent leaned so close to her it was . . . it was — *Oh, dear God in heaven, help me!* It was kind of nice.

He looked so worried, and he was so handsome.

"What am I doing lying on the floor?" Grace sat up so quickly they almost bumped noses. She didn't add "next to you." The words were just not ones she could force out of her mouth.

"Grace." Daniel studied her face so intently it distracted her from why she'd come to be here and how she'd come to be here and when she'd come to be here and . . .

"Where am I?"

"I'm glad you're awake. I was worried about you."

They stared at each other for a long second, and then, in Grace's muddled mind, another memory clicked into place. "Parrish."

Daniel's expression softened. "No, you'll be fine. I kept you close by the fire all night. What were you doing in my wagon anyway?"

Grace tried so hard to answer that question she could feel her forehead crinkling from the effort. "Am I . . . This is your . . . ?"

She looked past his shock of white-blond hair, which he'd passed on to all his sons. She looked past his broad shoulders, which proved to be next to impossible because they seemed to block out the whole world.

Then she knew. She'd come calling when she'd started teaching. And it *was* a rat hole. The man and his family lived underground like vermin.

Still, she'd come. It was her duty as schoolmarm. She'd heard about the new family that had yet to send their young ones to school. She rode out here alone, on a rented horse she could ill afford, determined to urge the parents to educate their children.

She'd talked a skeptical Daniel Reeves into letting his boys attend school, and she'd been paying for that mistake ever since. But no mistake to do with the Reeves family made any difference to her life now. If she hadn't been fired from her job, she'd have had to leave anyway because of Parrish.

"I brought you home. Well, I didn't exactly bring you home." Daniel's eyes dropped to the space between them, which Grace noticed was minimal. He rolled up on his knees. She noticed he'd been stretched out on the bare dirt floor with no blanket while she had a stack of them. "More like I drove home, and when we went to unload the wagon, we found —"

"We don't need a ma none."

It looked for all the world as though Daniel had sprouted another head, a slightly smaller one coming out of his right shoulder.

"Good morning, Mark." Grace recognized the oldest of the triplets. She knew him by the fire in his eyes that the other boys couldn't fake and he couldn't mask. And it wasn't because the others weren't always in mischief — heaven knew they were. But this one had a diabolical bend. Grace had always been one step behind him. Oh, who was she kidding? She'd always been miles behind all of them.

Ike tended toward hard work and determination, traits he often used to cause problems, but he'd been the best behaved of the bunch. Ike had brought a kitten into the schoolroom one day and spent his noon hour fussing over it by the potbellied stove in the schoolhouse. Ike had actually talked to her a little that day as she found a soft rag to wash away a deep cut on the kitten's belly.

Abe, the oldest, was the leader, or so it seemed until she'd watched Mark for a while. Abe gave the orders, but he very subtly looked to his little brother for ideas, not being quite diabolical enough on his own.

John was the sweetest one, but only by comparison. He was still more unruly than any non-Reeves child in Mosqueros. He was a follower, but he followed with an enthusiasm that had left Grace stunned on many occasions. He was also a good student, for some reason taking pride in doing his work quickly and well. Grace had learned not to draw attention to that fact, though, because it embarrassed John and he'd act up extra for a few days to prove what a troublemaker he could be.

Luke was the toughest. Maybe because he was youngest, he'd learned to take anything anyone handed out and return it with interest. He never cried, he never complained, but he never forgot a wrong. He had a knack for paying back anyone who crossed him that had quickly taught every child in

Mosqueros, even those twice his size, to steer clear of him.

But this one, staring at her now, was the brains of the outfit. Mark Reeves was a creative genius. Grace had often thought if she could harness that brilliance, the boy could cure diseases and build great buildings and invent new wonders of the world.

Instead, he just tortured her.

"We don't *want* a ma, neither." Luke's head appeared over Daniel's other shoulder.

"I'm sure that's very interesting, Luke, but why are you telling me this?" Grace waited; all the potential heads hadn't even begun to sprout out of Daniel's shoulders.

"Because Pa brung you home to be our ma, but we don't want you." Abe appeared. "So thanks 'n' everything, but —"

"Your father *brought* me home to be your ma, not *brung* me home to be your ma." Grace thought about that for a split second before she added, "Your pa didn't bring me home to be your ma."

"You just said he did." A little furrow appeared between John's brows as he tried to make sense of her.

Grace wished him all the luck in the world, since she couldn't begin to make sense of any of this.

"Which is it?" Ike asked with a suspicious

76

narrowing of his blue eyes.

All six men stared at her, hanging on every word. She'd never seen a single one of them be still for this long. Maybe she should grab this chance to run.

"Why're you here, then, Miss Calhoun?" Mark's eyes seemed to bore into her brain. He was no doubt reading her mind. Finding out through supernatural means what would bother her the most so he could begin tormenting her.

She couldn't tell them about Parrish. She couldn't tell anyone, or she'd be sent back.

Daniel nodded. "Go on. Answer him. I want to know, too. Why *are* you here?"

Grace sat up and pushed the foot-high pile of blankets off her body then snatched them right back up to her chin. "Oh, good heavens."

"What?" Daniel looked around the room; then he looked back at her, studying her as if he expected her to collapse at any second. "What's wrong?"

"I'm wearing my nightgown."

Dead silence fell on the room. Daniel's blond eyebrows arched up until they disappeared into the scruffy overlong bangs that dropped across his forehead. "You are?"

"I can't be out here alone with you wearing a nightgown." Grace clutched the blankets until her fingers hurt, thinking of the scandal of it all. "It's not proper."

Daniel's fair skin turned an alarming shade of pink as he stared at her. "I'll bet it wasn't proper of us to sleep together, either."

"It most certainly was not." The deep voice from behind hit them at the same instant the cold did.

They all turned to face Parson Roscoe.

The boys wheeled fully around. Daniel sat up. Grace clutched the blankets to her chest and looked into the startled eyes of the kindly parson and, just behind him, his gentle-hearted wife, Isabelle.

"Parson, it's not what it looks like," Grace said.

"Oh, thank heavens," Mrs. Roscoe said. "Because it looks like you and Daniel spent the night together in this cave."

"Then it is exactly what it looks like," John said into a silence more frozen than Grace had been last night.

"Well, yes," Daniel said. "We did spend the night together, but —"

"Daniel," Grace gasped in horror.

Daniel looked away from the parson, his skin now fully flaming red. "Well, we did. Do you want me to add lying to the parson in on top of having you in bed . . . I mean, sleeping together . . . I mean, having you here without your clothes . . . I mean . . ." Daniel lapsed into silence.

"Pa brung her home to be our ma, but he tried her out for the night and he decided to return her," Mark said.

Parson Roscoe stepped fully into the cave. "Both of you get up immediately."

Daniel stood in a single, lithe movement.

"In front of the children, Grace? I'm shocked." Mrs. Roscoe came in and shut the door behind her. The plump woman clutched her hands together in front of her chest as if desperate to get away and spend an hour in prayer just to wash the shock out of her mind.

Grace climbed to her feet. She fumbled with the blankets. There were too many of them to hold. She tried to drop a few of them and managed to drop them all. She caught at them and almost fell forward trying to keep herself covered.

Daniel caught her before she pitched over on top of him.

Every bone in Grace's body hurt. Every breath cut across her chest like a knife. Her arms and legs were so stiff she wanted to cry out with pain.

"We saw the broken window in your room." The parson produced his Bible from his coat pocket.

Grace remembered now. She'd fallen out of her window. No, she'd jumped out of her window.

"The whole town is up in arms about what happened to you, Grace." Mrs. Roscoe crossed the room, all three steps wide, and rested her hand on Grace's shoulder. "Search parties have been out all night."

"Someone mentioned Daniel being in town yesterday afternoon." The parson took up the story. "We offered to ride out and see if he knew of your whereabouts. Now I see you must have . . . uh . . . settled your differences and . . . uh . . . decided to . . ."

Grace could see the parson striving to be diplomatic when faced with the very worst possible sort of evidence of immoral behavior between two adults.

"Plan an elopement." Mrs. Roscoe's kind eyes found Grace, and the intertwined hands begged Grace to go along with this wild stab at respectability.

"No, oh no, no!" Daniel said. "We didn't plan no elopement. I don't want to marry the schoolmarm. Sure, we slept together. That doesn't mean —"

"What's 'lopement, Pa? Is that like an antelope?" John asked. "Are we gonna eat

80

venison 'stead of dumb old steak all the time?"

"No, it's like an envelope, stupid," Abe sneered. "The parson wants to know if we've got any letters to mail."

"We don't rightly know how to fetch a letter around, Parson," Ike said. "We haven't had much schoolin'."

"And what we've had isn't much better 'n nothin'," Mark added, " 'cause Miss Calhoun was a mighty poor excuse for a schoolmarm."

Grace turned on Mark. "I was not a poor excuse for a schoolmarm, you little —"

"Do not tell me, Daniel Reeves," — the parson stopped Grace from grabbing Mark by stepping past the boys and the table until he stood toe-to-toe with Daniel — "that you expect to keep this young lady, a *respectable* woman from *this* town and a member of *my flock,* out at your home *overnight* and not *do the right thing.*"

"Right thing?" Grace forgot about Mark as she saw Daniel's Adam's apple bob up and down as he gulped.

Grace waited for the floor to swallow her up. If God really loved her, He'd just strike her dead right this minute. Then she thought of Parrish. If he found her married, would that negate any legal claim he had on her as her adoptive father?

Grace looked from Daniel Reeves and his multitude of sons to her future if Parrish caught up with her, something it now seemed inevitable he'd do.

Daniel or Parrish or death. Those were her only choices.

"Grace!" Parson Roscoe's voice interrupted her panic.

"I'm thinking!" Weighing her options carefully, she prayed, *C'mon, God. Death. I'm ready.*

The parson could be formidable without half trying. Grace saw that he was trying like the dickens right now.

In a voice that seemed to promise eternal flames, he said to Daniel, "Yes, the right thing. We'll get on with this. Call it an elopement if you will, and no one will have to know what exactly went on here last night."

"Miss Calhoun's reputation will be spared." Mrs. Roscoe scooted closer to Daniel. She laid a comforting hand on his shoulder and pleaded. "Otherwise she's ruined, Daniel. You knew that when you brought her here."

Grace wondered what the parson and his wife were imagining happened in the tiny cave with five children as chaperones. She felt her cheeks heating up as she considered what might be going on in their minds. Although truly she didn't have a clue what might be going on in their minds, because she had no idea what went on between a man and a woman.

"Well, Daniel, will you do the right thing by this young lady?" the parson asked in a hard voice. "Answer now, in front of God, your pastor, and your children. Think well before you speak."

Daniel looked at the parson. He looked at his boys. Grace saw him look at the stone roof only a couple of inches over his head. Then he looked at her. It was the look of a wild animal caught in a trap. He appeared for all the world to be considering the pros and cons of gnawing off his foot.

He turned back to the parson. "Nothing improper went on here last night."

"I won't hear another word," the parson thundered. "She's ruined, and well you know it."

"I don't mind being ruined," Grace said. "Surely it's better than being stuck with him!"

The parson turned his eyes on her, and Grace remembered his roaring sermons, all aimed straight at her. She was suddenly afraid to go to church on Sunday. And as soon as she spoke, she realized she *did* mind being ruined. She'd lived close to disaster for a long time, but she'd always clung to the highest level of respectability. With her background, it was terribly important to her.

The parson looked away from Grace, having silenced her. Grace took just a split second out of this living nightmare to envy the parson that glare and wish she could look at her students like that. Of course, she didn't have any students. She'd been fired, thanks to the King of the Rats, here.

"Daniel Reeves, don't make me ashamed of you." The parson gripped his big black Bible in both hands as if he needed to physically hang on to his faith in the face of this indignity. "You will stand side by side and make right this grievous wrong you've perpetrated on this innocent maiden."

"What's *per potato,* Pa?" John tugged on Daniel's sleeve. "Does the parson want to stay for breakfast? I'm hungry, and I'll be glad to start cooking if you —"

"As long as Pa brung us a ma for one night, don't it seem like she oughta do the cookin'?" Luke asked. "It's the least she could do after she and Pa shared the blankets overnight."

"That's *perpetrated,* idiot." Abe shoved John into Mark. "It's like Methodist and Baptist and Perpetyrians."

"What's an innocent maiden?" Luke asked.

Daniel jerked his thumb at Grace, in a gesture Grace found shockingly rude. "It's her."

The parson narrowed his blazing eyes. "Until last night."

"I been around her long enough to know she's not innocent at all," Mark said. "Why, she's a cranky old —"

"Answer me right now, Daniel!" The parson glowered.

Daniel looked at her again.

Grace looked back.

Mrs. Roscoe cleared her throat. "There is no decision to be made here. Begin the service at once, Irving."

"Do you, Daniel, take this woman —"

"Now just hang on a minute there, Parson." Daniel talked over the top of the parson, holding up both hands, his palms flat in front of him as if trying to calm a nervous horse.

Grace quit listening to the parson as she considered what seemed to be going on in this cave this morning. Forget nervous horse: Try runaway train. This situation was definitely out of control, and Daniel's flat hands didn't have a chance of stopping anything.

She leaned forward to stare at the boys. "You're confusing *perpetrated* with *Presbyterian,* Abe." Grace believed in teaching, and none of the boys had been more stiff-necked about learning than Abe. If she taught this boy one word, she'd call her entire life a success, because he seemed stubbornly averse to learning of any kind. "*Perpetrated* means —"

"Daniel Reeves, speak!"

Grace pulled her attention away from Abe. Daniel was staring at her, his eyes so wide Grace would swear the man had seen a ghost.

Daniel shook his head.

The parson started yelling again. He seemed prepared to call down lightning on all of them if Daniel didn't speak, and now.

"I don't even know how I got here." Grace flung her arms wide, narrowly missing backhanding Daniel in the face.

"I do." Daniel grabbed her hand to protect himself. "It's like this. I needed supplies. . . ."

Grace almost smiled. Finally, she'd hear the whole story.

"About time." The parson turned his fire-and-brimstone eyes on Grace and scared her into paying attention.

"No, I didn't mean —" Daniel dropped

her hand as if it had sprouted cactus bristles.

"Silence, Daniel."

Grace ran that tone of voice quickly through her head. She had to practice. How she'd love to be the proud owner of a tone of voice that could silence Daniel Reeves.

"Do you, Grace, take Daniel —"

Mark shoved between his father and the parson. "We told you we aren't keepin' her for our ma." Mark appeared to be the only one in the room with no fear of Parson Roscoe's close ties with the heavenly Father. He turned on Grace. "You want out of here as bad as we want you out of here, don't you?"

Grace nodded frantically. "I do."

"Hallelujah!" The parson raised his hands to heaven, reciting a blessing that Grace couldn't quite understand because she was too afraid to take her eyes off of Mark.

"I now pronounce you . . ."

Mrs. Roscoe threw herself, weeping, into Grace's arms, whispering something. Grace could only make out "Congratulations."

"What?" Grace turned back to the parson.

But what was there in this mess to be congratulated for?

The parson finished with a prayer that nearly shook the solid rock cave; then he tipped his hat. "I'll expect you all to be sitting in church together when I announce your good news."

Grace thought immediately of Parrish. He would hang around Mosqueros, trying to pick up her trail. "No —"

"Yes," the parson retorted. "You will be there. You'll accept everyone's congratulations and put this episode behind you decently and in order."

"Congratulations for what?" Grace then realized the parson and his wife could give her a ride back to town. Then she thought of Parrish.

Mrs. Roscoe clutched Grace's hand. "I've always had a feeling about you two. That's why, when you were missing, I insisted Irving and I be the ones to come out here and check."

"You've had a feeling about Mr. Reeves and me?" Grace had a feeling, too, every time she'd spoken to the man. Quite a few feelings, honestly: contempt, fury, disgust.

The parson, who Grace had always liked, and his wife, who seemed like such a sweet-natured woman in the normal course of things, swept out of the cave home. The door slammed shut on the seven of them.

"But I need a ride back to town," Grace called after them.

"You're not getting a ride back to town,

woman. You're married!" Daniel might as well have been a cougar trapped in this cave with her. She'd have felt no safer.

"I'm what?" Deafening silence followed her question. She thought of what had just happened. She'd heard no such talk of marriage. Had she?

"She's what?" Abe and Ike asked together.

Mark shoved himself to the front of the pack of boys. "To who?"

Grace looked at Daniel, and it hit her like that imaginary runaway train Daniel had tried to stop. She was the mother of five — including two ten-year-olds. And she was only seventeen.

She'd be in all the medical textbooks if word got out.

"I can run after the parson and catch him," John offered with frantic eagerness.

"There's no need, boys." Daniel's shoulders slumped as if all five boys had just jumped on his back.

"Why didn't the parson give her a ride back to town, Pa?" Luke asked.

All the boys turned to their father with curious expressions.

In a voice so tired Grace would have felt sorry for him if she hadn't had her hands full feeling sorry for herself, Daniel said, "Because I brung her home to be your ma."

Grace sank onto the floor and pulled all six blankets over her head.

"Irving, I'm ashamed of you." Isabelle Roscoe folded her hands over her ample middle and tried to look severe.

Her husband started laughing. "You played right along, Belle. Now don't try and deny it."

"We could have taken that poor girl home and no one would have been the wiser."

"Something needed to be done." Irving chirruped to the horses, unable to feel any remorse. "Miss Calhoun had nowhere to go, and the good Lord knows Daniel Reeves needed a mother for those poor children."

"Yes, something did need to be done. But I'm not sure forcing them to get married, right there on the spot, was for the best. That sweet girl could have lived with us for a while until she found another job."

"Yes, she could have. But why, when this solution is so obvious? Anyway, it was necessary. They'd been together for a full night. Nothing else would have suited the situation."

"Alone with five boys? Nothing sinful happened in that awful cave, or everyone would have known it. Those two don't get along, Irving." Isabelle shook her head; then a grin escaped.

Irving chuckled. "You're the one who said you'd always had a feeling about those two. Where'd you come up with that?"

"Well, I did have a feeling she'd left town with him. I just figured things had finally come to a shoot-out and we'd find Daniel's body somewhere along the trail."

When they stopped laughing, Irving clucked to his horses. "They're not going to have an easy time of it."

She waved away his worry. "What newly-weds ever have an easy time of it?"

Irving nodded. "Well said, Belle." They eased through the gap, out of the canyon, their team already wading through knee-deep snow. "This trail is going to fill. They'll be stuck in there together awhile. That'll help them sort things out. What do you suppose possessed Daniel to build in here anyway?"

Isabelle shrugged. "I've heard talk in town that no one knew this canyon existed until Daniel turned up living in it. Look at this narrow entrance. Why, I wouldn't be surprised if this canyon closes up so tight they'll be locked in here solid until spring."

"They'll be settled in by then. Maybe we'll have a baby to baptize before they get snowed in next winter. It'll all work out fine." The two exchanged a fond, if conspiratorial, look as the horses plodded toward home through the narrow gap, snow drifting heavily down on their heads.

SEVEN

Adam staggered against the wind howling through the mouth of Sawyer Canyon. He clung to his Stetson, his belly protesting his hunger. He'd been out all night and most of the day searching for Grace Calhoun. The sun had long since dipped behind the rugged hills, although a dusky light made it so he could still see. The cold wind blew all day, but only in the bottleneck of this canyon had it grown teeth.

Remembering Judd Mason and the standoff at this canyon that had almost gotten Sophie killed, he prayed again for forgiveness of his sinful heart, knowing God had saved him from hate during that dark time.

He caught the reins of his horse and turned his roan toward home, knowing he had to go in and get some rest before he collapsed.

Where is she, God? Where did the schoolmarm get to?

Crackling brush had him wheeling his horse toward the rugged incline that guarded the canyon, his eyes narrowing on an area strewn with rock and scrub mesquite.

He pulled his Winchester and jacked in a shell. With a cluck of his tongue, he urged his roan forward. He saw nothing, but he wasn't a man to dismiss an out-of-place sound. Could the schoolmarm be hiding from him? Why would she do such a thing?

He considered firing a shot to summon Clay, but the hands had fanned out wide, and it'd be a distance for Clay to travel. Anyway, as a black man who'd lived free all his life, and now ran his own Texas ranch, he'd learned to saddle his own broncs. If he really needed help, there most likely wasn't time for it to get here.

"Miss Calhoun, you in there? I'm here to help. No harm will come to you."

He heard a tiny squeak of fear that was human for sure. If she really was out here with no coat or shoes, she might be beyond responding. He swung down off his horse and inched forward in the gathering dusk. The bushes rustled just enough for him to know he was on the right track.

He reached for the winter-killed branches of the waist-high scrub and pushed it aside.

He looked into a woman's wide brown eyes so awash with terror they made his heart clutch. Then she screamed and leaped for his throat.

Daniel wondered if he hadn't ought to drag Grace out of there.

He'd fed the boys breakfast. They had beefsteak and eggs and potatoes and biscuits and milk. They'd gone out and fed the horses, milked the cows, gathered the eggs, and checked the herd. Grace had stayed under the blanket.

He'd made dinner, beefsteak and eggs and potatoes and biscuits and milk. And Grace stayed under the blanket.

He would have asked her to join them, except he couldn't get his throat to work. Not when it came to the woman huddled in the corner of his house.

They went back to work in the blowing snow, dragging windfall trees closer to the house to cut up for firewood. They took an ax to the ice that had backed up behind his spreader dam and threatened to overflow. They tracked down a cow that had calved out of season and took the pair into the barn, hoping the little one would survive the winter weather.

Daniel's boys toiled alongside him, doing

good work the way he'd trained them. And getting tired for bedtime, he hoped.

A heavy snow became blinding by mid-afternoon. The wind picked up, and as night came, the snow fell more heavily, and Daniel thought they might be looking at a blizzard. This far south?

The gap they drove through to get to these highlands might close them in tight, but surely these harsh conditions wouldn't last. He'd heard Texas winters just weren't that cold. At any rate, Daniel had supplies. He didn't need to go running to town every time he turned around.

He set the beefsteak and eggs and potatoes and biscuits and milk on the table for supper. And Grace stayed under the blanket.

"Well, so far she ain't no trouble." Ike held on his lap the cat he'd brought home from school. Daniel knew Ike wouldn't sneak the cat so much as a bite of steak. A cat needed to catch his own supper.

"Nope." Mark looked at the pile of blankets. "No help, but no trouble."

"Do we have'ta sleep without blankets again tonight, Pa?" John asked. "Is that what havin' a ma means? No blankets?"

Daniel sighed all the way to the soles of his feet. With a dejected shrug of his shoulders, he said, "So far."

"Maybe she's dead under there." Abe stared at the unmoving lump.

Daniel had lived twenty-eight years in a hard land. He'd worked for everything he'd ever gotten. None of it came by luck. So he figured he wasn't going to get lucky now. "Reckon she's alive."

"Well, I want my blanket back." Mark got up from the table and turned to his new ma.

Daniel braced himself to see her. He could almost stand her if she'd just stay under there.

Ike grabbed Mark and held him back with wide-eyed fear. "Don't touch her."

Mark jerked his arm away. "I'll touch her if'n I wanta touch her. She's my ma. I get to touch my own ma."

"But what if she starts talking and fussing like she does at school?" Luke said. "We're better off with her under there."

Grace pushed the blanket off of her head. Daniel could see that she'd been asleep most of the time. Or the shock had knocked her insensible, maybe.

"You can have your blanket, Mark." Grace pushed all the blankets away then looked down at herself, saw that blasted nightgown, and pulled them all back. Daniel had the feeling he could have somehow saved himself from getting stuck with her if she hadn't been wearing that nightgown.

"What in the world were you doing in my wagon wearing a nightgown anyway, Grace?"

"That's *Miss Calhoun,* Mr. Reeves." She pulled her knees up to her chest and wrapped her arms around them.

Daniel thought if she stayed that way and never ate, she wouldn't be much trouble. But he'd been married. He knew women were *always* trouble.

"No, Grace, it's *not* 'Miss Calhoun.' " Daniel had heard her say those words many times. They'd always set his teeth on edge. "It's *Mrs.* Reeves." Daniel added with angry triumph, "And guess what? I'm calling you Grace and the boys are calling you Ma."

Daniel pushed back his chair, and all the boys stood from the two benches that lined the sides of the table. Abe and Ike were on one side; Mark, Luke, and John on the other.

"And I'm the head of this house. Someone as proper as you should know that's the God-given way to run a family. And the first order I'm giving is for you to tell me *what you were doing in the back of my wagon.*"

Grace clenched her jaw and pursed her lips. Her hair flew around, as wild as a litter

98

of wolf pups. She jammed her fingers into it, making it even worse. Her eyes looked swollen from sleep.

So she'd been sleeping all day while he and his sons worked their fingers to the bone. He wanted to cut her down to size. He wanted to blast her for mucking up his life. He wanted to shake her until she wasn't his wife anymore, and she wasn't here in his home with her cool manners, and her snooty nose wasn't in the air, and her yammering mouth never again criticized his boys.

A tear ran down her cheek.

Daniel froze. He'd forgotten about crying. The boys all inhaled sharply and took a step back.

"What's'a matter with her, Pa?" John hugged up against his leg and whispered, even though Grace was only three steps away and could hear every word.

The cave was a single room, roughly ten feet by ten feet. *Everything* was just three steps away.

"I'll tell you what I was doing in your wagon, Mr . . ." Grace lapsed into silence. She dropped her head onto her knees and clutched the top of her skull with both hands. Her shoulders shuddered violently. He heard her breathing become rough and unsteady. Crying.

Daniel had to fight the urge to give her the house and the herd. He'd take the boys and make a run for the border. He wondered if Mrs. Roscoe ever cried. Surely the parson would understand.

He and his boys stood absolutely immobilized.

The wind moaned around the house, and Daniel wondered if he'd have to dig them out in the morning. They lived on fairly high ground. They got a beauty of a snowstorm once in a while, he'd heard. A blizzard might cut them off from civilization for a spell, if Mosqueros could be called civilized.

Then he realized there was no way they were going to get to church in the morning. Daniel liked church. He did. But once he showed up with Miss Calhoun in town, his marriage was a done deal.

And that's when he realized he was still trying to think of a way out of this. But Daniel Reeves was no fool. He could dream all he wanted. He was tied to this woman.

John whispered again, "Is she supposed to get all sad like that, Pa?"

"Yep, in my experience with wives, they're supposed to fuss about something all the time. I've never had me one that didn't cry up a storm at the drop of a hat."

Grace lifted her head and scowled through her tears.

Daniel was surprised at his urge to laugh. She really was a mess. The oh-so-tidy Miss Calhoun kept getting herself slopped up more and more. He wondered when she'd gather her wits together enough to care about that.

"Did it ever occur to you that you might be doing things to your wives that make them cry?" She pushed her hair off her soggy face with shaky hands.

"Nope." Daniel shrugged. "Never was nothing I did."

"Is she gonna cry all the time, then, Pa?" Abe edged closer. " 'Cause if'n she does it *all* the time, then I reckon it don't mean nothing. Reckon girls just leak."

Grace gave Abe a dark look, then lifted a blanket and handed it to him.

He snatched it and dropped onto the floor and wrapped up.

One by one the boys all got a blanket. And then the boys spread out along with the blankets, except the one wrapped around Grace and that blasted nightgown.

Daniel was looking at a long, cold winter.

He turned his back on her and lay down as far from her as the room would allow. They only missed touching by inches.

She tapped his shoulder, and knowing he'd regret it, he turned around. "What?"

"I'll tell you what I was doing in the wagon, but I wanted to tell you privately. That's why I waited until the boys were asleep."

Daniel felt all the boys' ears perk up. They were all playing possum. Not a one of them was asleep. Daniel decided right there and then that he'd wait until a very private moment to hear Grace's story.

It suddenly occurred to him that Grace might have been up to no good. Maybe, just maybe, she was *already* ruined and not the proper young lady she'd led the town to believe.

And Daniel knew what ruined meant. Babies. His stomach clenched as he thought about having another child. The first two had almost killed Margaret, and the last three *had* killed her.

She'd begged him to have another child. He'd absolutely refused. But his wife had done her best to tempt him, and he'd been weak. His weakness had killed his wife. And now he might have another wife with a child, and through no doing of his own. He'd vowed to God there'd be no more Reeves babies to come in packs and finish off some poor woman.

Daniel sat up and leaned as close to her as he could. Her eyes got wide, and he wondered what in tarnation she was thinking. He whispered into her ear, "The boys are still up. We'll talk another time."

He pulled back, and she nodded. Her hair bobbed and swayed like a tumbleweed blown along before the wind. Surprised by the little corkscrew curls, he couldn't resist the temptation to push a couple of them away from her eyes. She'd always had her hair pulled neatly back. Unable to stop himself, he touched her curls again, just to test their softness. Then he looked at her for a long time. The tears had etched their way down her face. Her eyes were swollen almost shut. Red veins traced their way across the whites of her eyes, and the strange sparkling golden color, an exact match for her hair, was shining with tears. She hadn't been sleeping all day. She'd been crying.

But crying because of a mix-up that had left her married to a man she didn't want? Or crying because she was ruined and in despair over how to explain a baby that came too soon? The bruise on her face had darkened to purple. Had she told some man the bad news and he'd laid his hands on her? Was that why she'd run?

There was one question he knew would haunt him if he kept it inside. "Just tell me one thing."

Her puffy eyes widened a bit at his severe tone. She nodded and silently waited, acting like an obedient wife should.

"Is there a baby?"

Her eyes went blank, as if he'd spoken the question in Apache.

"A baby," he repeated, "on the way. Is that why you hid out in my wagon? To trap me?"

She gasped.

Daniel heard the boys gasp, too, though he doubted they knew what he was really asking. She knew all right, because she unwound from the little ball she'd curled herself into and slapped him hard across the face.

The boys all jumped, but they stayed under cover.

Smart boys.

She packed quite a wallop for a little thing. His face burned. His temper rose.

Her chin began to quiver. The sparkle in her eyes blazed into fire. She pulled her hand back to paste him again.

He caught her hand with a smart slap of flesh on flesh, surprised at how furious he was. He should have been sorry. He should have been begging her pardon for asking such a thing. But he wasn't. And her anger might be over getting caught rather than being insulted.

"Sorry, Mrs. Reeves, but that's no answer." The sting on his cheek came out in his voice.

She jerked against his grip.

He held fast.

She raised her other hand — this one clenched in a fist — and he caught that, too.

He leaned close. "You are well and truly trapped, *Mrs. Reeves.* Just like I am."

Daniel tried to think of the men in Mosqueros. His stomach twisted to think of such a thing passing between this proper young lady and one of the rough-and-ready types who lived around here. There were decent men, of course, but none of them would have dishonored her.

Maybe he was wrong about her problem, but there was something here, something behind her eyes. She was definitely hiding something. What else could it be? Why else hide in his wagon? What else couldn't she say in front of his boys?

"We'll talk when we can have a private moment." He let her arms go and lay down with his back to her, cold, blanketless, and looking likely to stay that way for the rest of his life.

Let her pound on him all she wanted. He felt only contempt for this ruined woman. By dragging him into this mess, she'd ruined them both.

She didn't attack. He didn't know what she did. He ignored her and looked at the tense shoulders of his wide-awake boys. He loved them fiercely. He was so proud of them he'd like to burst when he thought of how fine they'd turned out, raised only by him.

She'd ruined them, too, and *that* was something he couldn't forgive.

EIGHT

Adam fell backward more from surprise than from the impact. He landed flat on his back, and the woman shrieked and scrambled forward as if she'd try to flee. He tried to regain his feet and grab her, and then something hard swatted him in the face. He fell flat again, and a boot caught him in the chin.

Adam grabbed at the worn dark leather encasing her wildly swinging foot, got smacked in the hand by what felt like iron, then noticed her ankle wore a shackle, and blood dripped from around the metal binding. He let go, not wanting to deepen her scrapes. Blood glistened against skin nearly as black as his.

A black woman. His heart clutched; he hadn't seen a black woman in years.

In the dark night, he only knew it was blood because of the damp sheen glistening in the sliver of moon peeking out of the scuttling clouds. And there was the smell of blood to confirm his suspicion. She was hurt, the poor, helpless little thing.

She sprang backward, screaming so loudly his ears hurt, and something hard and fast-moving whizzed past his face and caught him on the shoulder.

"Ow!" He stumbled to his feet. "Miss, please. I won't hurt —"

"No!" She slammed the heel of her hand into his nose.

He hit the ground again, and blood splattered down the front of his buckskin coat. He'd have just left her alone, except her arms were bare, and she trembled visibly from the cold. He had to help her. He advanced on her, trying to trap her flailing hands without doing any injury. Finally, he gained a firm grasp on one arm.

"Let me go, please!"

A dull clink of metal on metal pulled his attention to the fetter that dragged several links of chain. Chain she'd used as a weapon.

She wrenched against his hold like a wild animal.

To Adam, it appeared her fear had a grip on her mind and she wasn't capable of hearing.

She twisted frantically. "Leave me alone.

Let go. Please don't hurt me." Her terror was punctuated by thin, high-pitched cries of pain.

Adam knew he was bruising her. Then he saw more bruises. Even in the dark he could identify them against her mahogany skin. Old bruises, yellow and purple. Not the kind of bruises a person got in an accident. She'd been beaten. Equal parts compassion and fury nearly overwhelmed him. The one thing he couldn't do was add to her injuries. His heart thudding, he released her, not sure what he'd do if she ran — because he couldn't let her go.

He stepped away, his hands in the air. "I won't hurt you. I'm not restraining you."

"Don't make me go back." Stumbling over a mesquite bush, she flattened her back against the wall of rock behind her. She buried her face in her hands and began to weep, sinking to her knees.

She wore a drab brown dress hanging in tatters and button-up boots, her toes visible through holes. With her head bowed low, he could see her long, tight curls, tangled with sticks from the bushes.

"I can't leave you out here, ma'am. You're freezing. Let me take you to the ranch."

"No!" She looked up. Tears cut through dust on her face. She staggered to her feet.

"Just ride on. If you really want to help, just leave. I'll die before I go with you."

Regret, deep as grief, cut through Adam's heart at her panic. She was beyond rational thought. He was going to have to force her to come along. Then he felt blood drip off his chin and swiped at his broken nose and *hoped* he could force her. He spoke as gently as he could, hoping he could penetrate her fright.

She cringed and dodged his attempt to urge her toward his horse.

"I'm sorry, ma'am. I won't hurt you, I promise. And I won't let anyone take you anywhere you don't want to go. But I can't leave you out here." Flinching to prepare for her next attack, he reached for her.

Instead of fighting, she sank to the ground, screaming as if he were driving a knife into her heart.

Adam swung her up into his arms. Her hopeless tears hurt him worse than the beating he'd just taken.

Grace lay awake, numb from staring sightlessly at his back. His back. Her husband's back. Daniel Reeves. Her husband.

She was going completely out of her mind. She was trapped. He'd used those very words. Trapped. Both of them. All of them.

She heard the wind and knew there'd be no church tomorrow. That was a blessing.

She cut off the thought. *No, forgive me, God. It's not a blessing that there's no church. It's just a blessing that . . .*

No, it was *not* a blessing that she was trapped in a house with six men, all of whom hated her. All of whom were completely out of control. Rude, sloppy, ignorant.

And here she lay married to the rudest, sloppiest, most ignorant one of the bunch.

So what did that make her? No well-mannered, tidy, brilliant choices had brought her to this place. That meant *she* got the prize as the most ignorant one of all. No contest.

Of course, if they couldn't get out, Parrish couldn't get in. She knew the man. *Tough* was not a word she'd use to describe him, and facing a Texas blizzard took all kinds of tough.

So she was safe and in the middle of a complete disaster at the same time. No wonder she couldn't sleep.

She finally noticed another reason or two she couldn't sleep. She started to cry when she thought of it. She needed to go to the outhouse. And she was starving. How could her body make such mundane demands of her at a time like this?

She didn't even know where the outhouse was. She didn't even have shoes. She had to wake Daniel. She had to ask him for help and take the first step to being a functioning human being in this household. She wasn't going to be able to stay curled up in her ball forever. That was the only plan she'd come up with today.

Her body wouldn't let her ignore its discomfort anymore. Her arm fighting every inch-by-inch movement, she stretched out her hand and — shuddering all the way to the soles of her feet — touched her husband.

Daniel rolled over. His eyes were open, fully alert.

Grace thought of the sluggish way she woke up every morning and almost jumped at Daniel's reaction. Forcing the words past reluctant lips, she said, "I . . . That is, can you . . . Is there a . . . I need directions to the . . . the . . ." She was pretty sure it was too dark in the minuscule cave for him to see her cheeks go flaming red.

Daniel must've been used to the question. Of course he would be. The father of five would know about nature calls in the night. "I'll get the lantern and go with you."

"No, just directions, and . . . a . . . a coat."

"The snow's too deep for you to go alone."

Daniel didn't discuss it or try to change her mind. He got up, lit the lantern with a piece of bark he touched to the fire in the stove's belly, and pulled on his shoes.

He glanced at her. "You're about the size of a ten-year-old boy, I'd say." He rustled around in a pile of clothes by the door and tossed her a shirt, a pair of boots, and —

"I can't wear a pair of pants."

Daniel's eyes narrowed in the lantern light. He said with grim humor, "Wade through the snow barefoot in your night-gown for all I care." He turned his back to give her privacy.

Grace wanted to start crying again. She thought of the years with Parrish, and the recollection steadied her. She'd survived that. She could survive anything.

She turned her back on Daniel and slipped on the clothes. She pulled the pants on under her nightgown. They were too short, but they buttoned comfortably on her waist. The boots fit perfectly. She *was* the size of a ten-year-old boy. She just pulled the shirt on over her nightgown, unwilling to undress further in front of Daniel. She tied the boots, and he handed her a heavy coat, which she pulled on.

"Ready?"

She nodded.

He swung the door open the smallest slit possible, and they slipped through into the biting cold and driving snow.

When they got back, Grace was shivering all the way to her bones. The snow had come in over her boots, and sharp needles of ice had cut through her clothing to her skin.

She trembled as Daniel closed the door behind them. He hadn't asked her any questions outside, thank heavens. The weather was just too brutal for anything like that. But she was well aware that she'd just had her chance to explain things to Daniel and she'd passed it by.

She at least could have told him there was no baby. But she was still so insulted she couldn't bring herself to deny his charge. She was tempted to let him wait nine months and figure it out himself.

If they continued living like this, it might even be possible never to tell him. When would they ever have a moment alone? The thought cheered her considerably.

Now they were back with the boys, who surely had been awakened by the noise and the blast of cold air, though none of them moved.

"I would like a biscuit, please," she whispered. "I'm hungry."

"Suit yourself." Daniel lay down on the bare dirt floor.

Grace wanted to kick him, but what had she expected? That he'd serve her then stand at her elbow while she ate? She neither expected nor wanted that.

She grabbed the single remaining biscuit off the kitchen table. She had to move carefully because the boys' sprawled bodies covered the floor. How could they live like this?

She thought of Parrish and the conditions she'd lived in with him. She thought of the litany of work Daniel had ordered his children to do. Had she stumbled onto a family that ran much like hers? The boys were little monsters, but that didn't mean she was going to stand by and watch them be treated like slave labor.

She thought of Hannah and wondered if her sister was safe. Surely Parrish had focused all his rage on Grace. But without Grace's money, how long before Hannah and the children began to go hungry? And how long before timid, nurturing Hannah came up with one of her harebrained schemes to rescue her missing sister?

Grace knew she had to get a letter to Hannah as soon as possible so she wouldn't go crazy worrying. As the wind whistled outside the door, Grace knew it wouldn't be tomorrow.

Grace closed her eyes and prayed that God would tend to Hannah and the little ones. Grace knew it was a sin to ask. God cared for his children. He knew the number of hairs on Hannah's head. She was distrusting God when she didn't put her faith in His promises. But where was God when she and Hannah and all the others had been in Parrish's clutches all those years?

Distrust came easily.

She found a few inches of milk in the bottom of the pail. One tin cup sat in the center of the table next to the biscuit and the milk. She poured herself the milk, finished it and the biscuit, and went back to bed. She rolled up tightly in the coarse woolen blanket. She should share it with Daniel, she knew.

Instead, she ignored him. And comfortable, fed, and warm, she found herself once again staring at Daniel's back. Her husband's back. Daniel Reeves. Her husband.

She fell asleep before she could start crying again.

"My name is Adam."

The words pulled Tillie awake.

"I'm taking you home with me."

A black man held her. She hadn't seen a

black man in years, not since the war was over. And Master Virgil had kept only Tillie as a slave long after all the other slaves had been freed by law. Of course, she hadn't known the war was over and the slaves had been freed until just recently.

"No one will hurt you at home."

No black man would send her back to that nightmare, would he?

"You're too cold. You have to get warmed up. I can't leave you here."

She felt the world shift steadily along and realized she was on horseback, held by a man — a black man — with arms like iron bands. Those arms tightened in a way that told Tillie he knew she had roused. She looked up into the full dark. Barely able to see his face shrouded by the brim of his hat, she tested his grip and found no escape.

Black eyes gleamed in the night. He watched her. She could tell even with his face in shadows darkened by his ebony skin.

Panic soared in her stomach like a flock of frightened birds. If only the wings were real and could carry her away.

Maybe if she convinced him she was all right, he'd let her go. She stiffened her spine and forced herself to speak calmly. "Thank you for helping me. I was frightened at first. That's why I fought you. I apologize for hurting you."

"I'm fine. You didn't hurt me."

"Your nose is bleeding, and one eye is swollen shut. I'm sorry. I don't know my own strength sometimes."

He tilted his head so the moonlight revealed his astonished expression. "You'd have never touched me if I hadn't been so careful not to hurt you."

Tillie controlled her expression, though a soft sniff of disdain might have escaped. Still, he wouldn't have noticed it. She hoped. "Well, for whatever reason you *let* me hit you, I do apologize. Now, I really need to be on my way. Please let me down, sir."

The man — Adam — didn't even slow his horse. "It's Adam, not sir. And I'm not letting you walk away from me in the snow and cold. I'm taking you somewhere safe. My boss's wife and daughters will see to your injuries. We will protect you from whoever hurt you. I promise."

"I don't need protection. I can take care of myself. And no one hurt me."

"Uh . . . so that metal cuff on your ankle is . . . jewelry of some sort?"

She'd forgotten about that horrid binding. She couldn't get it off no matter what she tried. It made her explanations sound weak.

She looked up at Adam. His voice and the strength of his arms could be a sanctuary, but trust was foreign to her.

A horse snorted, and she realized she was being carried along on its back at a ground-eating pace. The animal's feet crunched on the snow, its bridle jingling when it tossed its head, white breath whooshing out of its nose as it hurried along.

She became aware of a coarse blanket surrounding her. She wasn't so cold anymore. She'd been cold for so long that this blanket qualified as luxury.

"The McClellen place is just ahead, miss. You'll be safe and warm there. We'll tend your wounds, get you a hot meal and some warm clothes, and give you a soft bed for the night."

It sounded like heaven, back when she believed there was such a place. What choice did she have anyway? Since her escape attempt had turned to this disaster, she hadn't eaten, hadn't slept, hadn't been warm for days and days.

"What's your name?"

The chain on her ankle clinked, an eternal reminder of where she'd been, what she'd left, what awaited her if she was taken back.

"I won't tell you."

He made a sound, soothing, maybe prayerful. One strong hand held the reins while the other supported her back and gently caressed her shoulder as if she were a fretful child. But he was a fool if he prayed to a God who had forgotten one of His children. A God she'd believed in for so long, only to be betrayed. The knowledge that all of her years and years of prayer had been whispered into nothingness — because no God could have heard her prayers and left her with that madman — was worse than finding out the war had been over for years. It had nearly destroyed her.

Adam suddenly pulled his horse to a stop. "We're here. You'll be fine. I'll carry you into the house."

Tillie had vowed when she ran from Virgil that never again would someone tell her where to go and what to do. That vow had lasted less than a week, because now Adam was taking charge of her life. But not for long.

"Clay, get over here and take my horse!" Adam swung down to the ground with her still in his arms, his gentleness in vivid contrast to the brutality of Virgil.

His last beating had come with words that cut her to the heart. Virgil had sneered at her that there'd been a war. The slaves had been freed. But not her, never her.

She looked away from Adam to see a cabin, tiny compared to where she'd lived, but neat, with smoke pouring out of the chimney and lights glowing in each window. She saw a looming barn to her right. Wooden corral fences stretched away from the barn, and in the moonlight she saw grazing horses and other outbuildings.

A man strode toward them from the barn and caught the horse's reins.

Adam immediately started for the house as if he was afraid she didn't have much time.

"I heard they found the schoolmarm eloped with Daniel Reeves," the man called after them. "Did you catch up with Mrs. Reeves making a break from Reeves Canyon?"

"No, it's someone else. She's hurt. Sophie, open up." Adam strode along, taking her somewhere against her will.

Her whole life had been lived against her will. "I can walk."

Adam smiled down at her as his spurs clanked. "I've got your feet all wrapped tight. I'll put you down when we get out of the snow." He climbed a few steps to a porch, and a door opened and swung wide.

"What happened?" A very pregnant blond woman stepped back to let Adam in.

He entered the house as an equal, not submissively.

Tillie looked away from the woman by reflex. She'd learned well not to look a white man or woman straight in the eye.

Children filled the room. A bevy of little girls came up to Adam, trying to take a peek. Tillie turned her head so they could see her and felt the fear ease. The pretty smiles, bright lantern light, and warm home were so different from where she'd been.

"Bring her into the back room, Adam. It's the warmest. Mandy and Beth can share a bed tonight."

"I don't want to share a bed with her! She kicks!" the oldest girl screeched.

There hadn't been children in Master Virgil's house. She stopped herself. No, she wouldn't think of him as "master." But the name was branded into her mind.

The girls bickered, full of life and energy and courage, as Adam laid her on a feather bed. The chain on her ankle clinked against the wooden frame.

"What in the world is that?" Sophie reached for the chain, then stopped and looked sharply at Adam. "What's going on here?"

Adam would drop his gaze now. He'd back down and start saying, "Yes'm," and

"No, ma'am," in the face of the lady's upset.

Adam didn't blink. Instead, he actually glared at the lady. "I don't know. But it's coming off." He wheeled and headed out of the room.

"Wait. Her ankle is cut up from this thing." The lady — Sophie — looked at Tillie. "What happened to you? Adam, go for the sheriff. He can be out here in an hour. They can arrest —"

"No!" Tillie hadn't meant to shout, and she had to fight not to cringe. But her cringing days were over. "Please, don't call the sheriff. Please."

A tense silence stretched out. Sophie stood with her hands on her hips, obviously unsettled. Adam was holding on to the doorknob, looking eager to go for the law. Tillie was hoping, even praying, until she caught herself and stopped, that they'd let it drop.

Adam stepped back to the bedside. "Whoever did this broke the law. The days of chaining up another human being are gone." Adam's jaw clenched until Tillie wondered if he'd grind his teeth down.

Sophie patted Adam's arm and spoke quietly. "Get the tools and tell Clay to quit fighting with the girls and get in here to help. While you're finding the tools, I'll talk to her."

"Thanks, Sophie."

Tillie's mind almost couldn't wrap around the way the white woman touched Adam without landing a blow or issuing a harsh command. And Adam's response was even more astonishing. Respectfully, he'd backed off, but there was no bowing or scraping.

His eyes met Tillie's, and a thousand questions wanted to rush from her lips. Who was he? How had he found this life? Was he truly considered an equal by these people?

The girls screamed in the background, and a man who must be Clay hollered at them to be quiet. It sounded like the same man who'd taken Adam's horse, almost as if Clay served Adam. Except the girls were calling him Pa and they'd called Sophie Ma, so this must be their home and their family with Adam as a guest.

The fighting changed to giggling.

Sophie sat on the side of the bed and looked up at Adam. "Ask Clay to bring in some of the stew for her. It's still warm. Then go eat a bowl yourself. You've been out all day. It'll be a few minutes before I'm ready to have you work on the shackle."

Adam nodded then looked at Tillie. "I'll be right in the next room if you need me.

Sophie won't hurt you. Promise me you won't try and run away again."

Tillie hesitated, but Adam looked as if he wasn't going to leave unless she gave her word.

Sophie looked at Adam, and her eyes narrowed. "What happened to you?"

Adam jabbed a finger at Tillie. "She fought me when I found her."

Sophie looked back at Tillie, her eyes wide with amusement. "You really gave him a pounding. Good girl."

"Hey!" Adam's chin came up, and his eyes blazed bright as if his very manhood had been questioned. "I was being careful. I just didn't want to hurt her, so I didn't defend myself."

Sophie laughed then took Tillie's hand. "You're my kind of woman."

Tillie felt a spurt of amusement that shocked her. She couldn't remember the last time she'd been tempted to smile.

Adam snorted. "I'll get the soup. But watch her like a hawk, Sophie. She doesn't seem to have the sense to realize she can't go walking in the middle of a Texas snowstorm with no food and no horse and no coat."

Sophie waved her hand at Adam. "Shoo! She needs to eat, and you do, too. Get her some stew; then get something in your own stomach."

NINE

A foot landed in Grace's stomach.

Her eyes flew open as her . . . son? — Mark — tripped and landed smack on top of her.

If she could have breathed, she'd have breathed a prayer of thanks. There were bigger feet than Mark's in this family. And she imagined it was only a matter of time until they all stomped on her one way or another.

"Hi, Ma!" Mark shouted like a banshee.

Why did this family say every word at the top of their lungs? He scrambled up off her, then tripped and toppled toward the red-hot stove. She lurched up to rescue him, but he managed to evade disaster at the last second.

Hollering all the while, he leaped toward Luke, who skidded to a stop and missed stepping on her by inches.

The front door — the only door — hung wide open. Snow gusted in, pushed by a wicked, moaning wind.

"One of you boys shut the door," she said in her teacher's voice. She recognized it plainly.

So did they. They ignored her just like always.

Luke dived at Mark's ankles. They crashed to the floor, slamming up against the cast iron legs of the stove, which weren't as hot as the belly, thank heavens. Luke pounded a huge fistful of snow into Mark's face as Mark howled loudly enough to bring down the rafters.

Grace looked up. They had no rafters.

Mark crawled and rolled until he could regain his feet. The shrieking and threatening never paused. The two of them disappeared out the door.

"I told you boys to close that door."

Grace had been about to say that, but Daniel saved her the trouble as he came in, dragging snow inside with every step. The boys ignored him, too. He set a bucket down. Grace could see it was brimming with milk. He yelled, "Breakfast in just a minute," out the door that was swung inward, hanging from leather hinges. Daniel shoved it shut across the frozen ground.

Grace had just a glimpse of the swirling white world outside. The snow was scraped back from the cave a few feet, and footprints had battered it down somewhat past that.

Grace heard the whoops and hollers of a thousand marauding Apaches outside.

"Those scamps." Daniel shook his head and laughed as he picked up his bucket and turned to the stove. He saw her and froze as surely as the cold winter world outside this gopher hole. "You're awake."

Grace didn't point out that he was stating the obvious. She started to push back her blanket and then clawed it back, remembering her nightgown. And that's when she realized she was dressed. Brown broadcloth pants — of all things — stuck out from under blue flannel. A heavy brown and white shirt buttoned down the front. She even had boots on.

She'd crawled back under her blanket last night without giving her attire a moment's notice. Now she noticed. She felt her skin burn with embarrassment as she saw the way the too-short pants hugged her ankles.

"You're going to wear those until I can get to town and buy you something else. And they're the only spare pants Abe has, so you'd better appreciate 'em," Daniel ordered.

"So you've taken up mind reading, then?" Grace snapped. She held tight, for one last

129

precious second, to any thought of modesty. It showed in the clinging grip of her hands on the blanket. She looked at her white knuckles sunk into the coarse gray deer hide; then, sick with humiliation, she thrust her cover aside.

She stood up, looked at the ridiculous sight of herself in a long nightgown, pants, and a shirt, and said, "I'll need you to step outside while I remove my nightgown."

Daniel glared at her. "I've got breakfast to get on. I'm not going anywhere. I'll look away for exactly one minute." He wheeled around. "Sixty, fifty-nine, fifty-eight . . ."

Grace opened her mouth to protest and just generally scold the man for his very existence.

"Fifty, forty-nine, forty-eight . . ."

He meant it. Grace whirled away from him and dragged the shirt off. She tore the nightgown off over her head and thrust her arms back into the shirtsleeves.

"Thirty-seven, thirty-six, thirty-five . . ."

Grace buttoned the shirt with scrambling fingers.

"Twenty-three, twenty-two, twenty-one . . ."

The pants were indecent. Tight all over. After a shaky moment of indecision, she left the shirttails hanging out in hopes of maintaining a shred of decency.

"Ten, nine, eight, seven . . ."

The shirt covered her nearly to her knees. It had to be Daniel's. She couldn't walk around dressed in a strange man's clothing. She couldn't. . . .

"Three, two, one." Daniel turned around and started plopping steaks directly on the cast-iron top of the stove.

Grace gasped, "I am horrified that you wouldn't give me a moment of privacy. It is completely inappropriate for you to —"

"D' ya know how to make biscuits?"

"Your manners leave me speechless. I cannot live in a place where —"

"Speechless ain't as quiet as it used to be, that's for sure. How about the biscuits, wife?"

Grace did *not* know how to make biscuits. She braced herself for the ridicule when she admitted it. "No, Mr. Reeves, I'm afraid I don't. . . ."

He didn't disappoint her. "So I got stuck with a wife who's so worthless she can't even make a biscuit. Looks like my luck is holding. You ever heard tell of a woman giving birth to *four* babies all to onest?"

"Four babies at once?" She didn't even try to keep the horror out of her voice.

"If it can happen to anyone, it'll most

131

likely happen to me. No need to concern yourself. We won't be risking young'uns, no way, nohow. Get over here and keep an eye out for these steaks. I'll mix up the biscuits."

Grace edged between the table and the stove.

Daniel thrust a fork her way and, without giving her so much as a look-see, slipped by her and went to a canister sitting by the front door. He began scooping out flour onto the table.

Grace looked away from him when a flame jumped up from inside the stove through a slit in the lid. It flared nearly to the ceiling. Grace screamed, jumped back, and dropped the fork.

Daniel placed both hands on her waist, shoved her none too gently aside, and sneered under his breath, "Consarned woman'll manage to burn down a house made'a rock and dirt."

He stooped to pick up the fork. The tines had stabbed into the packed dirt floor so that the fork stood straight up. Daniel plucked it off the floor, swiped it front and back on his pant leg, and expertly flipped seven steaks with fire dancing madly all around his arm. He turned, still not looking at her.

She jumped back to keep him from tripping over her.

He went to the door, flung it wide open, and roared, "Ike, get in here and help with breakfast." Daniel left the door open and went back to the table and his biscuits.

Finally, a job I can handle. Going to close the door, she leaned outward into a world that was pure white: ground, trees, mountains, air all around, and sky up above.

Ike jumped down — from on high apparently — and almost took her arm off. With a shout of raucous laughter, he stomped into the house, making a damp floor even worse.

His cat raced in on his heels. Had the cat, no longer the skinny animal Ike had rescued, come down from overhead, too? Grace didn't have the courage to ask. The unflappable cat, as wild as the Reeves boys, seemed content to live the rough-and-tumble life.

"I thought Ma was gonna do the cookin' now. Why in Sam Hill'd'ya git 'er if'n she weren't gonna do nothing? You done mighty poor by us, Pa."

Grace wanted to point out that it was rude to talk about people as if they weren't there. Honesty prevented her from actually denying Ike's words, though, because Daniel *had* done mighty poor by his boys when he'd gone and gotten himself married to her.

"Mind the steaks." Daniel's voice shook the room. He always seemed to talk at a near shout, except when he shouted, which was extremely loud, so Grace knew the difference.

Grace went back to the door just as all four boys still outside came flying down from above.

Mark first, then Abe, then Luke, with John right on his heels. Each landed on a snowdrift and rolled out of the way so the brother plummeting down next wouldn't crash-land on him.

The boys wallowed in the snow, kicking a drift back into Grace's face. She paused long enough to make sure they were all alive. Wrestling, pummeling each other with snowballs, shrieking through mouths full of snow, she judged them to have survived. Fine. They plunged from the sky and lived. She slammed the door.

Ike played in the fire behind her back. "Pa, why're we cooking? Why're we doin' women's work now that we've got us a woman? Pa, I wanna go back outside 'n' play. It don't snow much, an' this is our chance to . . ."

"Can you get over here, Grace, and pay attention?" Daniel didn't seem aware that

134

his son was talking to him.

And Ike didn't quit carping or insulting his new mother, even when his pa talked over top of him.

"You may not know a lick about cooking, but maybe we can learn you something. You just take five or six fistfuls of flour. Boys have appetites. . . ." Daniel threw flour around until the air in the cave turned as white as the world outside. "That jar there," — Daniel jerked his head at the floor in a direction so vague Grace wasn't sure if it was a lame effort at pointing or if he had a crick in his neck — "you put a glug or two of that . . ." Daniel quit throwing flour, grabbed up the milk pail, and glugged away, slopping some milk straight onto the pile of flour on the table.

"If she's not going to cook, what's'a use of her, Pa? She's just hogging up the blankets near as I can see."

The door slammed open, and John charged in. He hurled a snowball at Ike, then whirled and ran out, whooping and hollering every step of the way. Ike roared like a rebel charging down the slopes at Gettysburg and ran outside.

"Get back here!" Daniel kept mixing while he yelled.

Grace covered her ears against the pain of

Daniel's thunderous bellow, afraid for her hearing. The flour was now a lump of dough.

Daniel went back to talking in his normally deafening tone. He didn't seem to notice Ike was gone. Well, he noticed. He'd yelled loudly enough, but he didn't do anything when Ike ignored him.

Grace pulled the door shut again. She'd found her place in the family. Door-shutter. She'd be busy from morning till night.

Daniel set the bucket of milk aside. Had he said something about some unknown number of glugs again? Daniel went to the stove and flipped the steaks through the roaring flames. Then he quickly stacked an enormous mountain of meat and reached for the lump of dough. He tore off knots of the white goo and dropped them directly on the stovetop, beside the steaks. He flattened each with his hands, adding dough until the stovetop was covered.

Daniel flipped open the small stove, and with a long-handled ladle he'd snagged from behind the stove — Grace was fairly certain it had been on the floor — he fished around inside the roaring fire until he began pulling out blackened lumps that looked like coal. He tossed them on the table and they rolled, but none went onto the floor.

Grace decided whatever he was doing, he was an expert at it.

He clanked the stove door shut, used the fork to prod the biscuits around until he could turn them, shoved them to one side, pulled a bucket from under the table, and began cracking eggs onto the stovetop. When he had a dozen or so broken, he went to the door, pulled it open, and bellowed, "Breakfast!"

By the time the ringing in Grace's ears subsided, the boys came charging in, skidding through the wide-open door on the packed snow. Abe got there first and slammed into the table. The coal started rolling, and before Grace could react, Abe and Daniel caught the lumps and held them down, corralling them with their forearms. Ike came swooping in next. He careened into Abe, who shoved him. Ike nearly crashed into the stove.

"Watch the food, Ike. You're eating 'em whether you knock 'em on the floor or not." Daniel set the milk bucket in the center of the table.

John came next, with Luke right on his heels. The two of them knocked into the bench that sat alongside the table. With deep-throated laughter, they dived out of sight then popped up on the other side of

137

the table, clambering onto a bench and reaching for the coal.

Daniel whacked at their hands with his fork.

They ducked the slapping utensil, snagged the coal, and began chewing on it.

Mark came in last. "You better not've eaten my share."

Grace backed as far as she could from the earsplitting child. She pressed up against the wall and stayed there.

Daniel threw the fork at Abe.

Abe caught it in midair. He stabbed a steak from the top of the tower of meat and handed it to Mark. Mark took it off the fork with his bare hand and started gnawing on it as he rounded the table, making sure to stomp on Ike's toe. Mark got shoved toward the bench. He sat down next to his brothers.

Ike took the next steak for himself and started eating as he stomped to the bench seat directly across from his triplet brothers. Abe handed a steak to Luke and John. He was getting near the bottom of the pile. Abe forked the next one and threw it to his father, who caught it. Abe took one for himself then stopped short.

"You made too many, Pa." Abe looked at the steak with pure greed shining in his eyes.

"Nope, had to make Ma one." Daniel pulled the single tin cup forward and poured it full of milk directly from the bucket that sat in the center of the table. He downed the milk then poured again. He handed the cup to Ike, who was sitting next to him.

The cat landed in the middle of the table and made a dash for the milk.

"Scat, you." Abe swatted at the cat.

The cat, obviously a master at self-preservation, leaped off the table with a yowl.

"Don't you hit my cat," Ike raged as he punched Abe in the shoulder.

Grace prepared for an all-out fight, no goofing around this time.

Abe shoved him back. "If I'd'a wanted to hit that cat, he'd've been hit."

That seemed to satisfy Ike, or he was starving. For whatever reason, this once the twins didn't end up tussling on the floor.

Abe gave Grace a glowering look, as though he was considering fighting her for the meat. Grace would have backed up more, but the wall held her in place. With a shrug of disgust, Abe forked up a steak and took it for himself, then poked the last one and raised it, stuck on the utensil, in her direction.

"I . . . I don't eat . . ." Her voice started

to fade. She hadn't seen the smallest sign of plates or silverware, besides the fork and ladle of course. The fork that had been sticking straight down into the dirt floor just moments ago.

"She don't eat?" Abe looked from her to Daniel, his eyes shining with hunger. "If she don't want that steak, I claim it."

"She's eating it." Daniel jabbed at Abe with a half-gnawed steak bone. "Put hers on the table. It was on the bottom of the stack, direct on the stove. It'll need to cool."

Abe turned from Grace and plopped the sizzling meat directly onto the tabletop. Then Abe began breaking biscuits in half, shoveling a hard-cooked egg into the middle of each, and handing the biscuits to Ike. Ike passed them on around. Each of them got two biscuits with eggs inside and one plain biscuit, besides the enormous steak.

Grace could see now that the coal was really baked potatoes.

Abe was almost finished when he looked at her. His surprised expression told her he'd forgotten his brand-new ma again. He tossed two eggless biscuits beside her rapidly cooling steak. Blood ran off the steak and onto the floor, and fat began to congeal on the table.

The milk kept getting passed. After everyone had a drink, the tin cup would start another circuit. Grace gulped when she saw Mark fish around in the milk with his unwashed index finger, snag something, swish it out and flick it onto the floor, then guzzle down the rest of the milk.

"We coulda stood some'a them apples, Pa. Didn't he have none left?" The din of conversation, all at full volume and all with mouths stuffed full of food, went on only briefly. The food — meat to the equivalent of half a cow, a small mountain of potatoes, a whole . . . stovetop full of biscuits and eggs, and an entire bucket of milk — vanished.

The boys shoved and pummeled each other as they ran back outside.

And Grace still stood, stunned, against the back wall of the tiny cave, with the door wide open to the bitter winter wind.

"S'pose it's beneath your dignity to help clean the kitchen up." Daniel scowled at her and began clearing.

Except Grace noticed that there was nothing to clear. The boys hadn't made a mess. They'd barely let the food cool and certainly never let it sit on the table. They'd even taken their steak bones out with them.

Daniel scooped the empty milk bucket full of snow and set it on the stove. He picked up another bucket half full of water that was tucked behind the stove, poured a little water into the milk cup, swirled it around, and then tossed the water out the door. Daniel shut the frigid day outside and set the milk cup back on the table — the table that was now perfectly clean except for Grace's cold, bleeding meat, with its pair of biscuits standing by its side.

"Eat when you want. Warm it up if you've a mind." Daniel grabbed the bucket of water and went outside without a backward glance.

TEN

"Ain't she *never* gonna do *nothin'* but stare or hide under a blanket, Pa?" Mark tugged at Daniel's sleeve while he fed some grain to the four milk cows. Mark seemed the most determined to return Grace.

"As long as she keeps outta the way, we'd better count our blessings, son." Daniel watered the cows with the bucket he'd carried from the house; then he went to the chicken coop to scatter cracked corn.

Mark carried his own, smaller bucket of corn and slogged along behind, setting his small feet in the tracks as Daniel broke a trail in the deep snow, trudging through the snow back to the barn. Mark nagged him every step of the way.

Abe and Ike had taken off on horseback to ride herd. Luke and John were in the woods that climbed the hill behind the cave — the one the boys liked to slide down on their bellies and go flying past the front door. It was Mark's turn to stay close to the place and help with the barnyard chores.

Daniel climbed up into the haymow and grabbed up the pitchfork.

"Couldn't you've done a better job of pickin' a ma?" Mark shouted from down below where he wrestled all three baby calves into the pens with their mamas.

After the Reeves family got their milk, the babies got to suckle the rest out for their own breakfast. The calves bawled and rushed for their mothers, who crooned deep in their throats to their babies. Then there was silence as the calves started feeding, their little tails jerking in time to their feasting.

" 'Tweren't no big rush about it." Mark trailed Daniel up the ladder and grabbed armloads of hay to throw down to the fat cows below.

"When we told you we wanted a ma, none of us never said you had to go off half-cocked and bring home the first ma you run across."

The kid hadn't stopped yapping since he'd come outside. Daniel pitched hay down, trying to work fast enough that — Daniel shook his head. Fast work wouldn't make him go deaf, and that was his only escape from Mark's harping about Grace.

The cows started crunching away at the hay, but the noise didn't drown out the boy. "Maybe if we took her back and told the preacher real nice that she weren't good for *nothin'*."

Mark's prattle was wearing on his ears to the point Daniel was tempted to leave the rest of the chores to Mark and go inside. Except "inside" was plumb full of that useless, prissy woman. She was most likely still standing there, holding up the consarned wall.

"Just tell him that she hasn't done nothing, 'cept'n sleeping with you. . . ."

Daniel cringed and forked faster.

"Maybe he'd take back your I do's. Just kinda erase the whole stupid thing. I'd be glad to tell Parson Roscoe that so far going to bed with you is the only thing she's good for. If the parson knew that —"

"Don't try and help me out with this, son. It ain't a job for young'uns." He worked beside his carping son in the dry, sweet-smelling hay. After he had the milk cows' feed bunk full, he moved to the opening above the hogs and gave the sows their share. They rustled their snouts into the growing pile in their low manger, their babies squealing and nudging the sows' fat udders for milk. Then he moved on to the pen with one older calf. The little heifer was weaned but too young to go out with the herd. He finished with the pen of older pigs from last summer's farrowing. The greedy little beasts squealed and bit at each other as if they were starving to death. Last he pitched some hay down to the cow with the new calf he'd found yesterday. They seemed to be doing well, but Daniel knew he'd have to keep them inside until the cold weather broke.

The barn was bitter cold, but the doors were tight and the frigid wind stayed outside. It was about a thousand times nicer place to be than that dark, musty cave. Daniel wondered again why he'd never got around to building a house. He craved the thought of having a bedroom for his new wife. She could hide in there forever if it suited her.

Daniel would just shove a steak under the door three times a day and be done with it. And he would build himself a room, too — as far from Mark's nagging and Grace's finicky manners as he could get. In fact, for a moment, Daniel toyed with the idea of just moving himself out to the barn. Sure, he'd freeze to death, but that was the only flaw he could see in the plan.

Mark kept pestering. He wasn't driving

the boy hard enough. He'd never get too tired to talk at this rate. The work his other boys were doing would half kill them, Daniel thought with satisfaction. They wouldn't get all the way killed. He'd trained them up right. Another ten or fifteen hours of hard labor mixed with wild, reckless play, and his boys would sleep like the dead. Now he only had to wear out this chatterbox.

"Mark, brush the horses when you're done here; then start fetching pails of snow into the house. Leave 'em long enough to melt; then water the animals. I gave the cows some, but I shorted 'em, so you're gonna need to —"

"That's right. With this much snow, we won't have to chop a hole in the crick er nothin'." Mark beamed at him. "It'll be fun feeding the stock snow."

"Don't forget the chickens. I'm gonna saddle up and see to dragging windfalls in closer for the night. John and Luke can't gather enough wood to last for long."

"I'll be ready to chop it for you by the time you're back."

Daniel jammed his fists on his hips and turned to face his son. "What'd I tell you about the ax?"

Mark's eyes narrowed.

Daniel held his gaze. It was a showdown.

He had one about twice a day with Mark.

Finally, his son caved. "All right, Pa. You think I'm too young for chopping."

"I don't *think* you're too young for chopping. There's no *I think* about it. You're *too young for chopping,* period. You're only five. I keep that ax as sharp as an Apache tomahawk, and it's every bit as dangerous. I've only been letting the older boys work it for a couple of years."

Mark glared.

Daniel had to hold his frown firm. He was mighty proud of all his boys, but Mark was the biggest handful. Maybe not the smartest, because all of them were smart, but the craftiest for a fact. Daniel loved that about him. It'd take Mark as far as he wanted to go in life — as long as it didn't take him to the ax. "Your chance'll come. After the watering, you can fetch around sticks with John 'n' Luke then break up the ones you brung in." Daniel held Mark's gaze for as long as it took.

Finally, Mark kicked at the nearest mound of snow, sending a plume of white into the air to be swirled about by the wind. "All right. I'll leave it be."

"You know better 'n to lie to me, boy. Right?" Daniel waited. Mark might cut a corner time to time and mislead a body with vague words, but his son knew not to lie straight to Daniel's face. Mark had learned that lesson over Daniel's knee.

"I know." Mark stomped his foot hard. "I promise."

"Good boy." Daniel ran his gloved hand over Mark's heavy fur cap, almost knocking it off his head. Daniel leaned close.

Mark gave him a suspicious look, the one he got if Daniel ever did something so foolish as hug him. Daniel stooped quickly, grabbed a handful of snow, and smeared it into Mark's face. Mark shrieked and dived toward the ground, caught up a ball of snow, and threw it back. Daniel laughed, and the fight was on.

By the time they were done, Daniel was almost too warm in his furlined buckskin coat and his long scarf, wrapped five times around his neck. His already-battered Stetson had been knocked off his head and trampled. Snow pounded onto his head had turned him halfway into a snowman. And he knew from the burn that his cheeks were glowing red with cold every bit as much as Mark's. Slapping his son on the back, Daniel said, "Get to it, boy."

Daniel glanced at the door to the cave. Normally about now, he'd go inside and slice more steaks. He brought a hank of meat in every night to thaw for the next day. They went through a cow and a pig about once a month, and he had the better part of a cow carcass hanging in the barn right now. He was glad he'd cut it down to size, because it was frozen solid.

He didn't want to go inside. "Bringing a new ma home for you boys was kinda an accident. But we're stuck with her now. There's no way back."

Mark sighed.

Daniel knew exactly how he felt.

"Reckon we'll just have to make the best of it, huh, Pa?" Mark crossed his arms and shot a hostile look toward the cave.

Daniel well remembered Grace's scathing comments about his sons when she'd been their teacher. And she'd been particularly hard on Mark. He didn't blame his boy for being unhappy. Daniel said, "Remember last summer when the McClellens were attacked and almost killed by those murdering renegades who were running the hills?"

"Yep, 'twere a mighty close thing."

"Well," — Daniel picked up his hat and whacked the snow off it against his leg — "having Grace come live with us can't be any worse than that."

"The McClellens got to solve their problems by shooting folks." Mark gave their home a contemplative look.

"No, they didn't. No one got shot in that mess, although it looked to be shooting trouble for a while. They solved their problem with their smarts. They worked it out. Grace . . . uh . . . that is, your ma . . . is here to stay. So we'll use our smarts to figure out a way to get along with her."

"And Miss Calhoun is smart, too, or leastways she kept acting like she was."

Daniel shrugged his shoulders. "She might be smart. No sign of it anywheres I can see. And besides, there's smart and there's smart."

"What's 'at mean, Pa?" Mark scooped up a handful of snow and seemed to be studying the house.

Daniel had to bite back a smile. "It means . . . smart is what you do with it." Daniel nodded his head at the house. "I've known a few real educated men, got through high school 'n' everything, who didn't have a lick of sense. And I've knowed some men who couldn't read nor write, who didn't have a day of book learning, but I'd trust 'em with big decisions about real important stuff, like my cattle, even."

"So we'll just see what kind of smart Ma turns out to be."

Daniel sighed again, and this time the

sound seemed to come all the way from his toes. "Yep. The good news is, since we're stuck with her for life, she's got a lot of time to learn."

Mark hurled the snowball at the cave door. It splatted harmlessly against the rough wood. "She's got the rest of our lives."

Daniel nodded, thinking that the menfolk in his family leaned toward long lives. He envied the boys getting to grow up and move away.

Then Mark perked up. "You know what?"

"What?" Fear skittered down Daniel's spine like an eight-legged creepy crawler. He'd seen that wily look on his son's face before.

"She don't have the rest of *our* lives. She's only got the rest of *her* life." Mark tipped his head sideways in a way that was purely cheerful. "Gotta get to the chores."

Mark went off toward the barn whistling, almost as if he knew Grace's life wasn't necessarily going to be very long.

ELEVEN

She was going to die. If she was lucky, it would happen soon.

Grace pushed herself away from the wall. "And when in my life have I ever been lucky?" The whispered words echoed in the burrow she now called home. She might as well plan on making a hundred years old. She moved hesitantly toward the steak — expecting the bloody thing to make a run for it.

It just lay there, taunting her. It turned her stomach, but she was hungry. After a dozen or so nervous looks at the door, which she expected to crash open any second, she got tough. The one thing Grace knew how to be was tough.

She picked up the fork Daniel had washed up and set aside, speared the steak, and tossed it on the stovetop. The steak sizzled and sent a savory plume of smoke toward the roof of the cave, all of twelve inches over her head. Grace picked up the egg and biscuit sandwiches and began gnawing on them as the steak turned to a more edible color. The dry bread and cold eggs stuck in her throat, but they tasted like heaven.

Daniel and the boys had downed all the milk, and Daniel had left the bucket, now filled with rapidly melting snow, on the stove.

She looked at the communal tin cup, remembered how she'd lived with Parrish, and decided this wasn't so bad. She dipped herself a drink of cold water to wash down the crumbling biscuits. When the biscuits and eggs were gone, she used the fork to lift the brown steak, now dripping clear juice. Unable to find a more ladylike way to dine, she proceeded to eat it hanging from the fork with all the manners of a hungry wolverine.

Grace ate the whole steak, which was at least an inch thick. She'd been hungry for a very long time, eking out a living on the two dollars a month she kept from her teacher's salary. She thought enviously of the blackened potatoes. She could've had one if she'd been on her toes.

She licked the fork clean, considered what to do with the steak bones, pitched them out the door as the boys had done, and washed the fork. She found a rag and wiped the blood from her steak off the table and looked around her home with satisfaction. There wasn't going to be a lot of housekeeping to do. That was for sure.

As she tried to wrap her mind around her current circumstances, she remembered the foul accusation Daniel Reeves had made last night. Equal parts fury and humiliation flooded through her as hot as the blood in her veins.

She had learned how to walk and dress like a lady. She'd learned how to speak correctly, remember her manners, and always behave properly — all without help. To be caught in this compromising situation by the parson then accused of flagrant sin by that worthless Daniel Reeves — Well, it was as if the last two years of struggle for respectability were for nothing.

With a pang of fear that overrode her anger, she suddenly wondered if the condition of being poor and unwanted clung to her like an odor. Perhaps she'd fooled no one. Maybe the whole town had turned up their noses at her from the first. Maybe the school board had been looking for an excuse to fire her when Daniel came to them with his complaints.

The door crashed open. Daniel filled the

doorway then came inside carrying a huge knife.

He might be planning to kill her, but again she remembered that she'd never been lucky.

Daniel closed the door and set a bucket on the stove. He went to a dark corner of the tiny room.

In the shadows, Grace noticed half a beef hanging by one skinned leg. How odd that she hadn't seen it before. Of course, she'd been in a daze since she'd awakened in this house. "Daniel . . ." Grace figured there was no point in putting this off. They definitely needed to talk.

"Huh?" Daniel hacked away at the meat without so much as glancing at her.

"Umm, I . . . I think — that is, we need to . . ." Grace had no idea what to say.

Daniel turned to face her with a stack of meat in his hand. "Talk? We need to talk? Is that what you were going to say?"

Grace nodded, her tongue as frozen as the world outside. She saw the fury in him. She saw the despicable suspicion clearly written on his face. She wanted to deny his accusations. She wanted to demand he treat her with respect. She wanted a different husband. Or better yet, no husband at all.

Into the silence, Daniel said with a sneer,

"We could talk about the fact that you are now my wife, even though I neither want nor need a wife."

They probably really did need to talk about that. "Well —"

Daniel cut her off as if she were just another steak. Of course, he didn't use the knife. His sharp tongue was enough. "We could talk about the fact that you hate my sons. Not a good thing when you're now their ma."

"I don't —" Grace stopped. Daniel had a point. She wouldn't have gone so far as to say *hate.* Hate was a little harsh. It wasn't Christian to hate anyone. Sure, she thought they were crude, grimy, smelly, noisy, rowdy, and rude. But hate? No.

Daniel snorted at her silence as if she'd just admitted to hating his boys. "We could talk about the fact that I've got no time for you, no place for you, and no interest in you."

Grace wanted to say, "Same here," but Daniel didn't give her a chance.

"Or we could talk about the really interesting question. The one that really might answer all the others." Daniel glared at her. The silence stretched. He finally said in a voice that could have blown in on the icy wind, "What were you doing hiding in the back of my wagon? Were you hiding from someone? Or were you planning exactly what happened? Did you need a husband and you heard I owned a nice stretch of land?"

"As if" — finally he'd asked a question she could answer, so she crossed her arms and lifted her chin and glared right back — "I'd pick *you.*"

Daniel's fair complexion mottled with red. "You might. You might if you found your-self . . . needing to be married right quick."

Daniel's blue eyes flashed bolts of light-ning. "Desperate times call for desperate measures. What's his name, Grace? I'll deliver you and his" — Daniel glanced significantly at her stomach — "*mistake* to his door."

"Daniel Reeves . . ." Grace jammed her fists onto her hips. The coarse cloth that touched her hands reminded her she was wearing pants. She was embarrassed, vulner-able, and so insulted she wanted to slap him. "There is no man. That is a dirty lie you made up to shame me. Don't you ever —"

The door flew open. Didn't anybody ever open and close the door slowly in this place?

Mark came in carrying a bucket of snow. He stopped short and looked between the two of them, reading their expressions.

Daniel relieved him of the bucket and handed him the other one, the snow inside now melted.

Grace had to step back to let Daniel pass her.

"Mark, get back outside and stay there. Your ma and I have to talk a few things over. Don't come back in here till I tell you to."

"Are you fixin' to return her now, Pa? I can hitch up the team for you whilst you get her out of Abe's clothes and back into the nightdress. It'll be plumb nice to have her gone. You won't have to share your blanket anymore, nor lie with each other. I'll be glad to tell the parson she did nothing but sleep with you the whole time she was here."

"Quit helping me!"

Mark pointed to the floor. "There ain't no room for her. The two of you was so crowded you 'bout had to lay right smack on top of her. Now that you've tried her out, you can tell Parson Roscoe and the whole town she just weren't no good."

"Mark!" Daniel's roar made Grace jump.

"I'm only trying to chip in and return her. It's what we all want. Her, too, I reckon." Mark glanced at Grace.

She remembered those eyes. This one was

always thinking.

Mark swung the bucket of water.

"Get out. Get your chores done," Daniel ordered.

Grace didn't like the tone of Daniel's voice. She felt sorry for the little boy. No wonder he was so difficult.

Parrish had been able to scare children into submission with just his voice, too. Although he didn't always confine himself to yelling.

"Get to work and stay busy until I call you in for dinner. Go!"

Mark glared at Daniel then turned his eyes on Grace. With enough stubborn grumbling to save himself from being obedient, he finally turned and marched out of the cave, leaving the door wide open.

Daniel shut it without comment.

"You leave that little boy alone." Grace surprised herself. And she wasn't done yet. "How hard do you make him work?"

"Until he drops over if I'm lucky." Daniel gave her an unreadable look. He was probably trying to decide how much hard work he could get out of her.

"Children aren't slave labor." Grace stepped right up to his face and wagged a finger under his nose. "It's no wonder they acted up in school. They're used to this kind of treatment. They think this is normal to be worked like dogs from morning to night. When I treated them decently, they probably —"

"Do not" — Daniel brushed Grace's scolding finger aside and leaned down until they were nose to nose — "tell me how to raise my sons."

"Well, somebody needs to. You have them shoved in this" — Grace waved her arms in a wild gesture that took in the tiny cave as Daniel ducked so she didn't catch him on the chin — "hole-in-the-ground. You feed them on a table with no plates or silverware as if you were throwing scraps to a pack of dogs." She jabbed him in the chest. "They have no clothes, no privacy, no manners, and no hope of ever getting any with you for their father."

Daniel grabbed her wrist so she couldn't poke him anymore. "You're about one wrong word away from sleeping in the barn with the animals."

"And that would be different from living in here, how?"

"That's the word." Daniel jerked her forward.

She jerked back.

They tripped over a stack of bedding that stuck out from the side of the wall and fell over in a heap.

He landed on top and knocked the wind right out of her. She gasped for air, but catching her breath was impossible with his weight. She shoved at his shoulders, but he was already scooting off.

As if he refused to do anything that she thought of, he stopped moving and settled down. His eyes flashed. His hands sank into her hair. "Tell me what you were doing in my wagon."

Grace felt something close to panic at being so controlled by Daniel. She'd sworn never to be under anyone's thumb again. But for all his fury, she didn't fear Daniel's fists. She wasn't sure why; probably just bad judgment on her part.

She looked in his eyes and knew she couldn't tell him the truth. He hated her. He'd hand her over in a heartbeat. But she could tell him enough, maybe, to stop his horrid accusations. Maybe if she did, he'd get off.

"I was hiding. A man . . . a man frightened me. I didn't choose your wagon. I was running —"

"Some man in Mosqueros was chasing you?" Daniel's eyes changed. The fury faded, replaced by worry. "Why didn't you go to the sheriff?"

Because the sheriff would have sided with Parrish. He would have held her until Parrish got there. "I didn't have time. He was coming. I just saw your wagon and climbed in. I didn't know it was yours. I didn't *choose you.*" The very thought made Grace shudder.

Her trembling caught Daniel's attention, and he seemed momentarily distracted. His hands, which had held firm in her hair but never pulled, loosened now until her head rested on his flexing fingers as if they were a living pillow.

Grace swallowed and tried to remember what they were talking about. Oh yes — terror, hiding, freezing nearly to death. "I was afraid to move, and I was afraid to tell you I was there because you'd take me back to town and leave me where he might find me."

"I'd have found him and taken him to the sheriff for you." Daniel removed one hand from her hair. His eyes were concerned.

Grace was surprised to realize he meant it. He would have protected her. If this story she was telling him was true.

"I would have, Grace. We may not agree on my boys, but I wouldn't have let you come to any harm. Surely you don't think I'm that much of a low-down skunk."

Grace almost did believe him. She

couldn't let herself. "I just stayed quiet, thinking to wait until you were out of town where it was safe. The cold was too much. I . . . I guess I fell asleep or passed out. I didn't t-trap you. There's no man with whom I have been . . . dallying. I'm not . . ."

Suddenly it was all too much. The fear of Parrish and this stupid marriage she'd been thrust into. Daniel's awful accusations. She felt the tears burn in her eyes. This man had reduced her to tears twice now. And Grace hardly ever cried. She'd learned long ago that it just didn't do a lick of good. "How could you think that of me? I am not a woman who —" Her voice broke.

"Don't cry." Daniel sounded a little desperate.

She tried to stop. She breathed raggedly. "I'm sorry. I don't blame you for thinking the worst of me." She reached for her cheeks to wipe the tears away.

Daniel's rough thumb got to the tears first. He wiped at her cheeks with surprising gentleness. She looked up to thank him.

Their eyes caught. Their breath caught.

Daniel rolled off her as if he'd been burned. He jumped to his feet, threw some potatoes into the stove, tossed the steaks on next, and asked, "Can you make biscuits?" He didn't look at her. In fact, he kept his back squarely to her as he worked around the kitchen.

She could tell her tears had disgusted him. Parrish had always punished her for crying. She quickly dashed them away. Then she thought to breathe again.

She'd seen Daniel mix the biscuits up for breakfast. She thought she remembered. How hard could it be? "Yes, I'll do it."

"Make a lot. Watch the steaks. If they catch fire, be careful. Hold back on the eggs until we show our faces." Daniel grabbed the bucket of now-melted snow off the stove and opened the door.

Grace saw another bucket heaped with snow sitting there.

"I wonder how much of that Mark heard?" Daniel muttered. He put the bucket on the stove and crossed to the door. As he left, he turned back toward Grace. "Maybe you didn't trap me a'purpose, but we're well and truly trapped just the same. But there's trapped and there's trapped. No woman's ever gonna die giving me another child. That's a kind of trapped I won't be a part of." He walked out, slamming the door behind him.

Grace wondered what on earth he meant by that. It wasn't for the first time she realized that she knew nothing about men or

165

marriage — or being a woman, for that matter.

And she set out to prove she knew nothing by making biscuits for the first time in her life.

TWELVE

"Come for supper." Hannah Cartwright whispered out the door into the bitter cold of the dusky Chicago afternoon. They just had to survive until spring. Everything was easier when the weather didn't try to kill them.

She didn't hear the children, but she knew where they were. Trevor huddled next to Libby near a grating, a warm spot they'd discovered across the alley from their little shed. The little boys sometimes found the energy to play hide-and-seek or toss a rock back and forth between them, but not today.

The children liked to be outside. Hannah didn't blame them. The little shed was dreary, and it smelled terrible, as if the owner had used it to store rotting potatoes at one time.

Hannah only came inside when the cold was too much to bear. The wind cut through her thin dress, and she stepped in to save as much of the precious warmth from the burning barrel as she could.

Stepping back from the shed door, her hands quivering with cold, she opened the letter from Grace. Pulling out eighteen dollars, in weary-looking one-dollar bills, she asked the empty room, "How much do schoolteachers make anyway?"

Afraid the answer was twenty dollars a month, Hannah stared at the cash. Grace was holding back two dollars for herself. That wasn't enough to buy food.

Hannah knew teachers didn't make much, and this must be the lot of it — again this month. "Grace, how are you living?"

Grace's letter spoke extravagantly of the meals she ate with her students' families and the warm, cozy room she'd been given as part of her salary. Even with little or no money, she should be able to get by, but she'd have nothing left for a proper schoolteacher's dress or any other necessities.

Trevor came into the shed behind the blacksmith's shop, helping Libby, with Nolan ahead of him and Bruce bringing up the rear.

The boys were all thoughtful and too quiet for Hannah's peace of mind. They didn't have food enough in their bellies to laugh and play.

Always so careful of Libby, who never spoke a word, they took their time walking beside her, supporting her as she limped on her slow-healing ankle. The instant they got inside, they carefully closed the rickety door to preserve the heat.

It was so different having brothers. Parrish had always preferred girls for some reason. Hannah and Grace believed he enjoyed terrorizing girls more than boys. Maybe they cried more easily when he laid the belt to them.

"It's time to eat." Hannah waved them toward the bucket of water to wash. "Mr. Daily set the bread out."

"I found this, Hannah." Nolan pulled a dented can out of his pocket. The label was gone, but there would be food of some kind inside.

Trevor went to work on it with a rusted can opener.

Bruce's hands were full of trash to burn. When he set it beside the barrel, to be fed in slowly all night, he shoved his hand deep in his pocket and pulled out a penny.

"A lady over by the train station gave me this." Bruce reached over to set it behind the barrel. From his other pocket, he produced a good-sized rag. When he spread it out, Hannah could see it was a shirt the right size for Libby, with an arm torn away.

Bruce glanced up at them with defiant eyes. Only six, he'd come into their shed one night and crawled up to the heat, looking at them as though they might attack him. Instead, Hannah had given him a full share of their bread and let him join the family. Bruce brought a wallet home with him the next day with five dollars in it.

Grace's money had run out early that month and the boys were starving on the bread. Hannah had a talk with Bruce about God and sin and what the police did to children who were caught stealing. But, though she'd never picked anyone's pocket, she'd swiped a few apples off a grocer's cart when they were starving. She was no innocent.

The eighteen dollars from Grace each month should have been enough to buy good food for all of them, with enough left over to rent a room and buy warm clothes. Hannah had written to Grace just once and never hinted that they were anything but comfortable. But paying off Libby's doctor bills to treat her ankle used every penny of it. Thank heavens they'd found this empty shed, or they'd have been sleeping on the street.

Every day Mr. Daily, who owned a diner

three blocks over, watched for Hannah, and when she came, he slipped outside and gave her two loaves of bread. A generous, Christian man, he was careful not to let his wife catch him.

Hannah could hear Mrs. Daily shouting from inside the diner anytime she happened into the back room. Carefully Hannah would crouch in the alley near the back door, knowing Mr. Daily would leave the food whenever he could.

"What's for supper?" Trevor smiled.

She couldn't smile back at her fourteen-year-old brother. She lifted the envelope so Trevor could see inside.

Lips curling down into a frown, he asked, "What's she living on? Did she write? Does she ever mention buying herself a new dress or shoes? Is she eating?"

Trevor had never met Grace, but Hannah had told stories of her brave big sister until they all felt as if she were out fighting the world for them.

"You know Grace. According to her letter, everything is fine. All she talks about is how comfortable she is and how bad things are for us here. Of course, she doesn't know about you boys, and she's dead set against adoption, so I didn't tell her I found homes for the little girls, but she's adamant that none of us work. I'm too old for school now, and maybe I could get a job, but I don't think Libby can stay at home alone while I work yet."

Trevor gave Libby a long look. He had been the one to find her, curled up in an alley, living alongside the rats, fighting them for food thrown in the trash, dragging her broken foot behind as she hopped or crawled after food. He'd brought her home, and because the little girl didn't speak and was too little to write, Hannah had taken to calling her Libby. Libby was tough, and Hannah and Trevor both well knew that the painfully thin three-year-old could survive alone in this shed all day. But neither of them wanted it that way.

"Grace hated seeing children put to work. She trusted me to look after the little girls when we got them away from Parrish. The one promise she demanded of me was that they'd stay in school and never be put back into that mill. They've all found homes now, but the same promise applies to you boys and Libby. Protecting us from the mill and from Parrish matters more to her than a new pair of shoes."

Trevor dragged his ragged woolen hat off his head. "The eighteen dollars would rent us a room, except —" He glanced at Libby for a split second then looked away before the tiny girl noticed.

Hannah thought about the doctor bills. They could pay them only because of Grace's money. And Libby needed to keep being doctored until her foot healed, if it ever would.

Bruce went straight to the barrel and threw in paper and other burnable trash he'd dug out of the alley. Kneeling by it, he reached out his hands to soak up the meager warmth. The elbows of the gray sweater he wore hung in tatters. Hannah saw the holes in the soles of his shoes. She'd found both in the trash and been grateful for an actual pair. Nolan's were mismatched.

"Yes, Trevor, 'except.' That about says it all." Hannah thought the last operation on Libby's leg had finally fixed the problem, and Hannah wasn't above cheating the doctor out of his money — she'd done worse things to survive. But they had to pay him because they might need him again.

"Well, since that money is all spoken for and we're eating bread — only bread — for the fourth day in a row, I'm not listening to Grace or you anymore. I'm doing things my way."

"Not a job, Trevor." Hannah caught at his arm. "You need to stay in school. Just three more years and you can get a real job, something good that will be safe. That mill is a trap that you'll never get out of without schooling. I'll gladly let you work for the rest of your life once you're graduated."

"It's not child exploitation if I do it to myself."

Hannah flinched when she heard Grace's most hated words — *child exploitation.* Grace had taught those words along with reading and writing. Wanting to argue with her brother, who had come sneaking out of an alley a year ago and joined the family, Hannah instead remained silent.

At last she said, "I think I'm going to exploit myself, too."

"No, Hannah." Trevor shook his head. His dirty brown hair hung too long on his forehead, and he shoved it aside impatiently. "You need to be here for the little ones."

Libby hovered near the burning barrel, turning her hands back and forth to warm both sides.

"I can earn money, too." Nolan slumped beside Libby, his face lined with the defiant expression all street kids had, acting as if they didn't care about anything. "If all three of us work, we'll earn enough to be comfortable."

Nolan had never worked in the mill. He'd

been on the street from his earliest memory. It was hard to explain to him the difference between Grace's schoolteacher job and work at the carpet mill. He'd never seen what it was like. The bitter cold in winter, the vicious heat in summer, and the roaring, deafening noise. Hannah still cringed when she thought of dodging the huge, dangerous machines, the cruel foremen wielding rods to whip slackers, always yelling and pushing them to hurry, work faster, work harder.

Hannah could see the determination on his thin, pale face. Nolan, ten years old, looked as though he was starving. No matter how Hannah tried, she could never fill the growing boy's belly. She knew Trevor went hungry, too. And heaven knew she did.

Libby backed away from the bit of warmth from the barrel and looked at Hannah with big, sad eyes capable of breaking Hannah's heart. The doctor had treatments for Libby's leg, but he didn't know what to do about her silence. He didn't think she'd had an injury to her voice. Instead, he thought Libby had seen something awful.

The doctor said that sometimes when people experienced something so dreadful their mind couldn't deal with it, they reacted in this way. He said that the words were locked inside her, and until she could face what had happened and speak of it, she would remain silent. There was nothing he could do. He warned Hannah that her little sister might never speak again.

Turning her freckled nose away from the meager heat, Libby limped to Nolan's side. Nolan pulled the little girl, hardly more than a toddler, into his lap and hugged her close.

Hannah shook her head. "Grace will hate it. She's sacrificing everything for us. Going to work instead of school is the thing she would hate the most."

"It'll be different for us," Trevor insisted. "We'll keep all the money we earn. You said Parrish always took every penny. I can't make twenty dollars a month like Grace, but I can make something."

"You'll be lucky to make a dime a day, Trevor. And you'll work seven days a week."

Trevor's eyes narrowed. "Well, that's ten cents a day more than we have now. Ten cents would buy us a little meat."

Nolan carefully lowered his eyes to look at Libby, but Hannah saw them light up at the thought of meat to add to their bread.

"With what Grace sends, we can save up and go find her. The five of us and Grace can make a home together."

Hannah smiled even though her heart was

heavy. Grace didn't know what a change had overtaken the family. Hannah hadn't told her about how hard she'd worked finding families for the little girls. Sneaking around, peeking in windows at night, Hannah had inspected each family to the extent she was able to make sure the girls would be safe.

Grace hated the whole idea of adoption because of Parrish. But Hannah knew there were good people in the world, and she'd set out to place the little children in homes. The only trouble was, as quickly as she found a home for one child, she found another on the street who needed her.

Grace had never stayed in one place long enough for it to make sense to write a letter. Now she seemed settled in Mosqueros, and Hannah had spent a few precious pennies to write and tell Grace that everything was okay, but she'd given no details. If Grace had heard Hannah was putting the little sisters up for adoption, she'd have quit her job and come rushing back to Chicago, trying as always to mother all of them.

For that same reason, Hannah didn't tell her about the new children. Grace would only worry.

Once Grace settled in Mosqueros and looked to stay there, she'd write for them to come. She'd send eighteen dollars a few more times, and no doctor would make a claim on the money. They'd always been an all-girl family, but Grace loved all children. She'd be happy to see the boys, too.

"I'm going to pound the next boy who comes slamming through that door." Grace piled flour on the table and used the family fork to mix up the first batch of biscuits in her life. There hadn't been much time to develop womanly skills when she worked twelve hours a day in a carpet mill.

The steaks blazed away happily. She went to them and turned them, doing her best not to catch herself on fire.

Back to the biscuits. "He put . . ." She tried to imitate the amount of flour Daniel had thrown into the bowl. His hands were bigger, so she threw in a couple of extra fistfuls.

"Then there was milk . . ." Grace looked at the bucket on the stove. Water. They'd finished the milk for breakfast. Daniel knew that. She shrugged. "If I'd needed milk, he would have said something." She poured water into the flour.

She looked around. He'd added something else.

The steaks waved flames at her. She

awkwardly shifted them away from the fire, except the fire seemed to follow the meat.

She spotted the jar on the floor next to the flour canister. She unscrewed the lid. She jerked her head back and almost dropped the jar. "Ewww."

Switching over to mouth-breathing, she held the jar as far away from her nose as she could. It wasn't far enough. She set the jar down on the table with the dull thunk of glass on wood and backed across the room. She stared at the foul mixture of rotten . . . goo.

She looked around the cave. "He must have used something from another jar." There were no other jars. She closed her eyes and tried to picture Daniel's quick, efficient movements. She opened her eyes again and stared at the strange bubbly concoction. "He used that."

She tried to sneak up on it. It seemed to be staring at her. She lifted the jar, breathing through clenched teeth, and poured — she didn't remember how much. But it was so awful, the less the better. She quickly clapped the lid back on the jar and returned it to its dark corner where it could fester in peace.

The steaks, looking far less bloody than they had this morning, thank goodness, shot fire most of the way to the ceiling. She took a moment to be grateful that her home was made of dirt and rock — nothing flammable.

She decided it was time to stack the steaks the way Daniel had.

She stirred the biscuits. The dough was too thick. She added water. It was too thin. She added flour. The dough stubbornly refused to settle on the right consistency. By the time she hit a thickness she could live with, she had a huge supply of biscuit dough and the table was coated with a sticky layer of it. Daniel had left the table as clean as when he started. The dough smelled like that nasty jar of stuff. She didn't remember the biscuits smelling bad when she'd eaten them.

Daniel had picked up the dough in his hands, but it was a bit too runny for Grace to make that work. Instead, she picked up a small handful and turned to drop it on the stove before it oozed out between her fingers. The blobs of dough ran together slowly — not as if the dough was really liquid, but more as if it was just being uncooperative — until they formed one big biscuit instead of a dozen small ones. She watched it, not sure what she'd do when it was time to turn it. She armed herself with the fork and waited.

At first the dough threatened to run down the side of the stove, but Grace was quick and kept scooping. The dough eventually hardened and stayed put next to the steak mountain.

After what seemed like forever, she lifted the corner of the monster biscuit. It was dark brown on the bottom. Very dark brown. She poked at it and struggled to flip it, and it broke apart.

She was inspired. "You know, why does it have to be whole anyway? I actually *want* it to break. She sawed little biscuit-sized sections loose and flipped them. The first ones fought her, but by the time she was done, she was getting to be handy at it. There were crumbs everywhere, and the biscuits had gone from brown to black about halfway through, but they were all flipped and cooking along nicely.

She saw that the bottom steak was on fire again. Her forking arm was exhausted, the stack of steaks was teetering a little, and no room was left on the stovetop, so she decided she'd eat the bottom one herself if it was overcooked.

The door slammed open.

As if a dam had burst, a flood of males rushed in. All six of them filled the room.

The triplets and Ike made straight for the table. Grace shut the door, almost catching the cat's tail, and waited for them to thank her for making them dinner.

Daniel fished the potatoes out of the stove's belly and barked, "Abe, fetch the steaks from your ma."

Grace decided she wasn't going to put up with his abuse of the children. That was the first change she was going to make around here. "Before we eat, I want to —"

"What'd you do to the biscuits?" Daniel backed away from the stove.

Abe grimaced at all her hard work. With a grunt of disdain, he started grabbing steaks and pitching them to his brothers.

Grace backed out of the line of fire.

"You made a mess of the table, too." Daniel grabbed a rag and swiped at the layer of clinging dough until it was gone.

"Ick, what is this?" Abe finished with the steaks and, with a look of disgust, began tossing biscuits across the room.

The boys howled as they caught the biscuits.

"Are they safe?" Mark bit into one and said, "Bleck." He took another bite.

"They'll likely break my teeth." Ike gnawed away, risking his teeth with abandon.

John gagged as he alternated a very black steak with his burned potato, which was mealy and white inside. He choked — loudly — swallowing his hardened biscuit.

Luke waded through the food, occasionally crashing his shoulder into John or Mark on either side of him. Grace found herself holding up the back wall again.

"Where'd you learn to cook a mess like this?" Daniel complained around a mouthful of food. He said to Ike, who was gulping milk with an air of desperation, "Hurry with that milk. I'm choking on this."

She might have answered, except the other boys were talking and choking, too — far more than was called for in Grace's opinion, even if the biscuits and steak were a little . . . tough.

"No eggs, Pa." Abe kept handing out biscuits. When the stovetop was cleared, except for a thousand crumbs that he scraped onto the floor, he cracked a dozen eggs onto the cast-iron top. "I'm cooking 'em hard. I don't think these biscuits'll break apart for a sandwich."

The cat dashed over to the scattering of crumbs then, after a few cautious sniffs, turned up its nose and went to sit by the door.

"Cat's lucky," Mark said.

"Why'zat?" Ike turned to look at his pet.

" 'Cause he can gnaw on a live rat 'stead of having to eat this."

All six of them nodded together, looking with blatant envy at the cat.

"Burn 'em good," Daniel said, gulping down a cup of milk and handing the cup on to Mark on his right. "It'll go with the rest of the meal."

The boys howled with laughter. Abe threw a hardened little circle of egg. They were coated with burned biscuit crumbs that had stuck to the stove, but at least the cast-iron stove top was clean now. Abe set an egg beside a black biscuit for Grace and snagged the last one for himself. Sitting down on Daniel's left, beside Ike, he began eating.

Luke, in the middle across from the twins, dropped out of sight, and his big brothers almost tipped over backward on their bench.

"Luke, leggo my boot." Abe made a concerted effort to kick Luke in the head, from what Grace could see going on under the table.

All five children laughed.

"Knock it off," Daniel roared. "Finish eating. We've got a long afternoon of work."

The boys ignored him. He didn't seem to mind. The chaos went on for about fifteen minutes. They insulted her and ignored her as she cowered in the same place she'd stood at breakfast. Her heart crumbled worse than the biscuits as she listened to them mock her hard work.

They all got up and left, taking the bucket with them.

Daniel said, as he left the room, "Next time use more sourdough and less milk. And for Pete's sake, don't burn them steaks up like that. The triplets still have their baby teeth. They'll break 'em off. I'll be back to cut the supper steaks later in the afternoon."

Somewhat amazed, Grace realized that Daniel, who'd enjoyed getting her fired as a teacher, wasn't going to fire her from cooking. She wanted to let him go. If she would just keep silent for another minute, he would. "Daniel, wait!"

He had the door almost closed. She saw him freeze. She could almost feel his longing to ignore her.

But she couldn't let him. Some things were just necessary.

He came back into the room. Standing in the doorway, letting the snow swirl in, he asked, "What?"

"Last night, when you . . . uh . . . led me outside." She fell silent, waiting for him to get it.

He didn't.

"I don't know where we went. I mean, it was dark, and I just trailed behind you to find . . . the . . ."

"It's an outhouse, Grace. Is the word too crude for you to say?" Daniel seemed very tired for some reason. She didn't know how he could be. He was making the boys do all the work.

"Come on, then. I'm in a hurry." Daniel stepped out the door. "Got to get the boys to work on windfalls."

Grace wanted to scold him. She looked at his impatient expression and decided to postpone it. She trailed him to the outhouse.

When she got there, Daniel said with heavy sarcasm, "Can you find your way back?"

Since it was only about twenty feet from the front door, she didn't bother to answer. She just went in the little house and shut the door with a sharp click.

When she came out, he was gone.

She hadn't seen where she lived before. When she'd been inside, it had seemed like a cave.

That's because it *was* a cave.

All she could see from where she was standing was a wooden door set into the side of a snow-covered mountain. A plume of smoke curled out of the hillside where the stove's chimney emerged.

Even with the snow still falling, she could see where the boys had left tracks sliding down this morning. Her heart quavered at the long, reckless ride they'd taken. Then, at the end, they'd become airborne for another ten feet before landing in a deep drift. She could see the battered-down drift just in front of the door. Daniel had trampled the snow back a bit and broken a path to the outhouse, but everywhere else it was standing in fluffy drifts higher than her head. The cave door swung inward, or they'd never have gotten it open.

This wasn't like a Chicago snowstorm. There the snow came heavily, and the weather was viciously cold. Wind battered the tall buildings endlessly in that big, dangerous city. The snow was dirty and flattened by the clattering wheels of countless delivery wagons and carriages.

It was bitter cold here, but it didn't cut through her clothes and into her skin as it had there, at least not today. And this Texas snow was pure white, almost blinding — beautiful.

Reluctantly she went back to the house. The door was closed because she'd been the last one to use it. She went inside and wished she could stay out. The dark cave didn't appeal to her. There was nothing to do. The boys had taken their steak bones and potato skins with them. A new bucket of snow melted on the stove. And there was a neat little pile of food at the end of the table closest to the stove. Her dinner.

She noticed they'd left her a potato this time and almost smiled. She washed her hands with water she scooped out of the bucket on the stove, ate her lunch with no utensils . . . and enjoyed the quiet. She actually went so far as to sit on Daniel's stool. The biscuit was so awful she didn't finish it, and she wondered how the boys could have.

"Use more sourdough." She looked down at the ugly little jar pushed up against the wall beside the flour and a bucket of eggs. Sourdough, huh? That sounded about right.

Enough light sneaked in through the stovepipe hole and the edges of the door that she could see, although the room was murky. She looked around, remembering she'd missed the hanging beef this morning. The stove was in one corner, but small as it was, it took up most of one wall. The ladle she'd used to pour water out to wash her hands hung on the wall behind the stove. There was a stack of clothing and blankets beside the stove.

The door was in the wall opposite the

stove. The beef was in one corner beside the door, and the table was in the other, although they couldn't exactly be called corners because the walls were uneven and the room was more round than square. The table took up a quarter of the room. A lantern sat on the floor beside the table. There was nothing else. No more surprises.

She was tempted to do a practice batch of biscuits, but she didn't dare waste flour. She threw her scraps outside, lingering in the crystal clean world. She wondered how long this snow would last. With a little smile, she decided at least it would keep Parrish away. She enjoyed the cold and soaked up the purity of the white world. She couldn't help but be glad she had on boots and pants. Her legs had never been this warm before.

The cold finally drove her back toward the house. She wondered how the boys and Daniel stood it all day. Of course, Daniel was driving them with hard work. She looked over at the nice barn. A building five times the size of the house. She saw a little chicken coop, too, but the chickens must have taken refuge from the cold and stayed inside.

If hard work kept Daniel and the boys warm, it might work for her. She was tempted to go see if there was any work she could do outside, but there was no one to be seen around the place. Her . . . family — she could hardly make herself think the word. Her husband and . . . children — her stomach swooped as she forced herself to face facts. They were nowhere to be seen. She went back inside reluctantly and sat down to wait out the afternoon.

THIRTEEN

Sally sat on Adam's shoulders, and a giggling Laura hung from one ankle as though Adam were nothing but a tree to climb. He'd had Laura in his arms most of the way, but that hadn't suited her and he had the broken eardrums to prove it.

Mandy and Beth tagged him, yammering up a storm and kicking the snow out of the way with their boots. The girls were all red-nosed and buzzing with energy from sledding. He tried not to pick up the pace any more as he headed for the porch steps. He was next thing to trotting now.

Clay had as good as thrown him out of the house because his hovering was driving Sophie crazy. But the woman he'd rescued was Adam's responsibility. He'd found her and brought her home. No reason all the work should fall on Sophie.

He swung Sally down headfirst over his shoulder, pretending to drop her just to make her scream. Her head would knock on the low porch roof if he left her perched up there. Then he hoisted little Laura into his arms. Sally dashed inside. Mandy snatched the tyke away from him as she charged into the house. He stepped back to let Beth pass then walked in.

The injured woman sat at the kitchen table, quietly slicing a hank of venison into steaks while Sophie kneaded bread and talked. Both women looked up. Sophie smiled. The other one frowned.

"You're feeling better, then?" Adam flinched at his stupid question. Of course she was feeling better. She was awake and sitting up. Sophie had her wrapped in a warm shawl, and though the woman was a sight taller and a whole lot thinner than a very round-bellied Sophie, she wore one of Sophie's riding skirts.

Adam could see a flash of her ankles swathed in thick red socks. The ankle where she'd been bound was thicker because of the bandaging Sophie had done. The bit of red showing in the toe holes of her boots reminded Adam of how close she'd come to real danger in last night's cold. But not so close she hadn't managed to slug him solidly. His nose was swollen to double its normal size, and one eye opened only a slit.

The woman nodded then focused on the venison as if the job were a matter of life and death.

Adam took a second to stare at her. She was skin and bones, but under Sophie's blouse and riding skirt, he saw strength, too. Her hair was streaked here and there with gray. Last night he'd judged her to be a young woman, considering her strength. He rubbed his aching nose tenderly. Now he thought she was older, maybe close to forty, only a few years younger than his forty-five.

She'd pulled her hair back and pinned it into a knot low on her head. He could see the long and graceful curve of her neck. Her hands worked with steady competence, every move so feminine and dainty he could almost hear music.

After her staunch refusal to talk about how she'd come to that remote place, Adam knew it was a waste of time to question her, but he had to try. "Can you talk about what happened to you?"

The woman's hands paused. She looked up, shook her head, and went back to slicing.

"Now listen here. . . ." Adam jerked his Stetson off his head and crushed the brim beneath his buckskin gloves.

"Leave her alone, Adam." Sophie waved a

hand towel at him as if she were shooing away a pesky fly. "She'll talk when and if she's ready, and she doesn't need you badgering her."

Adam slapped his thigh with his hat and saw snow sprinkle down onto Sophie's floor. "I want to know —"

The girls picked that moment to erupt from the bedroom, their warm sledding clothes shed. The girls started chattering and giggling.

Mandy had Laura on her hip and went to sit down by the newcomer. "Want to trade jobs, Tillie?" Mandy offered Laura to her.

"Tillie?" This was the first time Adam had heard her name. Maybe she'd confided in Sophie about everything.

"Let me take your coat." Beth came up beside him, always the caretaker.

Sally gave him a huge hug around his waist.

The woman's eyes widened as she looked between the baby and the girls tending Adam. She looked stunned and almost broken. He thought he saw tears brimming in her eyes.

"What is it?" His question was between the two of them. The girls were too busy chattering to notice, though he suspected they and their ma didn't miss much.

"They . . . touch you." She shook her head as if she was dazed then dashed the back of her wrist over her eyes. Tillie stood from the table. "I'll be glad to hold the baby. Let me wash up."

Mandy giggled. "You'll be sorry you said that soon enough. I'd rather chop on a dead animal any day than have to look after Laura. She weighs a ton!"

Tillie's full lips curved into a smile. She went to the dry sink, and Sophie handed her a bar of lye soap and poured warm water over her hands. Tillie gave Sophie a startled glance. "You don't have to wait on me, Miss Sophie."

Adam figured it all out then. He'd never lived as a slave, but he'd known men who had. Of course, Tillie had spent time as property to someone else. His life as a free-man from birth was the exception rather than the rule among black folks. She was stunned that white children would touch a black man. She couldn't believe Sophie was helping her wash up.

And that shackle told the rest of the story. Oh, it was possible she was an escaped prisoner, wanted for some crime, but that didn't seem likely. Adam suspected her own war for emancipation had just been waged, and she didn't trust anybody to back her should the man who owned her come hunting.

Tillie washed her hands and took Laura as if she'd been handed a pot of gold.

Adam smiled. He could see her uncertainty with the condition of freedom. She needed guidance and help.

And he was just the man to provide it.

Parrish looked at the gap. He'd ridden through it just a day ago, following Grace cowering in the man's wagon. Parrish was sure the man had no idea he'd been carrying a stowaway. Parrish had camped out in the nasty weather so no one in town would see him so soon after Grace's disappearance. He'd had to talk to the blacksmith to rent a horse, but he'd kept away from folks otherwise.

Now he was back to finish his business with that snip of a girl so he could get out of this wretched country. Solid snow packed the gap straight up a hundred feet. Absolutely impassable. He was so furious that his rage threatened to choke him.

He took his temper out on the worthless nag he was riding. The blacksmith hadn't given him the same horse he'd rented Friday night. This one was balky, even more uncooperative than the last. The blacksmith had given Parrish a harmless look and said the other horse he'd rented was spoken for, although that same horse stood right there in the stall, plain as day.

That young punk Mike O'Casey stood coated in filth and sweat from working over his stinking forge, with no respect for his betters. Parrish wanted to beat the arrogance out of him. But the Irish trash, with his freckles and red hair, had arms like corded steel. He weighed a hundred pounds more than Parrish, and he looked as though he'd welcome a fight. And even if Parrish won, which he figured to do if only by using the revolver he carried, he'd still not have a horse.

Parrish had gritted his teeth and taken the nag.

And now here he was. Grace as far from him behind this snow-filled pass as if she perched on the moon.

He knew he should just ride away. Texas didn't suit him. He missed the anonymity of Chicago and the street urchins who made such easy prey.

But his temper goaded him. He hungered to make her sorry for what she'd done. The image of her cowering under his fists kept him awake at night and rode him like a spur all day. He'd been out of prison for a year, and he'd yet to sleep a full night through. And when he did fall into a fitful sleep, he had brutally satisfying dreams of making her bleed and crawl.

"There has to be a way into that canyon." He rode to the left and the right, but not trained in the ways of the wilderness, he couldn't think of how to get past that solid wall of rock and snow.

He looked back at Mosqueros. If he showed up there acting as though he was passing through, he could scout around and find a way in, but it would take time. He shivered from the wind-whipped snow and ached from the rough ride on the slow-moving nag.

How could he stay in Mosqueros? He was down to his last few dollars. If he *was* passing through, he'd steal something and high-tail it as he had in a string of towns as he followed Grace's trail. But he'd found her now, and he had to stay put until he got his hands on her.

Then he laughed. His laugh turned into a snarl. His fists rose in the bitter wind. *Mosqueros needs a schoolteacher!* He'd driven the one they had into the hills. There'd be no one else to handle the job. He'd been a schoolmaster in his youth before he'd found children to make his money for him.

He turned the horse back toward Mosqueros. He'd keep an eye on the gap and scout the land on Saturdays and Sundays looking for another entrance. And the rest of the time, he'd bring a little learning to the children of Mosqueros. He might not be able to get this stupid horse to mind him, but he'd always had a knack for instilling fearful obedience in children.

All but Grace.

He might even find a few children who'd be likely members for the new family he'd need to start once he worked his fury toward Grace out of his system.

He kicked the horse savagely to make it move. The hag crow-hopped and kicked up its hind legs. Nearly unseated, Parrish didn't kick the animal again. Nothing in Texas acted the way it should. Nothing!

The cave was warm — she'd give Daniel that. The door slammed open. She had already realized she needed to give the door a wide berth in the tiny house. She braced herself.

Ike came dashing into the house, bent double as if he was in pain. He actually closed the door, which sounded an alarm to Grace.

"Ike, is everything all right?" Grace stepped back so he didn't knock her over.

"I gotta get warm." Ike dropped on his knees in front of the stove. Grace knelt beside him, worried that his hands were frostbitten, since he'd tucked them inside his coat.

Slowly, on a soft breath, Ike pulled out his hands.

Before Grace could see what he'd done to himself, the door slammed open again and Luke rushed in, carrying the cat. It yowled and wriggled until Luke dropped it.

"Close the door, stupid." Ike pulled her attention back.

He opened one hand, and Grace saw two tiny furry things; his other hand opened, and there were two more. Kittens. So tiny they still had their eyes closed.

"Where did you get them?"

The cat came up to Ike on the side away from Grace. Rising up on her hind legs, she sniffed at Ike's hand. A much smaller cat than she'd been just last night.

"Your cat had kittens?"

"Out of season. She should have had 'em in the spring." Ike lowered his hand so the cat could see her four babies. "She must have just birthed 'em last night. I found them in the barn, but it's too cold. They'll

200

freeze to death."

Ike glanced up, and Grace remembered the day the two of them had doctored the cat at school. Despite the fact that none of the boys wanted her for their ma, accord passed between her and Ike.

"They'll be okay." Grace patted Ike's shoulder. "You'll take good care of them, and their mom will feed them. Before you know it, we'll have five cats in this family."

Luke shoved himself between Grace and Ike. He jostled Ike's arm.

"Watch it, stupid." For the first time in history — as far as Grace knew their history at least — one of the boys got bumped without hitting back. Ike held the kittens too carefully. He didn't even yell, out of deference for the babies.

"Sorry, Ike. Can I help?" Luke leaned down until he almost touched the kittens with his nose. He reached his hand toward one.

"Just one finger, Luke. They're really fragile. You shouldn't touch a baby kitten at all. Their mother might abandon them. But I had to bring 'em in." Ike looked sideways at Grace for a second, a furrow cutting between his brow. "I know I shouldn't have touched them. But she born-ed 'em right out in the middle of the barn. It must be her first litter. I reckon she don't know how it's done yet. You think they'll be all right?"

"I think you had to take the chance." Grace silently prayed they would survive, hurting for Ike if they didn't. He'd blame himself. "They'd never have made it if you'd left them there. You had to do it, Ike."

Ike nodded, frowning but with an assurance that Grace had seen before when he tended animals. Ike said to Luke, "Touch it on its head and draw your finger gentle-like down toward its tail."

Luke did as he was told. "It's so soft. Softest thing I've ever felt."

Ike's expression lifted as he smiled at his brother. "Yeah, it is. Let's see if we can get the cat to feed 'em."

Ike glanced at Grace. She nodded and knelt beside the fretful mother cat. She petted the cat, gently urging her down on her side. Ike laid all four kittens on her belly.

The mother, her yellow fur soft and thick with winter growth, twisted her head back to study her babies. The babies started a high-pitched mewling, and the mother's purr sped up.

Grace had no trouble keeping the cat on her side. She seemed to know that was where she needed to be. The kittens' tiny paws waved and pushed at the fur. Their bellies were on the ground, and their feet could only inch them along.

Ike and Luke — who still used but one finger — nudged the kittens toward food. One by one they found what they were looking for and their heartrending cries quieted. It was only moments later that all four babies were eating.

The mother cat kept looking at them, giving them an occasional lick with her pink tongue or caress with her quivering nose. The babies drank steadily. Their paws, tipped with claws so fine that they were translucent, kneaded at their mother's stomach.

Grace knelt there stroking the cat's fur in a moment of peaceful joy with two of her sons. Ike and Luke just watched, looking up at Grace to smile every now and again.

Finally, Ike broke the silence. "They're gonna make it, aren't they, Ma?"

Grace smiled back. "You know, I think they are. Now there are enough cats so everyone can have his own."

Ike said, "Nope. They're all mine."

Luke nodded without comment.

"You know, I just thought she was fat." Grace sat back on her knees.

Ike snickered. "Me, too."

Daniel came in carrying an armload of

wood. He kicked the door shut. "What ya got there, boy?"

He dropped the heavy pieces of split oak in one corner then crouched down beside the cat. "Kittens, great. They'll keep the mice down. But they should be in the barn. No room for five cats in here." Daniel sounded strict, but he pulled one glove off his left hand, reached out, and rubbed the cat's shoulder. His heavy hand rested gently on the new mother.

"I'll move 'em out just as soon as I can, Pa. She didn't even make a nest for 'em. She had two in one spot and the other two just laid out alone. Reckon she's too young to be a ma yet."

Daniel thought about it. "How hard did you hunt, boy? A mother cat has six kittens most times."

Ike jumped to his feet. "I looked pretty hard, but maybe I'd better go over the barn again."

Daniel nodded. "Just to be on the safe side."

Ike rushed out with Luke on his heels. Ike took a second to close the door.

"That young'un is the animal doctorin'- est boy I've ever seen." Daniel kept petting the cat. "Luke's got the talent for doctoring but not the same soft heart for animals as

Ike has. That soft heart of his will get him in trouble."

Grace couldn't help but smile. "I wonder where he got that soft heart?"

Daniel jerked his head up and scowled as if he'd forgotten Grace was there.

Well, to whom had he been talking, then?

"I'm not softhearted."

The cat stopped purring at Daniel's disgruntled tone.

Grace just barely kept from rolling her eyes. "No, of course not . . . excuse me. You're just as hard-hearted as they come." She glanced at the cat, which Daniel still petted.

With a heavy sigh, Daniel said, "I reckon we just got ourselves four more house cats. When Ike brought that kitten home, I told him, 'No cat in the house.' That didn't even last an hour."

"Five house cats. You ever have a mouse in this house, Daniel?"

"No, but what self-respecting mouse would want to move into this place?" Daniel's mouth turned up on one side, nearly a smile.

Grace grinned.

"We did have a badger pop out through a hole in the ground in that corner." Daniel pointed to a spot right behind Grace.

With a squeak not much different than that of a hungry little kitten, Grace wheeled around on her knees toward the corner.

Daniel was still laughing when he closed the door on his way out.

The kittens moved into the tiny cave with the rest of them. When they survived through a couple of nights and the mama cat seemed to catch on to just how to mother them, Daniel insisted they be moved back to the barn.

The mother, in full power as a parent now, moved them back to the cave, carrying them by the napes of their necks, one at a time.

Daniel declared war with the mother cat and moved them back.

They'd been fighting it out for three days.

The snow started melting. The winter blizzard had come and gone, leaving cool but tolerable weather.

Grace's biscuits showed meager improvement, or else the menfolk were truly starving. Either way, the people survived just as well as the kittens.

As she stood, wondering how to pass this afternoon in the dark little home, even the kittens were currently, if temporarily, outside. She, on the other hand, had been made to feel decidedly unwanted outside.

The door slammed open. She braced herself for the onslaught.

It was only one small onslaught — John.

"Hi, Ma."

"Close the door, John."

John stopped short. He stared at her.

"The door," she said again.

He still looked.

"What's the matter?" she asked.

He shut the door.

A surge of triumph went through her. Suddenly she realized that it didn't take much to make her happy. A burned steak, warm clothes, an occasional split second of obedience from her son.

"How'd you know I'm John?"

The question surprised her. "How could I not know? You boys are nothing alike."

"We're exactly alike. Everybody says so."

Grace shrugged. "You're John. You sit in the middle at meals. You're a good reader." She leaned down and whispered, "And I think you're the nicest one of the bunch."

He gave her a look that made her wonder if she'd just insulted him.

"Am not. Mark's best."

"At some things he's best," Grace agreed. "At other things Luke is best. You've all got talents."

John studied her as though she had just

sprouted a second head. "No, we all know Mark's best, then Abe." John looked down at the floor and kicked at it.

He was so overly nonchalant that Grace knew what he was going to say next was very important to him.

"I'm worst at things. It's okay."

Boom! An explosion shattered the quiet of the cave.

FOURTEEN

Something slammed into the roof so hard the whole mountain shook.

Grace screamed and stumbled into the back wall. John shouted in terror. His fear hurt worse than her own. He fell against her, and they crashed to the floor in a heap.

Rocks from the ceiling pelted her back. John jumped up. Instinctively Grace grabbed him and sheltered him with her body. A sharp stone ripped her shirt with a loud tearing sound.

The door blasted open. One leather hinge at the bottom of the door snapped. Snow erupted into the opening. The door wedged into the ground and stayed standing.

The red-hot stove shook. It tipped sideways onto one leg, falling straight toward them. Grace shoved John against the far wall, mere feet away from the stove. With a sharp rending of metal, the stovepipe shattered into pieces and tumbled to the floor, rolling toward Grace. She flung her arms around the boy. Glancing over her shoulder, Grace saw the blazing stove teeter.

She lifted her feet and braced them on the wall as a piece of metal clattered toward her, keeping her body between the pipe and John. When the pipe stopped rolling, she kicked it away. The stove tilted back, rocked twice more, and stayed upright.

The outside rumbled and exploded around them. Dirt and stones from the ceiling continued to crumble, filling the house with choking grit. The savagery went on and on. Minutes passed. The cave went pitch-black except for the fiendish red glow from the fire.

Grace felt as if she were being swallowed, gulped down into the deep, dark belly of a monster. The noise became muted. Snow cascaded through the hole in the roof left from the broken pipe. The snow sizzled on the stove then clogged the small opening and stopped.

John sobbed in her arms, and she whispered comfort to him without knowing just what she said.

As suddenly as it began, it stopped.

The silence filtered into her mind. She slowly lifted her head. Dirt and rocks fell away from her back. The air she breathed was thick with dirt. She glanced overhead. The ceiling hadn't collapsed. The stove still burned. She looked down at the frightened boy in her arms. "John, it's over."

His face was buried against her chest.

"It's really over, John."

John lifted his tearstained face and looked into her eyes. His expression beseeched her to say they were all right.

He said between trembling lips, "Wh–wh–what happened?"

"I don't know." She lifted herself to a sitting position, and slashing pain tore across her back. She wanted to cry out, but John's terror forced her to be calm. "But we survived it, whatever it was."

She moved slowly, afraid the world would erupt again. John clung to her. She pulled him with her as she brushed the dirt and rocks off her back. Her back protested. A stab of pain ripped across her chest. One of her shoulders didn't want to move. She suppressed a groan of agony.

She got to her feet, John's arms sliding from around her neck to around her waist as she stood. She was too unsteady to do anything but stumble to the nearest bench. Careful to avoid the hot stovepipe, she lowered herself onto a seat and pulled John onto her lap.

He hurled himself the few inches between them and wrapped his sturdy arms around her. Her bruised body protested, but he felt so good — so solid and healthily and miraculously alive — that she hugged him back fiercely. She buried her face in his soft blond hair, and when he started to cry, she couldn't hold back her own tears.

The emotional storm passed, and John's shoulders ceased their shuddering. He lay exhausted against her for long minutes.

She had no idea what had happened. She wished John were safely away from this living tomb. But she was treacherously glad she had him with her in the awful, cramped, dark little world.

At last his arms loosened from her a bit. She lifted her head from his white-blond curls, and they looked at each other.

She wasn't ready for his question. "Are Pa and my brothers all right?"

Grace caught herself before a cry of fear could escape. She'd only had time to think of herself and John. What *had* happened?

Grace looked down at John's frightened little face. The stove lit up his eyes. The slits in the stove door glowed like devilish teeth, bared in an evil smile. They were trapped, buried alive. She had to take care of him. She squared her shoulders, straightened her aching spine, and began taking stock.

"Hop down. Let's see what's going on."

John got up, but he caught hold of the baggy shirt Daniel had given her and stayed tight up against her side.

She went to the door and pulled. It dragged against the floor and reluctantly swung open. They were faced with a solid wall of white. Even in the darkness, the white was so vivid they couldn't fail to recognize it. Snow. The door was buried in a snowdrift.

"There must have been an avalanche," Grace said. "Has this ever happened before?"

She looked down at John. He shrugged. "We just moved here this spring. We've never had a winter before."

"Well, I suppose your pa is just going to have to dig us out." Grace had a vision of a mountain of snow burying them hundreds of feet deep. Had Daniel and the other boys escaped the avalanche, or were they out there somewhere under this snow, crushed and dead?

She turned her mind away from such dreadful thoughts. She kept the fear out of her eyes as best she could. "I guess we can help. Let's start digging."

John seemed to become calmer when she

suggested a job for him to do. She was a little steadier herself. They went to the door and began pawing through the snow.

They pulled the snow inward and shoved it off to the side. At first they felt a feverish rush as they dug, but after a while the hard work began to tell on them, and they calmed down and worked steadily. When their fingers got too cold, they went to the stove and warmed them.

As she and John stood side by side at the stove, Grace realized that the crimson teeth weren't so bright as they had been. "We're going to need to add kindling. The fire is going out."

John bent down to the woodpile beside the stove while Grace, using her shirt to protect her hand, turned the squeaking little knob and lowered the cast-iron door. Burning wood nearly tipped out into her hands.

Grace realized that the stove didn't need more fuel. So why was the fire going out? She slammed the door with a sharp clank of metal and said, "Let's don't add wood yet. It's still got enough and we're warm."

John looked at her. "Okay." With perfect trust, he dropped the sticks back onto the woodpile.

The fire was dying. Grace looked up at the sealed opening where the stovepipe belonged. Where a fire couldn't live, people couldn't. They were running out of air.

A light sweat broke out all over her. She steadied herself and looked down at John's trusting eyes. She had to think of something, for him.

"I'll tell you what, let's say a prayer." Since she'd escaped from Parrish, she'd attended church as was proper. But right now she needed more than proper. She needed a miracle.

"Okay," John said. "But don't be all day about it like the parson."

In her heart she prayed, *God, what do I do? I need help. Not for me, God, but for John. He's so young. He trusts me.* She stared at the stove, aware of John's chubby little hand catching hold of hers.

"God, take care of us and take care of the rest of the family." She smiled down at John. "How was that?"

She backed up, thinking to sit and hold him again. Working made you breathe hard, and that *must* take more air. They needed to save it for as long as they could.

As she stepped back, Grace tripped over the stovepipe. She looked at the snow-packed hole. It dripped steadily onto the stove. If it was melting slowly now, maybe it would melt faster with the stovepipe carrying hot air directly to it. She didn't know if she'd thought of it or God had told her, but she thought the timing of her "idea" was directly related to her prayer.

"We'd better see if we can get those pipes back into the hole." She bent to pick up the first cylinder. "The stove won't burn well if it doesn't have an airhole."

John went right to work. They gathered four pieces of the cooled pipe and fitted them together in a column about as tall as Grace. As the hollow metal clinked, Grace heard John whimper softly.

Trying to keep both of them encouraged, she said, "You know, you're wrong about Mark being better than you, John. I think you're terrific." She wasn't saying it to make him feel good. She had always thought John was the best behaved of the rowdy Reeves boys.

"Nah, I'm not. I'm dumbest and smallest and slowest."

"You did really well in your classes, John. Better by far than Mark. You weren't dumbest."

"Yeah, I was, 'cause Mark knows how to do everything. He just doesn't do it, if'n he don't want to. I wanted to do it, 'cause I thought it was fun, mostly. But if he'd'a wanted to, Mark woulda beat me for sure."

Grace shook her head as she settled the pipe into the hole in the center of the stove. "That's not how it works, John. Smart is as smart does."

John helped her brace the stovepipe. "What's that s'posed to mean?"

Grace smiled in the fading red light. She could imagine the little furrow in John's forehead. He and Ike were the only ones who ever doubted themselves for a second. "It means if you're smart inside your head but you never act smart, then you're not so smart after all."

"Mark acts smart."

"Not in school things," Grace pointed out. "He got bad grades."

"But in other things," John insisted. "In real things that matter, like hunting stray calves and handling the horses."

Grace's jaw tightened as she thought of such young boys doing so much work. They needed a chance to be children, and they needed to respect education. She wanted to shake Daniel.

Then she thought of him out there some- where and realized if she could get her hands on him right now, she'd be so glad to see him — because it would mean he was alive and she was unburied — she'd give him a hug instead of shaking him. And she also had to admit that she was glad she had a steady little worker like John beside her in this tight spot. And who had trained him to work but Daniel?

Metal scraped on metal as she raised the pipe to the ceiling. She struggled but couldn't get it to go into the snow-clogged hole. The fire dimmed now until there were no flames at all, only glowing embers. Grace knew they didn't have long.

"John, what you're saying is making my point. Mark is better at some things, and you're better at others. That's just what I said."

"Yeah, but school is dumb and animals are important."

Grace fought down her panic as she wrestled with the stubborn pipes. Goaded to hurry, she lifted the whole thing off the stove and set it on the table. "I've got to clear some of that snow and stick the pipe out first, then set it on the stove hole."

John worked beside her. He pulled up a bench and held it steady.

She clawed at the snow and let it fall with a hiss on the stove. Her arms reached up higher and higher into the hole. The snow burned at her hands as they became encased in the bitter cold. If the hole was just a bit bigger, maybe she could squeeze through and dig them out through the roof, but the hole was so small now that not even John could wriggle through. When she'd cleared it as high as she could reach, she said, "I'm ready for the pipe now."

John handed the awkward tube to her.

This time, fitting the pipe into the hole overhead first, she got the whole thing put together neatly. As she climbed down off the bench, she heard water begin running down the pipe.

The fire in the stove sputtered wildly.

She had latched onto the fire as proof that there was still some air to breathe in the cave, and her heart fluttered with fear at the thought of its going out and leaving them in the pitch dark. Then, as the embers hissed, it occurred to Grace that putting out the fire might be a good thing. That might leave more air for them.

"Let's build the fire up some more," John suggested. "It looks kind of low."

Grace wondered how far the pipe had to melt before the smoke could escape and let fresh air in. She knew if she threw in more wood, it wouldn't burn. "Not yet. There's plenty for now until the snow stops melting." Grace sank down onto the bench.

John sat on her lap without being urged.

They sat there and listened to the water

run. The embers continued to fade. There was plenty of wood for a roaring fire.

Please, God, help us.

"We should pray again, Ma." John turned from the captivating red and looked at her.

Grace couldn't help but smile. "I was already praying in my heart. But let's pray out loud."

John bowed his little head, and Grace remembered the unruly Reeves boys tearing around in church every week. She'd judged them very harshly for their behavior. But they'd been there, worshipping. She should have given Daniel credit for that.

"Help Pa to be okay. Bless Abe, Ike, Mark, Luke, and John." He reeled off the names, including his own, as if he'd done it a thousand times. "And God bless Ma."

He was silent, so Grace spoke into the darkness. "Take care of the whole Reeves family." John had prayed for himself. She opened her mouth to add, "And me," then realized she'd already done it. She was part of the Reeves family.

Suddenly she didn't have to forcibly keep her fears to herself or her spine straight. She wrapped her arms tightly around John. "You just did something wonderful for me, John."

He looked up at her. "You mean praying

220

for you?"

That pulled Grace up short. No, she hadn't meant that. But maybe, just maybe, praying was what it all came down to. She settled John firmly against her. "Praying for me was wonderful. Thank you. And you did something else for me, too."

"What's that?" John rubbed his head against her neck when he looked into her eyes.

She glanced at the dying fire and heard the dripping of the melting snow. She felt a pang of regret that she hadn't been able to do more to save this precious little boy. She felt even worse to think that she would never have the pleasure of being his mother. Her chin quivered, but she held it steady. "You reminded me of who I am."

"The teacher?"

Grace shook her head. "No, before I was a teacher."

"You worked somewhere else?" John shifted his weight around as if getting comfortable for story time.

"Oh yes. I worked very hard somewhere else. But I'm not talking about what I did. I'm talking about what I was."

John shrugged and looked confused. "What were you?"

"I was brave."

FIFTEEN

John tilted his head and frowned. "Brave?"

"Yes, I was so brave when I was growing up." Grace nodded. "I had to be very strong for the work I did and for the children I took care of."

In a voice laced with fear, John asked, "You didn't cook for them, did you?"

Grace smiled. "You ate it."

"Yeah," John admitted. "But it helps if you're *real* hungry."

Grace laughed out loud. "Well, the truth is, I didn't cook for them. I worked at a really hard job, and when we'd get home —"

"Who's 'we'?"

"My sisters and I."

"Did you have a lot of them?" John bounced on her knee and swung his dangling legs.

Grace was glad he was relaxing. "I had more sisters than you have brothers. About twice as many."

"There were ten of you?"

"Yup, at least."

One corner of John's mouth curled up in confusion. "You don't know for sure how many?"

"No, it wasn't that. I lived with a man who adopted me. I was an orphan. And he adopted a lot of other kids, too. The older ones would grow up and go away." Run away — like she had. "And younger ones would come and take their places at the carpet mill."

"What's a carpet mill?"

"It's a big, noisy factory where they make rugs." Grace cringed when she thought of the deafening weaving machines, clacking hour after hour. "It's too hot in the summer and too cold in the winter. We worked long hours at hard labor and didn't get much to eat. Then we'd go home to our father, who took all our money and fed us . . . well . . . not much."

"And when you were doing that, you were brave?"

"Oh yes. I took care of all my little sisters. I had to be tougher than all of them, and some of them were really tough because they'd been orphaned and lived on their own. And I had to be tougher than the other kids at the mill who picked on us. And I was. I could face down anyone." Honesty forced her to add, "Except my father." She'd always been scared of Parrish. For good reason. But she'd stepped in many times to draw Parrish's beatings onto herself to protect a little sister. "Sometimes I was even brave with him.

"And I was a teacher to my little sisters. I didn't learn to cook, but I knew how to read before my own mother died, and I taught my adopted sisters how, late at night when our light was supposed to be off."

"Boring," John groused.

Grace ignored his all-too-common opinion. "Then when I was old enough, I got to leave my father's house and be a teacher for a real job. For you and your brothers."

"Till Dad got you fired," John reminded her.

She shrugged. "What's done is done."

In Chicago, she'd left Parrish by running away. But unlike her older sisters, she couldn't just go off and leave all those little ones in his brutal hands. No one would have cared if she'd told the police, "My father adopts children to force them to work like slaves."

But they'd listened when she said, "My father is stealing from the carpet mill."

With grim satisfaction at the memory, Grace said to John, "Oh yes, I used to be brave, but I forgot how . . . until just this minute."

Grace and Hannah had come up with the plan of making a home for the six younger children. Grace had lived with Hannah for nearly ten years. They knew each other too well. Grace had the nerve to run and lead Parrish on a wild-goose chase. Hannah had the natural mother's heart and would do best with the children. Besides, Grace was old enough to be a teacher. She could find work and send money.

"And now you've remembered?" John asked.

"Yes, I have." When the police came, thanks to Grace's anonymous information, she and her sisters had been ready. The minute the police took Parrish away, Grace and her little family of girls had run.

Grace had no intention of putting the children in danger by returning them to the orphanage where they might again be adopted by some parent as cruel as Parrish, so they'd vanished into the streets of Chicago. Grace had seen to it that Hannah was settled then set out to find work. Always in the back of her mind, she knew Parrish would come after her.

Grace had heard that mother birds sometimes pretended to be wounded, letting a wing hang awkwardly, when a predator came too near. The hungry coyote would come after the wounded mother, leaving the nest of babies safely behind. She had no wing to dangle, only herself, but Parrish was a coyote. If he got free, he'd come.

She'd stowed away on a train that took her to Kansas City. At first she'd cleaned houses and served in diners, sending money home to Hannah. Then, after only a few months, she'd caught sight of Parrish walking down the Missouri street. He'd either escaped from jail or used his connections to escape justice.

She hopped another train, weaving her way across the country, changing names and jobs as she went, trying to lose herself in the western lands. . . .

John nudged her out of her thoughts. "What made you remember?"

At last she'd seen the ad for a teacher in Mosqueros. Teaching — it was what she'd always wanted to do. By that time, she hadn't sighted Parrish in months and she was tired of running. She had no schooling, but she didn't mention that when she asked to be tested. She'd educated herself thoroughly while she studied with her little sisters, so she fortunately passed with ease and was hired by Mosqueros to teach at their school.

One bright spot Grace thought of — if Parrish was still hunting her, he wasn't adopting more children. She didn't tell John any of this. Instead, her eyes fell on a Bible, tucked into a corner of the room, on the floor like everything else. "I just had the strangest thought come to me, probably because we're trapped in here."

"What thought?" One of her sons was actually listening to her.

Grace had been blessed by having children listen to her all her life, with the exception of her brand-new sons. She hoped she had something worth hearing. "I remembered that God is faithful."

John's brow furrowed with concentration. "What's 'at mean?"

" 'It is of the Lord's mercies that we are not consumed, because his compassions fail not. They are new every morning: great is thy faithfulness.' It's from Lamentations. I used to read that one to my sisters."

"What does it mean that God is faithful?"

"Don't you ever feel like God is far away?"

John shrugged. "He *is* far away. He's up in heaven with my first ma. Pa says so."

Grace smiled. "Yes, God is up in heaven,

227

but He's right here, too," — she tapped John on his chest — "inside your heart."

"How can an old man be inside your heart?"

Grace controlled the urge to laugh. "Your picture of God as an old man is a common one, but that's not the picture I have of God. I think God looks like the wind."

"The wind doesn't look like anything," John protested.

"You can't see it, but no one doubts it's there. He has power like wind has power. You've seen the trees blowing in the wind, right?"

"Right."

"So you believe in the wind because of what it does. No one sees God, but everyone sees what He does. And the wind is air and the air is inside our chests when we breathe, just like our hearts. God is everywhere. And God never leaves us. God is faithful to us, even when we aren't so faithful to Him."

"Even if we're bad, God is still with us?" John asked with fearful eyes.

Grace knew her son. He had indeed, in his short life, been very bad. "Everyone is bad sometimes. 'For all have sinned, and come short of the glory of God.' That's why Jesus came and died. God sent Him to die in our places. Jesus sacrificed His life to save us."

John nodded with a serious face. "That's what Pa says."

"And what can be more faithful than that?"

"So God loves us and is faithful to us, even when we don't deserve it?"

Grace hugged him until he squeaked. The pain in her back and shoulder didn't seem important anymore. She pulled back and, in the dim light, saw a little boy who desperately wanted a mother.

Grace fell in love. She knew a fraction of how God felt because she knew she'd die for John. "God loves us *especially* when we don't deserve it, honey."

She gave him a noisy kiss on the cheek, which he wiped off with a growl of disgust, but he leaned closer to her. The disgust was all for show.

She didn't want to give him an excuse to climb down off her lap. She badly needed to hold on to someone she loved right now, when she might not be on the earth much longer. Every minute the stove dimmed.

"Let's read." The meager light from the stove would be enough. There was only one book in the house. John hopped off her lap and was back instantly with the family Bible.

She and John sat together, and she helped him sound out words. Slowly they worked their way through a sentence. She chose the book of John because her son liked knowing his name was from the Bible.

" 'In the beginning was the Word, and the Word was with God, and the Word was God.' "

John had taken to schooling. He'd picked up his letters and numbers right from the first. Now he read all but the hardest words. " 'The same was in the beginning with God.' "

And he kept improving. " 'In him was life; and the life . . .' " His reading slowed; his head nodded. " 'Was the light of men.' "

Grace knew they didn't have much longer.

She jerked awake when the Bible hit the floor. She realized it wasn't light in the cave anymore. John had fallen asleep in her arms.

With a nervous glance at the stove, she saw that the grating had become so dark that only the faintest glow of red still showed. The water hissed against the hot coals. She tried to stir herself to stay awake, but her muscles were heavy, her head cloudy and confused. She wanted sleep.

"This is it," she murmured. "The air is running out." She looked down at the sweet, sleeping boy in her arms. *God, forgive me for the coward I've been. Once I started running, I turned into a scared rabbit instead of the fighter I used to be. I thought . . . I guess I thought proper manners and the loneliness I've been living with were how respectable people behaved. Now I see I just held people away out of fear. I'm sorry.*

She used her waning strength to lift the Bible onto the tabletop. A loud splatter of snow dimmed the red glow until it was barely visible. With one hand holding her son and another resting on the Good Book, she prayed into the dark room, *Now that I remember how to be brave, if I had more time, I'd make You proud, Lord. Forgive me. Take John and me to be with You.* Her head fell forward.

A loud thud from the stovepipe startled her awake. Her heavy head lifted, and John stirred. A puff of white steam exploded from the grating.

"The snow must have put it out." John's voice quavered.

His fear was too much for her to bear. Yes, she'd been brave, and she was still brave. And she was married and the mother of five sons, even if just for another few moments. She refused to sit here and die without a fight.

She didn't like the idea of staying still and

doing nothing while they both suffocated in this dark pit. Her words sounded thick and stupid. "Let's throw some kindling on the fire. Maybe we can keep it going."

She and John tried to stand. She had to force her body to obey. John swayed and would have fallen if she hadn't steadied him. They both stumbled to the stove. Grace opened the grating door in the stove's belly. The wet wood in the stove mocked them.

Grace grabbed the fork and poked at the sodden black mess. She uncovered glowing embers. They tossed in kindling. Grace leaned down and blew gently on the smallest pieces of wood. And the stove blew back.

Grace jerked upright. "I felt wind."

She also realized her thoughts had cleared. "John, let's get some more wood on the fire. I think we've melted our way out through the stovepipe."

A little coaxing and patience and the first bit of dry wood caught. A curl of white smoke, full of steam, rose straight for the stovepipe, and then the shredded kindling burst into flames. Sizzling in protest, the wet wood even grudgingly dried and burned. The flame danced higher.

A draft from the stovepipe blew cold and fresh.

Shut in as tightly as they were, the cave

was very warm, and working on the stove had made their fingers nimble. That gave Grace the energy to turn to the door again. She stared at the solid wall of white. "I wish we had a shovel."

"Wishin's a pure waste of time, Ma," John said.

Grace thought John sounded a little too old, but in this instance he was absolutely right. She held the ladle up in front of her and studied it against the heavy snow. Setting it aside, she said, "Let's get back to work with our hands."

Grace and John scooped at the snow. With a steady supply of fresh air, they had the strength to work steadily, pausing to warm themselves as the fire leaped up and burned with a white flame.

John talked about his family and school and ranch life.

Grace was surprised at how much advice the little boy had for her about cooking. "Your pa taught you all how to cook?"

John shoved snow to the side. The pile grew until it reached the tabletop. It melted on the side nearest the stove, and the floor of the little cave became muddy. "I don't know about teachin' us, Ma. He just makes us do it an' we've had to learn or we starve, simple as that. We all started out cookin' "kinda like you."

"Um, you eat it," she reminded him again. She'd eaten it, too.

"Like I said, eat it or starve."

"So how do you make the biscuits stay separate, like your pa does? Mine all run together."

"First you take the flour and —"

Grace noticed the stove had stopped sizzling and the fire burned brightly. "Look at the pipe, John."

John turned away from the hole he'd been digging so diligently. "There's light coming in from around the edges."

"Grace, are you down there?" Daniel's voice echoed through the stovepipe.

She felt tears of relief burn behind her eyes as she ran to the stove and shouted to the ceiling, "Yes, John and I are trapped in here."

There was absolute silence. For a second she began to think she'd imagined hearing Daniel.

In a strangled voice, Daniel finally said, "John is in there with you?"

"Yes, we were in here when the whole world seemed to explode. We've been trying to dig our way out."

An explosion of another kind came from above the pipe. Daniel shouted, "John's in there, boys. He's okay."

Shrieks and hollers of glee rattled the pipe.

"Where'd you think I was, Pa?" John yelled.

Daniel's shouting turned to laughter. "I was worried about you, boy. I didn't know where you'd gotten to. There was an avalanche, and . . ." Daniel's voice broke.

Grace heard everything. He'd thought his son might be buried in the snow, just as she and John had worried about the rest of the family. Her heart turned over, and the tears spilled as she imagined what Daniel had gone through. "Are all of you all right?" Grace yelled.

"Yeah, sure. We were above it. I was afraid. I've been praying and working full steam ever since it happened, trying to get to you. Hoping John . . ." He fell silent.

"Are you going to stand up there and talk all day, or are you going to get us out of here?" John demanded.

Daniel spoke again, steady now. "We'll have you out in two shakes, son. I've been digging out front. When I saw smoke coming out of the stovepipe, I ran up here to see if you could hear me. We were dragging windfalls down, and they got away from us on the steep slope. I didn't think . . . I mean . . . an avalanche never occurred to me."

There was silence again. Then Daniel roared, "Get back to work on that diggin', boys."

Grace turned to John. "They made it through. They're coming for us."

John smiled. His lips wobbled, but he held them steady. "I was powerful worried about 'em, Ma."

She dashed the tears away with her wrist then hugged John's shoulders. "We'll be out in a minute," she said. "Let's scoot up to the stove and take a break until our fingers get warm."

Without waiting for him to agree, Grace sat down and pulled John onto her lap. He seemed to fit there comfortably. She hugged him close and thanked God for her family, even though they still scared her to death.

Parrish had always scared her, but that hadn't stopped her from being brave. Well, it was time to remember how to be brave again.

"We've rested enough, John," Grace said with a firm jerk of her chin. "Let's get back to digging."

Sixteen

A fist, delicate and lily white, punched out of the snow and smacked Daniel in the nose.

He jerked backward, his feet slipped, and he landed on his backside. He looked at the hole in the snow made by the fist and saw Grace's cherry-red nose poking out of the snowdrift. He suspected his nose was now the same color, and not because of the cold.

"Well, it's certainly nice to see you boys." Grace smiled and pulled her nose back out of sight.

"We got through!" Mark dived at the hole and began clawing with his mittened hands.

The other boys plunged in.

Daniel scrambled around on his hands and knees and began digging. The hole grew wider. He saw little boy hands and big girl hands digging from the inside.

"We didn't think you guys were ever going to get here!" John shouted.

The sound of his son's voice gave Daniel

such a thrill that his heart almost pounded right out of his chest. He'd been so scared. He'd been fighting off the urge to begin mourning. Then he'd heard Grace and then John through the stovepipe.

"We're sick of being stuck in here!" John yelled as if he were disgusted.

They all laughed as if that was the funniest joke they'd ever heard. John and Grace laughed, too. All of their spirits were so high that, although Daniel was exhausted from hours of hard work in the sharp cold, and he knew the other boys were, too, Daniel could feel them bursting with energy.

Daniel heard Grace's gentle laughter from under the mountain of snow. He didn't think he'd ever heard her laugh before. The music of it warmed him as much as the hard work.

Before long, John poked his head out of the widening hole, then dived forward and tumbled through into the outside.

"Hey, don't leave me behind." Grace's good-natured voice — something else Daniel had never heard before — was full of mock indignation. Nowhere did he hear the prim, overly polite schoolmarm.

Grace scrambled out next, laughing. She jumped to her feet, threw her arms around

John, and hollered, "We're free! We made it!"

John slung his arms around her waist, and she whirled him in a circle. Then, as John's legs flew out, she let go deliberately and tossed John into the feather-soft snow. She turned on Mark and did the same thing to him.

Mark landed in the snow beside John, who grabbed a large ball of snow and slammed it into Mark's head. Ike got tossed next as Grace wrestled with him.

The reunion turned into a riot. Grace tackled every one of the boys. They ran wildly away from her, screaming, only to turn and attack. John joined her side and lunged at anyone who got close to them.

They were all shouting and shoving at each other when Grace turned from the chaos. Daniel caught the wicked gleam in her eye just before she charged him. She ran smack into him with her shoulder and slammed to a stop. Daniel looked down at her, feeling her arms around his waist and seeing her upturned face just inches below his. She weighed just slightly more than the average feather.

"You're a moose," she pouted. "How am I supposed to knock you into the snow?"

Daniel couldn't help grinning down at her

impish exasperation.

"Boys, how about a little help?" Grace shouted.

In a split second, all five boys pounced. With a shout of protest, Daniel went down in a flurry of arms and legs and snow.

They continued the battle until they had nearly turned themselves into a family of snow-people.

Finally, Grace plowed a huge armload of snow into Daniel's face. "Give up, big man. We've got you. Admit it."

Daniel lay flat on his back with Grace straddling his stomach. Two of the boys were on his legs. John and Mark were clinging to his arms. Somehow Abe was halfway underneath him, with his arms wrapped around Daniel's neck. They were all laughing like loons.

Daniel made one more Herculean effort to throw them all off, chuckling through the mouthful of snow. He managed to knock Mark loose and tip Grace forward until she almost smacked face-first into him, eating a mouthful of the snow that she'd smeared on him.

"Mark, hang on. He's getting away." Her golden eyes sparkled inches from his. Her cherry-red lips curved in laughter and glistened from the gleaming snow. She filled his sight. For a moment the weight of her filled his whole world.

Then his boys were back in the fray and pinned him down again. He quit fighting them from pure exhaustion. "I give." He let all his muscles go lax and lay flat on his back, panting for air. "I give. You win."

Grace began giggling. "We beat him, boys."

All five of his sons cheered and jumped off him. They began dancing around in the snow like a tribe of Indians at a medicine dance.

Grace scrambled off him. Aware of every move she made, Daniel studied her. She didn't seem to notice what she was doing to him. Leaping up, she celebrated with the boys.

Daniel lay there trying to cool down. Then he remembered his son, and the long, frightening day, and the victory over death. He staggered to his feet, his energy returning, and he joined the riot, only occasionally noticing Grace's long, snow-soaked tendrils of hair and the glitter of gold in her hazel eyes. Only now and then, when she sassed him or laughed in his face, did he wonder how her smile tasted.

The snow had buried an overanxious prude. He'd dug up a little spitfire.

At last, with a final laugh, Grace sat right down in the snow. "That's it. I'm tired. Party's over."

The boys all collapsed beside her, and Daniel dropped down on his knees in front of the line of them. They all breathed hard for a time.

"Say, how'd you know it was me Pa threw off his arm?" Mark asked, breathing hard.

Daniel braced himself for whatever trouble Mark might cause, such as telling Grace to go away and putting out that pretty spark in her eyes.

Grace laughed and pushed Mark backward in the snow. Mark just flopped back. He didn't even try to fight.

They'd sleep good tonight, Daniel thought. As long as they didn't have nightmares about John being buried alive. John and their ma.

"Okay, boys, here's how it is." Grace got to her feet. Snow stuck to her front and back, head to toe. She turned to face them.

The boys were in a straggly row in front of her, sprawled back on their elbows while Daniel knelt in the pounded-down snow at Grace's right. He watched as she nodded her head at the boy farthest left and went down the row without hesitation. "Ike, Mark, John, Abe, and Luke." The she jerked her head sideways and looked down at him. "And this big one, who's so hard to get down, is Daniel. Am I right?"

Abe crossed his legs at the ankle and sat forward, plopping his elbows on his knees. "No one knows us apart. Pa's the only one who's mostly always right, but we fool him from time to time."

"You do not." Daniel tossed a handful of snow at his oldest son.

Abe smirked, and Daniel wondered what tricks these scamps had pulled on him over the years.

"Well," Grace said, studying them, "if you set your mind to it, I'm sure you could fool anybody, because you're a smart bunch. But when you're just being yourselves, I never have to think about it twice."

"But what's the difference in us?" Luke set his face into such stubborn lines that Daniel knew they'd turn into wrinkles before he was thirty.

Grace crouched down in front of Luke. "You've got a line right here." She drew a finger down between Luke's eyes. "It's there because you're always thinking, planning. You're the best planner of the bunch, I'd say, always keeping in mind what you've got in front of you to do."

Daniel knew the exact line Grace was talking about.

She turned to Abe. "You and Ike are as alike as two peas in a pod, but right here," — Grace touched the corner of Abe's mouth — "when you smile, this corner of your mouth curls up first; then the other corner follows."

"With Ike," — she turned to him and reached past John and Mark — "both corners turn up together."

She put her left thumb and index finger on Ike's mouth and pushed his face into a grin. She smiled at him until he smiled back. She leaned away. "Two great smiles, but as different as your pa is from me."

When Daniel thought of the differences between his wife and himself, it wasn't their smiles that came to mind.

"Now John I know because he's . . ." Grace hesitated.

Daniel knew why. John was the best behaved, the most polite. His son would die of embarrassment if Grace said that out loud, and his brothers would torment him about it forever.

"John's got this little arch in his eyebrow, right here." She touched him, and Daniel watched John enjoy that touch, leaning closer to Grace to make it last. She rested her cold, snowy hand on the side of his face.

Every touch she bestowed poured over the boys like water in the middle of a parched Texas summer. He saw them, each and every one, drink in the pleasure of her touch.

She'd left Mark until last. Daniel covered a grin, wondering what Grace would have to say about this rapscallion. He didn't think Mark's heart was tender, so she couldn't hurt him when she described him. But he could dig in deeper in his wish to have her gone.

"And Mark. Let's see — what do you think, Mark?" She dropped to her knees so she knelt beside Daniel in the trampled snow.

He felt as if they were together. Them against the kids. With Margaret, he'd always felt as though he was parenting mostly alone. Margaret had never been strong. Despite being large and looking hearty as a lumberjack, she'd spent a lot of time in bed, before and after the babies were born. They'd been married only six years, and the first babies had come along quickly. She'd been sick more than not that whole first year. For a year after the twins came along, she'd taken to her bed, mending from the birth. They'd had a couple of good years with the boys mostly tagging him around their Kansas farm. That had been a good time, and Daniel had been firm in his wish for there to be no more young'uns.

He hadn't been strong enough to resist his wife, though. She was a warm, generous woman, given to a lot of laughter and far and away too many tears, especially in the year after Abe's and Ike's birth. One night of weakness between them after nearly three years of holding firm and he'd given her another child.

Looking at Mark, Luke, and John, he corrected himself. He'd given her *three* more children.

"Just one this time, though, Daniel," Margaret had joked, but underneath she'd been serious. Who could have known they'd get three?

Then another year with Margaret either sitting in her rocking chair or staying in bed altogether. Daniel tended the twins, who were four at the time and starting to be real helps around the farm, doing his best to keep them away from their ma, who was more prone to tears than laughter when she was brooding with young'uns. And then the triplets came.

And Margaret went.

He was grateful when Grace interrupted his unhappy memories. It was Grace's fault he'd started thinking of Margaret. Because he could see that if he wasn't careful, there'd be babies between him and his new wife, too.

"The truth of it is" — Grace laid her hand on Mark's cheek — "I just know you by the fire in your eyes. Luke's the planner, figuring out how to make things work."

Daniel noticed she didn't mention planning revenge. That was Luke's greatest talent. But come to think of it, he did have a practical streak. Daniel knew that. He'd just never put it into words.

He watched Mark pretend to ignore Grace's soft hand. But he didn't pull away, and Mark was a boy who didn't put up with anything he didn't like.

"You're the idea man. You come up with one great idea after another." Grace arched her eyebrows at Mark, and he grinned at her, not a repentant bone in his body.

"You come up with them." She jabbed a finger at Mark.

She turned to Abe. "You throw in."

"Ike and John do the hard work to make sure your scheme of the day gets done, and you" — she turned to Luke — "make sure nothing gets missed, no detail is overlooked, and no poor, defenseless teacher or mother is left untormented."

With an indelicate snort, she shook her head. "My word, if General Grant had you boys on his side, the Civil War would have ended the first weekend. How could I not know you apart?"

Daniel looked at his boys. Yes, as alike as peas in a pod. Yes, as different as day and night.

Ike studied her. "No one else can tell between us."

Abe sat up straight. "You know, you've been telling us apart since the first day we came to school, haven't you?"

"She has," Luke said, nodding. "I didn't think much of it — figured you knew where we sat or something — but you've always gotten it right."

Grace shrugged. "It's easy."

"It's hard," Mark insisted.

"Not for me."

Luke said quietly, "For everybody."

Grace grinned at them all. Daniel thought she looked like a child herself down in the snow teasing his boys.

"Well, I'm not apologizing for it. You're as different as can be and that's that."

The boys stared at her with a mixture of fascination and fear, as though maybe she had some magic power that let her know who was who.

As he studied them, his boys so alike, he remembered how this whole snowball fight had started — a celebration of life.

Daniel reached for John and pulled him onto his lap. "I was mighty worried about you for a fact, son. I'm so glad you're all right." He wrapped his arms around John, and although it was completely against their family's view of proper behavior, John hugged him back.

"I'm sorry you was worried, Pa."

"I love you, son. I was so afraid the avalanche had got you." Daniel held his son and marveled at the mass of wiggling, lively, unhurt boy he had in his arms.

And Grace had kept him safe. She'd been there for John in that dark one-room cave. He'd have come out of there terrified if he'd been trapped in there alone. She'd protected his boy. Thinking about it shook him deep and hard. He had a wife now, a wife he didn't want and wished he could get rid of. And God had used her to protect one of Daniel's precious sons.

John, alive and chipper and snug in his arms. Grace, full of sass and vinegar from cheating death and so pretty it hurt to look at her. For just a second his eyes stung, and he caught his breath at the force of his love for his children and what a miracle they were.

Then he remembered who he was and, worse yet, where he was. He'd die before he let the boys see him crying. He broke the spell that had spun itself around him as he relished John's hug.

He pushed John away to arm's length and grinned at him. "Let's get the rest of this snow out of the way so we can get into our house."

He jumped up. With a laugh, he dumped John, none too carefully, in the snow. He turned to the cave and began digging with the shovel he'd brought from the barn.

Grace stood behind him, and he forgot she existed for the most part. But she was a woman, so of course she didn't let him forget for long. "We're not living in this cave. You are building us a proper house, Daniel Reeves, and you're doing it starting today."

Daniel quit digging and turned around.

Abe took the shovel away from him and kept working while the other boys pushed at snow with their hands.

He looked into Grace's sparkling eyes. "Did I just hear you right? Did you just *order* me to build a house?"

Grace plunked her fists on her slender

hips, wrapped in those silly-looking pants of Abe's. "Of course I didn't. Because you are a smart man, and you have already seen that we cannot continue to live in that cave."

Daniel wanted to argue with her. It seemed almost required, considering they'd done nothing but argue since the day they'd first clapped eyes on each other. Then Daniel looked over his shoulder at the steep, snow-covered hill above the door.

He turned back to her. "We haven't been here that long. I didn't know snow could bury the place like this. I . . . I'm so sorry, Grace." He took a step nearer to her, conscious of his snoopy sons and their sharp ears. He caught her upper arms, and she lifted her fists away from her hips in surprise. "Thank you for taking care of John in there. I'm sure it must have been dark and frightening . . . and . . . I just . . . I never thought . . . I dragged those windfalls right above the house. You could have been . . . John could have been . . ." Daniel thought he might disgrace himself.

She smiled and arched her delicate brows. "We made it out, Daniel. We're all right. Don't think up things to worry about that didn't happen."

Daniel nodded and returned her smile with a sheepish one of his own. "Heaven knows there's enough that *does* happen out here, we don't have to make stuff up."

"I'll bet that's right." Grace shook her head. "Now how about that house?"

Snow flew past him from the fast-moving shovel, burying his feet. "I don't see any reason we should wait another day to start building."

The boys, listening just as he suspected, began whooping and hollering loudly enough to raise the dead. The snow flew all the faster, as if they could begin building as soon as the door was clear.

He turned to them. "I didn't know you boys wanted a house."

Mark yelled, "Neither did we, Pa!"

"But it's a great idea." Ike jerked the shovel out of Abe's hands and started digging.

Abe yelled and dived at Ike, and the two of them rolled into Mark and John.

"Should the boys be playing right underneath where an avalanche just came down?"

"Reckon not." Daniel shook his head at the horseplay and left his boys to their wrestling. "We've got a nice thick stand of trees to use for lumber. In fact, we brought so many windfalls down that hill with the avalanche that we've got a good start on the logs."

"And since we've just had the snowslide and a nasty storm," Grace pointed out, "you'll have a real good idea of where to build out of the wind and drifts and away from the danger of a future avalanche."

Daniel was struck for the first time that he'd married a schoolteacher. She was a right smart woman.

He glanced over his shoulder at the mountain looming overhead of his front door. The hillside looked swept clean of most of the snow, but he'd never again allow his children to sleep in there.

"I don't like the look of that hill even now. We're not spending another night in that cave."

Luke jumped out of the cloud of snow he and his brothers were stirring up. "Are we gonna sleep outside, Pa?"

Daniel noticed the sharp-thinking furrow between his son's white eyebrows that Grace had pointed out.

"Nope, tonight we sleep in the barn with the horses. It'll be cold, because we can't build a fire in there, but the night isn't bitter and we'll cuddle up." He turned away from the treacherous hill above his home and looked back at Grace. He froze as surely as if he'd been turned to ice by the now-faded blizzard.

She smiled, her expression playful and warm.

And he thawed under the golden fire in her eyes.

He thought of the weight of her on his body, and he remembered earlier in the week when he'd fallen down on top of her. He had a wife. One who needed him to cuddle up to her in the night. How else could he keep her warm? He smiled back.

Then he remembered the price he'd paid for giving in to a man's weakness. He'd killed his first wife. He'd die himself before he'd kill another one. The smile faded from his face.

She looked confused and hurt when he backed up a step.

He tore his eyes away from her, the effort as painful as tearing his own flesh. He turned toward the cave. "That's enough, boys. Since we're not moving back in, all we gotta do is get our things out. Let's start by moving the table and benches to the barn. Everybody grab something."

He charged into that hole in the ground feeling as if he were running away from the devil himself. As he grabbed the table, he realized that he was doing exactly that. Temptation. Straight from the devil himself. He'd given in before.

Margaret had been too warm and giving to be resisted. But only a fool reaches into a fire after he has been burned. Daniel Reeves had been burned badly, and he was no fool. He began dragging the table. Ike and Abe got the other end and lifted. The three younger boys were wrestling over the benches, arguing and laughing.

Daniel walked backward, glancing just once at Grace's uncertain expression.

As he passed her, she said, "Daniel, did I do something wrong?"

"There're things in there you can tote, Grace," he said as he passed her, looking anywhere but at her. "Make yourself useful."

Abe and Ike looked at him and frowned.

Grace lost all her sass. "Of course, Daniel. I'll be glad to help." She gave him one last unhappy look and turned to the cave.

They moved the rest of their meager belongings in a matter of minutes.

Daniel made supper that night. He went in the cave and cooked it, then brought their steaks and eggs and potatoes and biscuits and milk to the barn for them to eat. Everything was cold.

Especially Daniel's heart.

Seventeen

She didn't know what she'd said or done to make him mad, but Grace's stomach twisted when she looked at Daniel's angry eyes. She let it bother her for about an hour, about the length of time it took for them to sit down in the waning light to eat their cold supper of steak, eggs, potatoes, biscuits, and milk. The meal was a vast improvement over the wretched meal she'd cooked at noon. Then she remembered what she'd learned today.

"Great is thy faithfulness." God had been faithful to her. She could only be faithful in return. For Grace, being faithful meant being brave, having the courage to trust God with her life.

Her bravery didn't extend to grabbing Daniel by the ear and twisting until he told her what was the matter. But it did mean taking charge of the boys. "All right, this corner of the barn is farthest from the wind.

Let's pitch some straw onto the floor. No reason the animals should have it better than we do."

The boys, subdued by their father's sudden bad temper and their own hard work, obeyed instantly. Daniel helped, too. They built a comfortable little bed for themselves and worked up a nice glowing warmth in their muscles.

Grace lay down, not willing to put on her nightgown and wear it in front of the boys. She had no way to wash anything out, either. She wondered how long she had to live in the same clothes night and day. Pulling John into her arms on one side and with Ike up against her on the other, she tried to relax.

She didn't look at Daniel, who had slept at her side until now. She had no desire to cuddle up to the cranky old bear. As they all cuddled together, they barely noticed the cold weather. The sun having long since set, they were all heavy lidded from the long day's tension and labor.

Lying awake, Grace heard the breathing of her sons all around her and the heavier breathing of her husband, about two children away. She gave a mental shrug. She didn't know what to make of the heat in his eyes, and she didn't know how to speak of it. The ways between men and women were a mystery to her.

The only man she'd really known was Parrish, and Daniel was certainly a step up from him. She'd done poorly being on her own as a teacher. She thought of going to bed cold and hungry every night. At least she'd been earning money for Hannah.

How would Hannah manage without her? She'd received one letter since Grace had sent the first money. Hannah had insisted she stop giving away every dime she made. She said they had found a safe place to stay and that generous people gave them food. All the children were in school and doing well. Grace hoped that meant Hannah could manage without eighteen extra dollars a month. Since she could do nothing about it, Grace committed Hannah and the little girls to God and forced herself to quit fretting.

All in all, moody husband or not, she decided she'd made an improvement in her lot in life.

She prayed before she went to bed, but her prayers were different than they'd been since she'd run away from Parrish. She returned to the prayers of her childhood.

Give me courage, Lord. Help me be brave. Give me wisdom. Give me strength. She thought that about covered what she needed to survive. She added, *Help me love these boys as my own children.*

As she said it, she smiled into the night. Sleep pulled her into the cold darkness. She didn't need to ask for that again. God had already given her an abundance of love for the little monsters. *Thank You, God.*

They awoke the next morning to the sound of dripping. Grace burrowed her way out of the straw in the murky morning light and realized that it was almost too warm buried in blankets and children.

She gave John's shoulder a playful shove. "Get up, sleepyhead. We've got a lot to do today."

John mumbled and rolled away from her. Then he sneezed and shoved a stick of straw out of his nose and sat up with a big grin on his face. "Mornin', Ma. Why's it a big day?"

"It's a big day because, starting today, your pa's going to build us a house." She announced it loudly, and by the time she was done, all her boys — all six of them, considering Daniel was acting like a child — were sitting up rubbing their eyes, and most of them — five to be exact — were grinning.

Scowling, Daniel shoved the straw away from his legs. The boys began climbing out of their makeshift bed, scattering straw far and wide, yelling and pushing at each other for no reason Grace could imagine.

Mark tripped over her stomach and raced, shrieking, out of the barn.

Grace looked at Daniel, who calmly stood up out of the cattle forage. "Why did he yell like that? He sounded like a wolf was chasing him out of the barn."

Daniel shrugged.

"He's getting first turn at the outhouse," Ike grumbled. Stumbling over feet that had started growing ahead of his body, he ran out of the barn, too, hollering loudly. The rest of the boys were on his heels.

Grace shook her head and stood up. She whacked at the straw clinging to her then looked Daniel in the eye. He didn't seem to have eaten vinegar for breakfast; his face wasn't all twisted up and sour. Cautious, so as not to set off his temper again, she asked, "How do you build a house, Daniel?"

Daniel cocked his head to the side with a little one-shouldered shrug. "Hard work, long hours, lots of slivers in your fingers."

Grace narrowed her eyes at him. "That could describe half the jobs on the earth."

"Why don't you let me show you? Talkin's

260

a waste of time." Daniel walked to the wide-open barn door and shouted until her ears rang, "First chores, boys, then breakfast. Then we cut down a passel of trees; then we build a house."

His announcement was met with more yelling.

Grace thought it sounded as though the boys were unhappy, but maybe the high-pitched racket was joy. She couldn't tell much difference in the sounds they made. Maybe she'd pick it up in time.

He looked back over his shoulder. "I'm gonna get the fire going in the cave and throw in the taters. Then I'll milk the cow. I don't want you going in there. I'm afraid of all that snow clinging to the hill overhead. You and the boys stay well away."

"I should be the one to go in," Grace said, striding toward him. "If another avalanche comes down, you need to be outside digging."

Daniel shook his head. "I'll go in prepared to dig from the inside. I'll be in and out quick. What I don't want is any of you stopping near the door. I can come out quick and get myself clear of the base of that hill, so I'll be safe. But no one is to hang around near the entrance in the meantime."

"I could go in and out quickly just as well

as you could," Grace said in exasperation. "And I could be cooking while you're doing chores. It'll save us time starting on the house."

"No, it won't," Daniel said flatly.

"Yes, it will. How can you say it won't?"

" 'Cause it'll slow us down trying to chew on those burned biscuits of yours."

Grace gasped and looked up at him, her feelings hurt.

He laughed in her face.

"You're just lucky I'm in a hurry, then." Grace spun around before she could smile back at him. His handsome smile did strange things to her insides — made parts of her melt while the rest of her shivered. She didn't understand it. She only knew that she'd felt this way yesterday, right before he'd gotten surly as an old grizzly bear. She decided she didn't want to risk that again. Odd that her being happy seemed to make him decidedly unhappy.

She said over her shoulder as she walked away, "Well, if you have to do it yourself, then I suggest you get a hustle on, Mr. Reeves. The sun's already lifting high into the sky." She marched away then stopped short and turned back to him. "I thought you said the boys were racing to the out-house." She pointed to the little building, standing alone.

Daniel snorted. "No, Ike said Mark was getting first turn at the outhouse. The other boys just —" Daniel stopped talking.

Grace watched his cheeks turn red on his fair-skinned face. His blond hair, badly in need of a trim, hung down his forehead and to his collar from under the Stetson he always clamped on his head.

"What's the matter?" She took a curious step toward him, amazed at the blush that colored his whole face.

Staring at the ground, he said, "Um . . . nothin'. It's just . . . well . . . uh . . . boys can, well they can use an outhouse or not." Daniel peeked up at her for one second, then turned and headed for the cave at a near run — a handy place to hide until he quit blushing.

Grace looked around. None of the boys was visible. It finally dawned on her what he meant. She turned and headed for the outhouse at a near run — a handy place to hide until she quit blushing.

EIGHTEEN

"Good news. They've hired a new teacher in Mosqueros." Clay rode in from his trip to town.

Adam paused with his load of sloshing water buckets.

"Wash day?" Clay nodded at the bucket.

When had Clay gotten to be so long-winded? They were water buckets. What else could they be for? Adam shook his head in disgust and didn't comment further on the obvious. "A teacher already? That was fast. Last I heard, they figured to close the school down until spring at least, while they hunted up a new instructor."

"A guy came through figuring to settle in for the winter. He's educated, so Royce convinced him to take over the school."

Adam lowered the buckets to the ground. This was his fifth trip back and forth to the spring on this cold winter afternoon. He was keeping ahead of Sophie, so a break wouldn't hurt a thing. "They just hired some drifter?"

Clay shrugged. "Surely the school board checked him out."

"How?" Adam crossed his arms.

Clay jerked one shoulder. "I'd like to talk to him myself before I let him take charge of all those children. I'll ask Royce about it at church."

Adam nodded and picked up the buckets. "If he don't shape up, we could just turn the girls loose on him."

Clay's hearty laughter followed Adam into the house.

The door swung open before Adam had to set the buckets down to grab the knob. Tillie greeted him with her shy smile and downcast eyes. She sure was a pretty thing.

He tore his eyes away from her and saw Sophie at the cookstove hoisting a steaming pail of water with a thick towel protecting her hands. Sophie was busy, but she still found time to smirk at him. He rushed over and relieved her of the pail.

"I can get it, Adam. It doesn't weigh a thing."

"Just behave yourself. I'd leave you to it if I wasn't here, but as long as I'm nearby, let me do some lifting for you."

Sophie sniffed in disdain, but she let him

have his way.

Mandy knelt in front of the fire with a wooden tub and the washboard, scrubbing away to the sound of splashing water. Her fine blond hair escaped from its braid and hung bedraggled around her damp brow.

Beth hefted a basket, woven out of slender branches, off of the kitchen table. It was filled with damp clothes to take out in the cold to line dry.

Sally stood by the table, wielding a hot flatiron on the stack of clothes Beth must have just brought in. A steaming tub of water took up the rest of the table.

Beth went out the door.

Laura giggled as she dashed around them all; then she toddled her way toward the fireplace. Adam set the pail on the floor and rushed to grab the baby. Sophie would have gotten to her in plenty of time, but maybe she'd worry and that'd wipe the smirk off her face.

He caught Laura high against his chest and bounced her until she started shrieking with joy. "Clay just came home from town and said the school will be starting up again right away. They found a new teacher."

The girls all groaned. "Ma, we don't want . . ." All three of them set to whining until Adam thought his ears would bleed.

"They found someone already?" Sophie, despite a belly that looked far bigger than normal to Adam, took Laura and walked to the hearth to scold the little girl about the danger of fire.

Between the whining and the scolding, Adam almost had Tillie to himself. He stepped up close to her and whispered, "I'd like to go riding with you, Tillie."

She'd been staring at the girls and him in the way she had, as if the whole family struck her with a sense of awe. When he spoke, she lifted her chin and started shaking her head.

Before she could say a word, he added, "I'd like to talk to you about my life here and the changes this country has seen since the war ended."

A quick glance around the room told him no one was paying attention. "I think I can put your mind at ease about someone coming after you and taking you back as his property. There are decent men hereabouts. None of them would stand by while someone abused a woman or took her somewhere against her will, no matter the color of her skin."

Her eyes widened, and her expression was equal parts doubt and hope. "Oh, if only that were true."

"Come riding. There is a lot you've missed and maybe a lot you need to say, especially to a man who knows some of what you've been through. Anything we talk about would be private. You have my word on that."

Tillie hesitated until Adam was sure she'd say no. Then her shoulders squared and her chin lifted. Adam had seen her do that before, as if she was having a talk with herself and reminding herself to be brave.

"I'd like that. Yes. You look cold. We could do it another time."

"I've been carrying water buckets for a couple of hours. I'm warm from all the exercise. There's no need to wait."

"Right now I need to rinse the next load of clothes."

Sophie came up beside them, stomach first. "No, you go ahead, Tillie. The girls and I can finish. Having all your help has put us hours ahead."

Adam looked at Sophie, and there was no teasing smirk this time. Only the kind eyes of a woman who was like a daughter to him.

Tillie insisted on staying. She could have stood up to him, but Adam knew she didn't have a hope of changing Sophie's mind once it was made up.

Sophie had her convinced in no time. She patted Tillie on the arm. "Take my coat."

Adam was careful not to look Sophie in the eye as he held the door for Tillie. He never could abide a gloating woman.

Adam led the way toward the barn, with Tillie fussing with the fur bonnet Sophie had provided.

Finally, as they entered the barn, Tillie looked up. A black woman couldn't blush so anyone would notice it. But Adam was sure Tillie had pink under those dark cheeks by the wariness in her eyes.

"I'm really sorry I beat you up, Adam. I hope you're feeling better."

His pride pricked at his temper. "You only got a hit in because I was being careful of you."

"But your eye was barely open."

"You didn't hurt me a bit." Adam stalked into the first stall and threw a bridle on the gentle mare the girls sometimes rode.

"And there was a bruise as clear as day on your —"

"I'm fine!" Adam forced himself to un-clench his jaw before his teeth broke.

The mare widened its eyes and danced sideways. He worked on getting both horses ready then went to boost Tillie into the saddle.

She swung herself up so effortlessly he had to reassess everything he'd thought of her.

Except he hadn't thought of her . . . much. Well, some. A lot, honestly. Constantly.

They rode single file out of the wide barn door and headed up the trail.

"I've got something I'd like to show you." Adam set a brisk pace, hoping the woman wouldn't have enough breath to spare to apologize yet again. He skirted along the bluffs north of the house, right along the tree line in the general direction of Reeves Canyon.

When he came to an arroyo that cut down out of the hills, he followed it, noticing with relief that it hadn't filled in with snow like Reeves Canyon had. He hadn't been up this way in the winter before. He wasn't sure just what to expect.

They rode up the mountainside through the gap, smoothed by runoff water, and entered a pretty valley slanting upward for several miles.

Adam stopped and stared at the snow-covered beauty. He still slept in Clay's bunkhouse, but come spring this would be his home.

"I've homesteaded this land." He swept his arm to encompass the whole valley.

Tillie gasped. "They let a black man homestead?"

Adam looked away from the site of his

dream for the future. His own land, near his beloved family, the McClellens. "Yes, they did."

"I can't imagine." Tillie looked from the land to Adam and back.

"There's a lot you've yet to imagine, Till." Adam turned his horse so he faced her, their legs nearly touching. "You're not the first slave that wasn't set free when the war ended."

Tillie's gaze locked on his. "I never said such a thing."

"They can't take you back. The law is on your side. But the best protection you've got is to tell me about it. What if they did try and take you —"

"They will."

Adam ached when he heard the fear in her voice. "If they did, I'd come and get you. I'd bring a posse along. Clay would come — a lot of men would. You'd better tell me about it so I know where to come look."

"If no one knows I'm here, Master Virgil —" She lifted her head, her neck stretched as elegantly as a swan. "I mean *Virgil.*" She spat the name. "I won't call that man master ever again. He can't find me."

Adam nodded. "I think you'll be safer if I know, but that's your decision. When you trust me enough, you'll tell me."

"I . . . I do trust you, Adam. It's not that."

"It's just a habit to keep things to yourself. And it's a habit not to make yourself vulnerable. I know the feeling." Adam nodded. "But maybe someday you'll be ready. And in the meantime, if something happens to you, even if you don't tell me where to hunt, we'll still find you. There are some first-rate trackers at the McClellen place, so we'll find you."

Adam leaned closer to her. "You're safe, Till. You're free. I've never been a slave, but my best friends in the world were. I ranched with them for ten years. I know the difference between slave and free. Once you begin to trust it, you won't believe how sweet the air smells."

Tillie's mouth curled down, and a breath caught in her throat. "Free. I've never really thought about it. I only knew about a month ago that the war had ended. He always kept me chained. I knew that the chain wasn't strong. I was sure with work I could break one of the rustier links. But I could never figure out what the point of running was. Run where? To what? Then he told me about the war." Tillie's hand went to her face.

Adam could still see the slight swelling.

"He needed to hurt more than my body for once, and Mas — I mean Virgil — gloated about it. I bided my time; then I broke a link in my chains and ran. I hid out in a baggage car on a train and rode a long, long way. I had as much food as I could carry, no money, and only the clothes on my back. I just found a spot and tucked myself away. Then they found me and threw me off. I walked until I found a wagon train with a big line of supply wagons and hid in there for days on end. They found me, too, and threw me off again. I've been walking ever since. I've been out of food for days. I . . . You saved me, Adam. I wouldn't have lasted through the night in that storm. And I thanked you for that by giving you a beating."

"You didn't give me a —"

"I'm so sorry."

Her apology was so kind Adam decided to let her have her way. For now. "Apology accepted then. Just don't make a habit of pounding on me, okay?"

Adam smiled, and Tillie smiled back. A glorious smile that lit up her whole face.

"How do you like my valley?"

"I love it."

"What do you like best about it?"

Tillie's smile widened, and Adam could

sense that she was really having the first moment of understanding what it meant to be free.

"I love that it's yours."

And that about summed it up for Adam, too. "Let's head for the ranch."

Daniel pointed to the canyon gap, visible in the distance, as he and Ike prepared to chop down another tree. "It's filled almost all the way to the top."

Ike turned and looked where Daniel pointed. He dropped his ax, missing his foot by an inch. "We'll never get out of here."

Daniel felt his stomach sinking. "I reckon not. We're socked into the 6R solid till we've had a good long thaw."

"But the rest of the snow is almost gone." Abe came up beside them, not watching where he walked as he stared at the canyon mouth.

Everywhere Daniel could hear the sound of running water. The steep mountainside where they were chopping trees was clear except on the north side of the trees where the sun never hit. When it melted, it ran off because, Lord have mercy, it was steep. Daniel found out that cutting down trees wasn't much work if gravity worked alongside you. All he had to do was pick the right tree and hack away. The tree fell all the way to the building site.

He'd been chopping trees for two days solid, barely taking time away to eat and sleep. By now the land around the cave and barn was clear; the bulk of the melting snow had run off instead of soaking in because the ground was sloped.

The house site was one of the few level spots on Daniel's property. It had taken a woman and an avalanche — to Daniel's way of thinking, one and the same — to make him carve out a real home for his family. The 6R was going to be a bona fide ranch once this house was up. He was glad she'd thought of it.

"Will we starve, Pa?" Ike picked up his ax.

Daniel wondered if he should be letting ten-years-olds handle something so dangerous as that well-honed ax. "Nope. We've potatoes and flour to last the winter and eggs, milk, and beef to last a lifetime."

Daniel waved at the longhorns that grazed far and wide in the vast canyon. "God's been good to us, boys. We're wealthy men. We've all we need to last forever. The only thing town has for us is luxuries, like apples until we can grow our own. But we can get along without anyone else, and that's something a man can take satisfaction in."

Daniel looked down over his valley and felt rich as a king. He had found this place while scouting the area, looking for good grassland.

"Remember when John found this place for us, Pa?"

Daniel pulled his head away from daydreams. He smiled down at Ike. It took young'uns to keep a man honest, it seemed.

"Sure I do. He'd got up to foolishness as usual."

"We were just playin', Pa. No harm in a little hide-and-seek."

"There's harm in it when one of you hides so well he can't find his way back to camp."

Abe and Ike laughed. Daniel grinned then laughed along with them. "John getting lost was the luckiest day of my life. Because when I trailed him in here —"

"Into what looked like a solid wall of stone," Abe reminded him.

"Yeah, I didn't see that notch in the wall until I was ten feet from it. Even then I'd'a missed it if John hadn't left footprints."

"It's still hard to see," Ike added. "Half the people in Mosqueros can't figure out where the 6R is because of the way the one side of the rock juts out farther than the other and the two sides blend together to look solid."

"And you tailed him into that cut and found our home," Abe finished with satisfaction.

The hidden gap had opened into this lost paradise in the rocky west Texas plateau country. Daniel had hurried to town, homesteaded one hundred and sixty acres, and then bought ten thousand more acres for pennies from the state of Texas. His home was registered as a mountainous wasteland on the surveyor's map. He'd registered his 6R brand, bought a small herd of longhorns, and still had most of the money he'd earned selling his Kansas farm.

"So God and this rich land He created gives us all we need and more besides." Daniel nodded his head. He breathed deeply of the cold pine-scented air. The damp soil and fresh-cut wood were better than the rarest perfume.

"An' you brought a heap of supplies with you when you brung Ma. It's a wonder you could manage to fit her in with the flour sacks."

Daniel wondered again exactly what Grace had been doing in his wagon. Had a man really chased her? "Yep, it was a tight squeeze, all right." He thought of how pretty she'd looked yesterday, wrestling with his boys, trying to tackle him, and sitting on him.

Daniel jerked his thoughts away from trouble and looked at the stand of trees. "We've got about another two hours of chopping, boys; then we'll have us enough to build a house." He glanced at his sons, still transfixed by the snow-packed gap. It scared him a little, too.

He looked on up the mountainside. He could climb out of here if he needed to, but it would be a couple of days of hard climbing on loose rock with hundreds of feet to fall if he missed his footing. Then if he got out, it was a fifteen-mile walk to town, which he could manage in a day, or about ten miles to the nearest ranch, where the McClellens lived. Then what help he found would have to make the dangerous trek back with him. If an emergency cropped up — say, if the boys needed a doctor — it would take a minimum of three days to get out and back in. He couldn't get help in time.

Daniel looked at his boys and the sharp axes, and his gut clenched. He almost ordered them to leave the chopping to him and go do the animal chores. He clenched his jaw to keep from saying the words of caution. He couldn't live his life like that.

Then he thought of Margaret dying. A

doctor couldn't get there in time to help her, either. He breathed a sigh of relief that he didn't have to worry about Grace and a baby. He believed her that there wasn't one on the way. He still thought she'd run from a man because she'd mixed herself up wrongly with him. But that didn't mean a baby.

Then he thought of her sweet smile and knew what his husbandly rights were. The Bible was clear about that. A woman was to meet her husband's needs. And since a woman inspired most of those needs, it was well and good that she met them. The way she smiled at him made him wonder if she wouldn't even welcome a child from him. Temptation made him shudder.

The Good Book said Jesus was tempted of the devil for forty days in the wilderness. So Jesus knew just how Daniel felt. He breathed a prayer for strength to withstand the temptation.

He looked back up the steep cliff and thought of the doctor and how far he lived from town. He looked at his boys. They weren't in nearly as much danger with those axes as he was with his brand-spanking-new wife.

"Let's get these trees down, boys."

Abe and Ike looked away from the gap

and lost themselves in hard work. Daniel did his best to sweat every ounce of temptation out of his body. Or at least make himself so tired he didn't have the strength to give in to it.

Daniel thought ruefully that he was a very strong man.

NINETEEN

As the sun set on the third day of chopping, Grace served supper to the usually riotous group. Their eyes were heavy with fatigue, and they could barely chew their food — and that was due to exhaustion more than her cooking.

Trying to hold her tongue in front of her sons, Grace wanted to berate Daniel for pushing them so hard. When she'd announced so boldly he was going to build the family a house, she hadn't meant to add yet another burden to the boys. She needed to put a stop to it.

She squared her shoulders. If Daniel avoided being alone with her all day, every day, they'd just have to have it out with witnesses.

"Mark, you little rat!" Grace covered her ears as Ike shrieked as if he were being murdered. He ducked under the table and almost tipped it over.

Daniel steadied it without so much as a pause in his eating.

She had to get Daniel to let up on the boys, and she had to teach these little monsters some manners. "Daniel, we need to talk."

No one heard her over the shouted insults being tossed back and forth between Ike and Mark.

Grace clamped her mouth closed. There was no point in discussing anything now. The boys were hungry and tired. They didn't have enough energy to listen — only enough to yell and fight. Or maybe she didn't have enough energy.

She forced herself to say nothing as Mark dropped from his bench and disappeared under the table for the third time during the meal.

The barn proved to be a more pleasant place to live than the cave. And now that the temperature was more moderate, they had gladly remained here even though enough snow had melted and no further danger of an avalanche existed.

None of them suggested moving back into the cave. The boys didn't show it, but fear haunted Grace, and at least John had to feel a bit of it. She'd lay awake at night and remember that glowing ember fading, dying from lack of air. Then she'd shake herself and remember to be brave.

Thinking she might calm the riot and then be able to bring up more important subjects, she tried to engage Daniel in polite conversation. "Well, have you picked a site for the cabin?" She'd learned about pleasant talk while waiting on people at the railroad diner. She'd mainly worked in drab, dirty little restaurants, moving from one cow town to the next. But that railroad diner was a clean, refined establishment. She'd stayed there until she'd found a place that would give her a job as a teacher.

Luke yelped with pain and jumped and knocked his stomach against the table so hard it upset the milk cup. Fortunately, it was empty.

Daniel set the cup to rights without comment.

Mark stuck his smirking face out from under the table and growled at Luke.

Grace breathed through her nose so the threatening words wouldn't explode.

John patted her on the knee and tilted his head toward his brother and sighed.

Grace smiled.

"There's only about one level place in this whole canyon," Daniel said. "It's just to the uphill side of the barn."

"Right by the stack of trees you've been letting fall down the mountain. Daniel, you won't have to worry about dragging them a long way."

"Yep, that's why I cut 'em there. Didn't you know that? The mountainside is covered with trees. I could have cut them anywhere."

"Well, you never said. I guess I was thinking you decided to let them fall there because it was well away from the ranch yard where the trees could come crashing down and kill us or the animals."

Daniel shrugged.

Ike screeched in pain and punched at Mark under the table, who laughed uproariously and popped up into his seat again beside Daniel.

"Gotcha," Mark said with a smug grin.

Ike seemed about to throw his steak bones at Mark.

Grace grabbed them and laid them out of his reach.

Ike didn't seem to notice or care about her displeasure.

"A man hadn't oughta hafta say everything out loud that goes on in his head, Grace. You should figure what I'm thinking and save us some time." Daniel began scooping white, mealy potato out of his charred, black potato skin with his fingers.

Grace tried to imagine a better way to cook the poor charcoal-colored spud. If only she had a pan. Of course Daniel wasn't even letting her cook much, which rankled her. He refused to start the stove in the cave unless he was there to do the cooking. He carried the only matches they had in his shirt pocket, and she didn't know how to light it without them. John said he knew, but his pa had forbidden him or any of the other boys to teach her.

She shook her head. "So we're building it on that level spot. I want to help, Daniel. I'll do anything you say." She looked at him.

"Anything?" He looked back, and after he'd looked too long, she shivered.

He suddenly turned rapt attention to eating his potato.

Grace tried to figure out what about the word "anything" had bothered him so much. She mentally shrugged her shoulders. As long as he let her help build, she didn't care. "You know, Daniel, the trouble with expecting me to read your mind is sometimes you aren't really thinking what I think you're thinking."

Daniel looked back at her.

The collar on her shirt — or rather Daniel's shirt, because she still wore the same outfit — suddenly fit too tight. Grace unbuttoned the top button so she could breathe and maybe cool off a little. And she wasn't reading his mind worth anything, because she wasn't conjuring up a single thought about the house.

"So do you start building tomorrow?" Excitement rose in her that didn't seem reasonable. *Of course, every woman wants a house,* she imagined. But the thought of its imminent construction made her breath come short and her heart race as she looked into Daniel's eyes. She remembered her promise to God to be brave, and somehow, returning Daniel's look took true courage.

Daniel flashed a look at her hot enough to cook the potatoes with neither pan nor fire. "I can work up the dirt on the house site for a while before dark."

He got up so abruptly he knocked his seat over. Snagging his coat and hat, he almost ran out of the barn. "I can use a hand, boys."

The boys bolted what scraps of food were left on the table, yelling as they gobbled and ran out after him.

Since it was already full dark, Grace didn't have any idea what he planned to do. Maybe he could work by starlight.

She sighed and cleaned up the supper dishes — that is to say, the cup and fork. It took thirty seconds. Then she followed after her family.

"So you've done a lot of teaching in your life, Mr. Parrish?" Royce Badje asked.

Parrish watched the banker puff out his chest. The arrogant little man looked as though he thought the world rose and set at his command. Parrish assumed his humble teacher's voice, even though it was all he could do not to jeer at the pompous little pigeon of a man. "Yes, sir. I've been a teacher all my life. After my wife died, I couldn't stay in Chicago anymore. I decided to go west. I've traveled around some and planned to spend the winter in Mosqueros. I wasn't thinking of finding work here, but the teacher's job being open seems providential. I'd like to settle and begin a new life."

Parrish already had the job, but he'd been asked to visit with a few folks after church, and he'd played his part and agreed easily. He'd led everyone to the schoolhouse.

"You'll have your hands full, Mr. Parrish." Clay McClellen sat a bit slumped in the undersized school desk. He should have looked ridiculous, but McClellen had watchful eyes. Parrish concealed his contempt even though McClellen was obviously a crude piece of western trash. This whole land was filled with the dregs of humanity as far as Parrish could see. But not by so much as a sideways glance or the least twist of his lips did he reveal his disdain for the coarse clothing or the uncultivated manners.

Sophie McClellen sat next to her husband. This should have been man's work, but she'd come along and no one had told her to leave. "The last teacher left because the children were unruly. They'll keep you on your toes."

The way Mrs. McClellen talked, Parrish knew she spoke of Grace. *So Grace quit, eh?* Did no one in this town even know she'd been fleeing when she left?

"She ran off and got married is what she did," Badje said, pulling his black greatcoat around him in the cold little schoolroom.

Clay and Sheriff Everett grinned.

Parrish sat up straighter. Grace, married?

McClellen, even though he was amused and sharing a joke with the sheriff, never quite stopped watching. The slovenly cowboy had noticed Parrish's reaction and narrowed his watchful blue eyes. Parrish forced himself to relax.

Sophie shook her head. "Those Reeves boys will eat her for dinner."

How had Grace gone into that gap, hid-

288

den in a wagon, and ended up married? Parrish considered how a husband would complicate his taking of Grace. His legal claim had just been severed — that was for dead certain.

Parrish's blood ran as cold as the winter wind. Everything would be more complicated now. He should just ride on. Then he thought of his night dreams and daydreams. He thought of Grace, begging and crying and promising, under the thud of his fists, never to disobey him again.

Parrish closed his eyes for a second and fought for control. He opened his eyes, wiping every expression from his face.

McClellen's humor had evaporated. "Where is it you say you've taught before?"

Parrish was prepared for this question. He produced five letters of recommendation from his pocket. A passing good forger, Parrish had been mindful to carry them with him at all times. Some of them were years old and showed it. Some were fresher. They were written in different kinds of ink on different types of paper. Most were from Chicago, where he'd been careful to use names of people who were dead. One he'd written himself only yesterday, dated for last spring, from a town far enough away that it would be impossible to check the authenticity.

He ruthlessly controlled a smile as he thought of how his former prison warden would feel about having his name listed as a proud school board member, recommending Parrish highly.

"I don't know anybody in Chicago. And I've never heard of this last town. There's no way to check these letters." McClellen tossed them to the sheriff with little more than a glance, as if to say they weren't worth the paper they were printed on.

Parrish saw Mrs. McClellen pick up on her husband's attitude. Her expression mirrored her spouse's.

He forced himself to smile. "Well, that's true enough. If you wish to test me, I'm sure I can pass any exam you have." He knew he could do it. He'd been a good student. And what he couldn't do honestly, he could cheat his way through. "That's the way most teachers are hired, isn't it? Do you often have someone with any experience take the job?"

McClellen and his wife exchanged looks. McClellen turned back to him. "No, that's true enough. Miss Calhoun was young."

Badje said, "The one before her, my wife, was young, too. This was her first job."

"Well then, gentlemen and lady." He nodded to McClellen's wife, the only woman present. "Test me if you like, or perhaps just give me a chance. If you like the way the school is run, you can keep me on. If not . . ." Parrish shrugged, careful to keep the look of a lamb amid lions.

"Sounds good enough to me," Badje said. "Any school is better than no school at all."

Three other school board members nodded. The McClellens didn't, but they didn't protest, either.

Parrish shook hands all around with the fools. He wanted to laugh out loud when they told him part of the miserable pay was the same room the former teacher had. He wished Grace would come home and find him there.

Welcome home, Gracie.

Daddy's here.

TWENTY

Daniel scraped a ditch the width of a tree trunk into the ground to set his biggest logs for a foundation. He glanced back and saw pretty little Grace coming out to help. He turned back to his digging. He was going to make the house big. If he had his druthers, he'd keep building day and night for the rest of his life. It helped to be exhausted.

A bedroom for the twins.

"You get down from there. Pa doesn't want us up there."

Daniel didn't even turn around when Luke started shrieking. He sounded jealous. Probably Mark had gotten to the top of the woodpile ahead of his brothers.

A bedroom for the triplets.

Ike and Abe were digging straight toward him. Mark, Luke, and John were fighting over which log was the biggest as they climbed over the tippy stack of lumber. They found one that teetered, and with a whoop of joy, they invented their own see-saw.

It rolled on them, and they had to scramble to get out of the way. Daniel heard Grace gasp.

A bedroom for Grace.

"Boys, be careful," she scolded.

The boys climbed around like monkeys, escaping death by a whisper. It was what boys were good at, after all.

Why was she out here?

"If you break a leg, we can't get out of the canyon to get to the doctor."

Daniel glanced over his shoulder and saw her with her hands fisted and planted on her slender hips. Hips encased in Abe's outgrown pants. He needed to get her a dress somehow, a big, loose-fitting dress. He looked long enough to see she had fire in her eyes. A fire that hadn't been there before the avalanche.

What about being buried alive could spark such a fire in a quiet, prissy woman? Because there was definitely a fire. It burned him hotter every day. He turned, half desperate, back to the trench.

And definitely a bedroom for me.

"Big. Build it big," he muttered and dug and dug some more. "I don't ever want to run across her by accident."

He worked until he was ready to drop, which was his plan. He and the boys dragged themselves back to the barn. Grace slept curled up in a ball to keep herself warm. She'd asked today about heating water to wash clothes and have baths.

Daniel almost turned back around to dig some more. Instead, he collapsed on the ground with the boys firmly between him and his very own God-approved wife, the one to whom he'd pledged himself.

He fell asleep dreaming about baths. He'd always hated baths. But his dream wasn't a nightmare, far from it.

He did the chores before first light because he was up and out of the barn early anyway. He made a quick breakfast of steak, eggs, potatoes, biscuits, and milk and was building by the time the sun came up.

"It seems kinda big, Pa," Abe said, scratching his head and staring at the immense rectangular foundation and all the smaller trenches that split the house up into rooms.

Daniel had to admit the boy was right. And he'd been toying with the idea of adding another couple of rooms. After all, the boys might want their own someday. And besides, if the house was huge, he could keep busy for the rest of his life chopping firewood to warm it. He'd never tried to build an upstairs any fancier than a crawl space in the rafters. He could do that here. That'd take awhile.

"It just looks that way now. Once we get the walls up, it'll be normal size. Besides, we're a big family. We need a lot of room."

"One bedroom for us boys and one for you and Ma oughta be enough," Ike said dubiously. "There're a lot more 'n two."

"Yep, we need two." Abe looked at the neatly arranged trenches dividing the house up into a kitchen, dining room, sitting room, pantry, and four obvious bedrooms.

"Well, I thought you two could have your own room, without the triplets in it to bother your stuff."

Ike looked at Abe.

Abe shrugged. "We don't have any stuff."

Daniel knew that to be the honest truth. "Well, maybe if we have enough room, we'll get you some stuff."

Abe looked intrigued.

Ike looked confused. "We got everything we need now, Pa. 'Cept'n I'd surely like an apple now and then. But the apples won't take up that much room."

"I'd kinda like to have my own ax," Mark said.

"No ax, Mark, and you know it." Daniel turned on his son. Stubborn kid. Smart, too.

Daniel didn't want him to start reasoning out bedrooms.

"This is enough digging." Daniel changed the subject before the boys could count the trenches again and ask about the other bedroom. The one on the far end of the house, as far from the bedroom Daniel had planned for Grace as he could get it.

In fact, he was thinking of putting a door to the outside of the house in that bedroom, and no door to the rest of the house. Maybe he'd be able to sneak in late and leave early and never see her again. He was from a long-living family of men, but he was almost thirty. He could keep up long workdays and full-time sneaking for fifty years or so.

He jabbed his shovel at the tree pile. "Let's strip the branches off those trees so they'll line up neat."

Mark jumped to his feet. Running eagerly to Daniel, he skidded up, slammed into Daniel's legs, and almost knocked the both of them over. "Let me help, Pa. Let me take a turn with the ax. I'll be careful. I'm getting on toward six now, and you know I'm smarter 'n every one of the rest of the kids. I'll be careful."

"You turned five in November. You're not getting on toward six. And anyway, you need to be ten. Don't ask again." Daniel held

Mark's stubborn gaze. "And don't you ever let me catch you playing with that ax."

"Aw right." Mark kicked the ground with the toe of his boot.

Daniel noticed the top was tearing away, and he could see some of Mark's sock peeking through the worn leather. And Grace was wearing the pair of boots set aside for the next triplet who needed shoes.

Daniel wondered if he could fetch home a deer and make moccasins tight enough to keep the snow off Mark's feet. He'd never done much boot making, but he could certainly tan a deer hide. He reckoned he'd put in some time practicing and learn that just as he'd learned everything else — by doing. Plus it'd keep him extra busy.

He and the boys tore into branches. He set Mark, Luke, and John to work dragging the scrub branches away to be saved for firewood and furniture and whatnot. Grace helped.

Daniel noticed that John stayed near her, talked to her, and seemed to side with her when the other boys got too rambunctious.

When they had nearly a mountain of logs stripped, Daniel hitched up his calmest horse to start dragging the trees into place.

"A few more steps, boys." Daniel waved Mark and Luke ahead. Abe and Ike walked on each end of the log to give a tug if it started plowing too much ground as it slid along.

Grace tagged along, holding John's hand. Daniel caught himself glancing at those joined hands more than once. He remembered his own ma and how much he'd liked holding her hand when he was a youngster. He couldn't help being glad for John that he'd found himself a nice mother.

Grace was treating the other boys well, too. She looked the same on the outside, but inside, the fussbudget schoolteacher had changed into a laughing, sweet lady. A very pretty lady. Of course, he'd noticed from the first that she was pretty. Even when she was so grouchy about his boys, he'd been able to see that her hair was a pretty dark blond and her eyes had the shine of pure gold. Her waist was slender and her ankles trim. . . .

He jerked his attention back to the log. "Hold up there, boys. That's far enough."

The boys gave him a funny look. He realized they'd already stopped the horse. He wondered how long he'd stood there looking at his bona fide wife. She was his, after all. God and Pastor Roscoe had said it.

"All right, let's get this log notched. Abe and Ike, come here and I'll show you how to do it."

"Pa, can't I —"

"Forget it, Mark." Daniel chipped away a squared notch in the top of the log. It was slow, tedious work. He glanced at the vast number of logs he'd cut down and the huge house he planned for his family. Building it would most likely wear him down to the bone.

Good.

With his jaw set in a grim line, he finished the second notch on the first log and said, "Okay, boys, let's get this log into the trench."

"Can I help, Daniel?" Grace stepped close, and even bending over to lift the log as he was, he could see her ankles plain as day with those stupid short pants of Abe's.

"Sure, grab ahold down at that end." He pointed to the far end of a long, heavy tree without looking up.

She sighed, and he wanted to stand up straight and find out if anything was wrong. He had to fight himself to keep from dropping the log and seeing to her happiness.

Working himself to death was the only way to save his sanity . . . and her life.

TWENTY-ONE

Grace had married a crazy man, and that was that.

"How can you see to build this thing in the dark? Come down from there, Daniel." The noises from on top of the house sped up. What was the man thinking?

The boys were all asleep, collapsed from exhaustion. They ate more and yelled more and, in general, just lived life as they always had — only more since they'd been building this house.

"I'll be down as soon as I lash these logs into place. Don't want them collapsing in a high wind."

"Daniel, this is the most sheltered spot on the face of the earth, let alone on the 6R. And you've built this house solid as a rock. The wind is not going to blow the house down."

"Until the roof is on, I'll worry. But lashing the top of the walls to the crosspieces of the roof will brace her up."

"Daniel Reeves, you get down here, or by all that's holy, I will drag you off that wall by your ear." She used her schoolmarm voice. "Now quit risking your fool neck by working in the pitch dark when you're so tired."

"It's not that dark. The moon is high and the stars —"

"Daniel," she barked. She really did bark. She was starting to sound like the coyotes that wandered these hills and howled at the moon. Since he was acting like a stubborn child and she was treating him like a stubborn child, she went ahead and added, "Don't make me come up there."

Her schoolteacher voice had made many a tough young man mind. True, it had never worked with the Reeves boys, but some almost as wild. She wondered if her tone would work on the biggest and, right now, wildest Reeves boy of all.

She heard Daniel grumbling as he climbed down. She had to force herself not to grin. He might see it and become mulish again and climb back on that roof. There was, after all, considerable moonlight.

She picked her way across what would one day be her front yard to meet him. Chunks of wood from Daniel's notching and limbs from a thousand sword fights and shoot-outs lay scattered around the yard.

Daniel scampered down the corner of the house where the ends of the notched logs stuck out like interwoven fingers. He had to be worn to a nub from his hard work, and yet he seemed as strong and energetic as ever.

When he got to the bottom of the wall, she was waiting. "The house is —"

Daniel yelped like a scalded cat. He whirled to face her. "What are you doing here?" His eyes practically burned her skin.

"I just talked to you. Of course I'm here." Grace crossed her arms over her chest. She chanted to herself, *Be brave.* She could handle anything with God at her side. She thought about reciting the Twenty-third Psalm, but really, a cranky husband wasn't exactly "the valley of the shadow of death." Surely that wasn't called for.

"Get to bed. I'll be in after a bit." He turned away from her.

She grabbed his elbow and pulled him around to face her. She was surprised she could stop him. He was, after all, huge. Over six feet to her five feet six, he outweighed her by sixty or seventy pounds, and his muscles felt like iron. She could feel the corded strength of him just by gripping his arm. His shining white hair caught the moonlight and glowed almost as if a halo had settled on his head. But Daniel was no angel. She could see the fire in his blue eyes even in the moonlight.

"Why are you so mad at me? What is wrong this time?"

"I'm not mad at you." Daniel jerked free of her grip. She expected him to storm away, but he didn't. He stood facing her, his shoulders heaving with temper and exertion and who knew what else.

"Well, that is just so obviously a lie that I can't even believe you said it." Grace stepped right up under his nose. "Are you mad because I wanted a house? Are you mad because John likes me a little?"

He probably was. *Be brave.* She jabbed him in the chest with her index finger. "Maybe you're just mad because I'm *here.* I didn't plan it, but I'm here now. I'm sorry if my presence inconveniences you. I'm sorry if I couldn't be polite enough to die in the avalanche. I'm sorry if you're stuck with me, but I'm stuck with you, too." She poked him again.

"Stop that." Daniel shoved her finger aside.

Her temper flared. He should stand there and take his poking like a man. "I'll do exactly as I want. That's what *you* do. You storm around and work yourself and the boys to death and ignore me or yell at me." Poke.

It occurred to her that this might be her only chance to talk to Daniel about the way he worked the boys. But somehow that didn't interest her at all. She dug her fingernail in a little the next time she poked him.

Daniel shoved her hand again. "Don't touch me, Grace. Get out of here. Go to bed."

"Not without you, Danny boy." Poke. That really bothered him. Good.

His breath heaved faster, and he moved closer.

She could see the flushed cheeks and the narrow eyes that had locked onto hers. She felt a thrill of satisfaction that she could goad him like this. Now, she thought with a surge of power, she was being brave.

"You're coming in, Daniel Reeves."

He leaned down closer. "Get away from me. I'm not some tame dog to be kept on a chain."

He was upset about the house. He blamed her for all his hard work. But they needed it, and that was the truth. She had no intention of letting him make her feel like this was her fault.

"I may have been the first one to talk about this house, but you know it had to be built. You don't need to take your temper out on me." She really needled him with her finger with the next poke.

Daniel's huge, work-roughened fingers closed around her wrist. His voice sounded husky. "I told you to stop touching me, woman."

"Why are you angry at me?" She jerked her hand loose and poked him again, even though she had the strangest feeling that he wasn't angry anymore, and she wasn't exactly angry anymore, either.

"I'm warning you." He caught her hand again. This time when she pulled against him, he didn't let go. He tugged her by her forearm until she bumped up against him.

"Answer me, then." She poked him with her free left hand. "What is the matter with you?"

He caught her left hand. He pulled her closer. He leaned over her. "Why are women like this? Why do they torture a man? Dear God, why?"

Grace had a second to think Daniel didn't sound angry at all. He sounded confused and desperate, and his question to God was a genuine prayer.

Then he lowered his head, and the stars and moon blinked out, hidden behind his burning eyes and his glowing halo of white hair.

She opened her mouth to demand he be nicer to her.

And he kissed her and pulled her hard against him and lowered her to the cold ground.

It was the nicest thing he'd ever done.

Grace awoke when she felt Daniel stir then stand and walk away from her. "Daniel?"

"Get out of here, Grace." He strode into a shadowed corner of the house.

The moon had set, and clouds must have come in, because the stars were blotted out. She couldn't see him in the dark interior of the roofless cabin. She saw him sink to the ground in a far corner and lean against the house's log wall.

"Come back here, Daniel." Slipping into her clothes, she wanted him to hold her again. She wanted to tell him she loved him. She wanted him to say it back.

"No."

She saw barely visible motion from the corner, and she could make him out as he stood.

"No, I won't come over there. Leave me alone."

Grace's heart clenched at the cruel rejection she heard in Daniel's voice. Earlier he'd been gentle, loving as he helped her understand what it meant to be truly man and wife. Now all that tenderness had vanished in the dark.

As an orphan abandoned by her parents, then as the adopted daughter of a man who made a mockery of the word *father,* she'd had plenty of practice being rejected. She expected it. She hadn't ever known much else. And now she found there were more ways to hurt. The pain of Daniel's rejection sliced through her not-so-tough-after-all heart until she wondered if when she looked down at her chest, she'd be bleeding.

"Daniel, what's the matter?" But she knew what the matter was. It was her. Something was missing in her. She wasn't a woman anyone could love. Why hadn't she realized that before and protected herself better?

"Get out of here, Grace."

Her real parents, her adoptive father, her husband, her children — none of them wanted her.

Except John.

"Be brave."

She didn't think it. She wasn't strong

enough to think that right now. It had been a whisper on the wind that flowed inside her and all around.

John loved her. And Ike was a little nicer these days. She got an occasional smile out of Luke. And one night the cat had sat on her lap.

She turned to her husband in the open doorway of their half-built house. She wanted to hurt him. She wanted to cut him as deeply as he'd cut her.

"Be brave."

Again the still, small voice. Not her own. Not her thoughts.

God.

She didn't hurl at him the awful words that came to her. True bravery wasn't spiteful and petty. God wanted her to be brave. She knew the brave thing she'd say to him if she could: "Daniel, I love you."

But she wasn't that brave. And it might not even be true, because she hated him right now just as much as she loved him.

"Yea, though I walk through the valley of the shadow of death . . ." Now that verse seemed appropriate, because she felt as if she were dying inside.

The bravest thing she had the power to do right now was say, "I won't bother you again. I'm sorry."

She turned and left the cabin.

From behind her, Daniel's anguished voice said softly, like a prayer, "I'm sorry, too. Dear God, I'm so sorry."

Beth hung her cloak on the nail where it always went. Feeling just a touch shy, she waited while Mandy set down the lunch pail so they could go inside together. Miss Calhoun had been prickly, though kind underneath. Beth wanted to get off on the right foot with the new schoolmaster. She'd never had a man teacher before, but Ma had said it was normal enough.

She exchanged a glance with Mandy, and it helped to know her big sister had some jitters, too. They went through the little entry area into the classroom and headed straight for their seats. Her eyes widened at the old man who stood up front slapping a ruler in his hand. Wrinkles cut deep at the corners of his down-turned mouth in a way that told her Mr. Parrish spent far more time scowling than smiling.

Nervous, Beth settled silently in her desk and noticed Sally whispering to one of the two other students in her grade, a boy.

"Sally." Beth kept her voice to a whisper even though several children were talking in normal voices.

"What?" Clutched against Sally's chest was the slate that Ma always sent from home.

"Sit down and be quiet," Beth hissed then glanced up at Mr. Parrish. He was staring straight at Sally, and his scowl had deepened.

Sally looked at the new teacher. A furrow appeared between Sally's brows at Parrish's glare. She fell silent and settled into her seat. The other children were soon settled and silent.

"My name is Master Parrish. You will remember that." He slapped the ruler against his hand. Beth's spine straightened almost instinctively. Her feet flattened on the floor. Her eyes were fixed on the teacher.

"My rules are behave, be quiet, be warned." He slapped the ruler with each rule. "No second chance will be given. Behave — I expect my rules to be followed instantly and completely or you will be punished. Be quiet — you are silent from the moment you're called back into class unless called on. That means the silence begins on the playground when I ring the bell. Be warned — this is your first and only warning. You will be punished for disobedience immediately. I assure you I have discussed my rules with your parents, and they assure me that they want order as much as I do. This school was run in complete disorder with your last teacher."

Beth had to admit that was the truth, but only when the Reeves boys were here. No one could make them behave. With a flash of loyalty to poor Miss Calhoun, Beth remembered how well the school had run before the Reeves. She wanted to defend her former teacher, but one look into Mr. Parrish's eyes scared her out of any thought of speaking up.

"That will not be the case in my school." His eyes seemed to come back again and again to Sally. Beth wondered why he would focus on the littlest girl in the room. She wasn't likely to be any trouble.

"And your parents have also agreed with me that if you come home complaining about school or about being given lashes, they'll back me and hand out double the punishment." He slapped the ruler on his hand again with a loud crack.

Beth knew that was true. Her parents had always said whatever punishment the girls received at school, they'd find awaiting them at home. Of course, Beth couldn't remember ever being punished at school — scolded a bit from time to time, but never given lashes with the ruler — so that rule had never been tested.

"Very often I've found children to be both stupid and naughty, and they need a lesson to see that I mean what I say." Mr. Parrish's eyes narrowed on Sally. "You, little girl, what's your name?"

"S-Sally McClellen."

"Sally, you were noisy entering this class-room. That's one lash. Come forward."

Beth looked at her sister and saw that Sally's eyes had gone wide with fear. "B-but, Mr. Parrish —"

"And now you're disobeying me. That's a second lash. Do you wish to continue disobeying me?"

Sally slowly rose from her desk. Her usually pink cheeks white, her chin tucked against her chest, she walked to the front.

"It is *Master* Parrish."

Beth thought he said the word as if he savored it, as if he were feeding on something delicious.

"You will speak my name as I order you to, or you will be punished."

Sally opened her mouth, then stopped herself and nodded.

Beth was afraid if Sally spoke, she might be breaking the quiet rule, and obviously Sally had thought of that.

"Extend your hand, palm up." Parrish

stood on the raised floor at the front of the room beside his desk. He towered over Sally. She raised her hand as ordered.

The moment stretched. Beth held her breath. Master Parrish stood like a looming vulture.

Please, God, help me be good. Help us all be good. Please, God, don't let Ma and Pa find out Sally's been bad.

The ruler crashed on Sally's soft skin.

Beth saw tears well in her little sister's eyes, but Sally was good. She took the thrashing with complete and utter silence.

TWENTY-TWO

The house was going up with lightning speed. Daniel worked until he wanted to drop every night and got up hours before dawn the next morning. He couldn't sleep anyway.

What if there was a baby? What if she died? He prayed long and hard as he worked the punishing days. *Please, God, please, please, I can't stand to bury another wife.*

By the end of the week, he'd finished the roof and the fireplace could be lit.

He laid a wooden floor. Splitting all those logs was a useless frippery, but it was hard work that took a long time, so Daniel insisted on it. When he got the floor done in the main room, the family moved in. He planned to put flooring down throughout the house, but since the boys only had blankets to sleep on, they could clear out of their rooms in half a heartbeat and he would work in there during the day. Grace avoided him, thank heavens. But as she carried a flour sack from the barn to the ridiculously large cabin, he knew he hadn't built it big enough. She was ignoring him, but he knew the ways of women, and now he didn't have anything to do to keep busy.

It took about ten minutes to settle into the house. Once they had a real home, Daniel realized that they really had nothing.

"Pa, aren't there some boxes up in the barn loft left from back home?" Abe asked one day.

Daniel had forgotten them. He'd wanted to forget. He hadn't wanted anything in Texas that reminded him of Margaret.

Grace heard Abe. "You've got things for a home stored away?"

"Sure. Let's go get 'em." Abe jumped up from where he sat on the floor in front of the fireplace. "I think there are some dishes in there and other stuff left from our first ma."

"Grace, I don't —" Grace was gone before Daniel could protest.

Daniel watched her go. She was too thin. Her ribs stuck out almost sharply. She was underweight and had a tiny frame. Margaret had been big-boned and built from sturdy Irish stock. And childbearing had been too much for her. He decided then and there

Grace needed to fatten up.

He stared out the door after them and saw them enter the barn to collect Margaret's things. Daniel wanted to call out that they were to leave those things alone. They were his, not to be toyed with or used or even seen.

He didn't because he would have had to speak to her, and he hadn't in nearly two weeks.

All he needed to make his life into perfect torture were Margaret's fussy belongings spread out all over this house.

The other boys went whooping and hollering after Abe and Grace. They liked Grace, all except Mark. He delighted in tormenting her. Mark didn't follow her like the other boys did.

Daniel looked down at his son. An expression had settled over Mark's face that Daniel suspected was an exact reflection of his own.

"We have to get rid of her, Pa."

Daniel didn't speak for a long moment as he looked out the open door. He wanted to agree. *God, there's no getting rid of her. What am I going to do?* He ached for her.

It was part of Satan's plan to bring mankind down. Daniel had to be strong. That was God's will.

316

Daniel glanced at Mark. His heart turned over at the anger and rebellion on his son's face. Daniel knew he was responsible for that. The other boys were giving in to their longing for a mother, but not Mark. Mark followed his father's example. And while Daniel didn't need a wife, Mark needed a ma.

The gentle ways of a woman were so pleasant to a child. He had loved his own mother fiercely. He could still hear the gentle way she sang a lullaby and feel the soft touch of her hand when she tucked him into bed at night. Yes, children needed a mother. So why did God let a woman die giving birth? It made no sense.

Daniel wrestled with his own dangerous feelings. He had to be a better example for Mark or the poor boy would grow up twisted inside. "Well, let's go help drag that old stuff out of the hayloft."

"We don't need it." Mark crossed his arms.

Only then did Daniel see his own crossed arms. He let them drop. "Sure we do. We didn't have room for anything to spare in the cave, but here we're rattling around. Let's get that house stuff out and use it. It's dumb not to."

Daniel headed for the barn, knowing he

had to set an example for Mark.

They met Grace backing down from the hayloft, balancing a small box in one arm. The boys were coming right after.

Grace turned to him and smiled. "There's a lot there we can use, Daniel." She always spoke nicely to him, considering he never spoke back.

"There are even some women's dresses. I can get out of these ridiculous boy's clothes." She sailed past him, not waiting for a response that he'd trained her would never come.

He caught sight of one of Margaret's dresses poking out of the box Grace carried. He thought of Margaret, bleeding and dying and begging him to save her. Her strength ebbing away as Daniel pulled child after child from her body. He was overwhelmed by three wriggling babies and two frightened five-year-olds.

Margaret's weak pleading had come close to breaking him. He'd tried everything, knowing nothing to try.

"Do something, Daniel. Help me."

His hands had been soaked in blood. It coated his clothes. He watched Margaret die by inches. The blood, the pleading, the fear, the hungry infants, and the crying toddlers had kept him awake every night for months. After she died, all he'd done was stay alive and keep the boys alive and his livestock alive so he could get milk for the babies. It took a pure miracle from God to keep the babies alive.

Now, five years later, he'd begun to forget. He hadn't jumped awake in the night, feeling Margaret's blood on his hands, for a long time. Until two weeks ago.

His nightmares were back, and he might have to live through it all again if Grace had a baby.

The rest of the boys followed after Grace, their arms full. He thought of Mark and the example he knew he needed to set and turned to climb to the hayloft. He had to treat her decently while the boys were watching.

On his way back to the cabin with his arms loaded with bits of fussy lace and cloth that he didn't remember from their other home, he said to Mark, "We're in the house, but we aren't gonna be settled for a long time. I need to build some furniture." He stepped inside. "You boys need beds."

With a sigh of relief, he realized he'd thought of a whole new big job to keep himself busy.

Sophie McClellen was delivered of twin

boys in the middle of a cold winter night, and after that, Tillie worked so hard she quit feeling guilty about putting Beth out of her bedroom.

Tillie heard the whispers coming from behind the chicken coop and almost went back to the house so as not to disturb the girls' privacy. She could collect eggs later. The days were getting longer as the winter wore down, and she'd come to fetch eggs without bothering with a wool coat she'd made, bought with money Sophie had paid her for nearly running the household since the twins had been born.

"You didn't deserve that thrashing." Tillie recognized Beth's voice and stopped her retreat.

"I'm telling Pa what Master Parrish did to you." Mandy's angry voice rose past a whisper.

Master? What was this? And thrashing? The schoolteacher had thrashed one of the girls? A shudder ripped the whole length of her body as Tillie remembered thrashings. She'd grown nearly to womanhood with her parents on the plantation in Virginia, and she'd never received one of the beatings the field slaves had endured.

And then she'd been sold south to Louisiana. She was the sole slave to a miserly man who lived in a decrepit, isolated mansion just outside New Orleans. Virgil was brutal, and nothing she did pleased him. She toiled all day in the thick heat, her legs cuffed with a short length of chain between them. Then she slept shackled in the cellar at night. He delighted in finding a reason to reach for the whip or a cane. When those tools weren't handy, he'd used his fists or a boot. And then to find out she'd been freed by President Lincoln years ago. The injustice of it infuriated her.

And the injustice of someone striking Sally set a torch to that fury. She'd never seen the McClellen girls receive more than a quick swat on the seat at home. They were lively but bright, with hearts as good as gold. She didn't even make a conscious decision. She marched around the chicken coop and saw the three older girls sitting on the ground.

"Your teacher makes you call him Master? Master Parrish?"

They all gasped, and their matching blue eyes shone with fear. Their reaction reminded her so much of herself that her throat nearly swelled with a sob.

"Y-yes," Sally said.

"I *hate* the word *master.*" Tillie jabbed a finger at the three of them. "No schoolteacher is going to thrash one of my girls. You tell me what's going on."

"No — you'll tell Ma, and then we'll get in real trouble."

Tillie knew just how it was to be in trouble not of her own making. She felt such a kinship with the girls she wanted to go fight the schoolteacher for them. Sophie and Clay were good people. But Sophie was so busy with her baby boys that she barely stirred from the house. And schooling seemed like a woman's business.

She briefly considered telling Adam. But he might tell Clay, and if her actions somehow resulted in the girls getting a beating from their pa, Tillie would never forgive herself. Before she decided what to do, she had to find out what exactly the trouble was.

Despite her doubts about the girls keeping this from their parents, she nodded firmly. "I won't tell unless you give me leave to. Now what is this man doing to you?"

They all relaxed. Mandy eased back from the circle of bright-colored gingham to make room for her. "Okay. Let us tell you about the mean man they hired to be our schoolteacher. Maybe you can help us figure out what to do."

TWENTY-THREE

Grace washed the supper dishes and caught herself humming. She had dishes. A whole set of china. Plain white clay pottery to be sure, but pretty enough, especially compared to a bare tabletop. A couple of pieces had chips here and there, and a fine mesh of cracks covered all of them, but they were beautiful just the same.

She might have a husband who didn't love her, but that was pretty much the same as her life had always been. At least now she had a roof over her head and a cloth for the kitchen table and one to spare. She had a nice set of silverware, enough so everyone could have his very own fork, and four spoons in case she ever learned to make soup out of steak and eggs and potatoes and biscuits and milk.

She even had a soup bowl, although only one. But since she had no idea how to make soup or porridge, it hardly mattered.

Washing carefully, Grace enjoyed the smooth sides of her very own paring knife. Daniel had used his whetstone to put an edge on it as sharp as a razor. She'd already nicked herself with it a dozen times, but she still loved that knife.

There were pots and pans so her potatoes didn't have to look like coal, although she was having a little trouble managing the heat and had a tendency to scorch the poor potatoes. But she'd learn. And her steaks could be cooked without being laid directly on top of the cookstove, although they seemed drier and there was no way to get six in the two skillets she owned. So she fried away on the stovetop much the same as always.

She had a stack of sheets that needed beds to go with them and tatted lace that she planned to drape over the backs of the chairs the menfolk were making.

There were several little combs and a necklace from which dangled a golden heart that misted Grace's eyes when she looked at it. A gift of love from Daniel to Margaret certainly, the most beautiful thing she'd ever seen. She set it aside immediately. Not for a second had she considered wearing the pretty necklace.

And best of all, she had clothes.

Women's clothes. They were far too big, but with the thread and needles found in the boxes, she had plans to alter them, if only she could figure out how to sew.

Life was good. She'd married an idiot — but a woman couldn't have everything.

Feeling as though her life was at last in order after a lifetime of one kind of desperation or another, she now had time to fix things with Daniel. And she needed to fix more than his attitude. She didn't like the way he worked the boys.

Until now she'd stood by while Daniel drove them like slaves to build this house. But the way he pushed them reminded her too much of Parrish. She wanted to tell him children should be children for a while, not slave labor. But Daniel, although outwardly polite to her, avoided her like a leper unless the boys were around. So how was she supposed to straighten out his crooked thinking when she could never get a minute alone with him?

With a long yell of pure frustration, Abe shook the chair he worked on. "Pa, help me fix this blasted thing."

"Abe, watch your language," Grace admonished.

Abe ignored her, which Grace expected, and held out the lopsided results of hours of toil. It had no back yet, but the seat and four legs were together.

The other boys had gone outside to play in the dusk, but they rushed to see what Abe had hollered about.

Daniel, sitting by the fireplace sanding a board to be used as a seat, turned from his work and picked up Abe's chair. "That's nice work, son."

The four boys fought each other to be the first one inside the door, plugging up the doorway until none of them could get through. Yelling threats at each other, they shoved and punched.

Daniel and Abe didn't look away from the chair.

Grace noticed Mark had a bloody nose. "Mark, what happened?" She rushed toward the clog of boys.

Ike crushed his little brothers enough that he finally got through. The rest of them came through like a gusher. They almost knocked her over, but she'd learned to be nimble since she'd become the mother of five.

"What happened to what?" Mark went to Abe's side.

"You're bleeding."

Daniel looked up from the chair then went back to work.

"Eww, get away." John shoved him. "You're getting blood and snot all over everything."

Mark swiped the back of his hand under his nose, coating his hand up to the wrist in mostly dried blood. Grace could see that the bleeding had already stopped.

"No, it's not nice work, Pa." Abe finally acknowledged his father's comment. "The legs wobble."

Grace had to admit the boy was right. The chair didn't look safe to sit on. She didn't say anything, but she vowed that if her son made a chair, she'd sit in it and say thank you with never a word of complaint until the day it collapsed under her. Then she'd sit on the floor and pretend she liked her chairs that way.

She firmed her jaw as Daniel inspected the job. She knew he'd never let up until Abe got it right. Of course, by then Abe would be able to build a proper chair, and that was a good thing. But the boy was only ten. Did Daniel have to push so hard?

Daniel, holding the chair with the legs sticking up, turned it over and set it on the floor. Sure enough, it teetered drunkenly.

Abe ran his hands through his white hair, leaving bits of wood shavings behind. "I've tried to cut 'em off even, but I can't get it."

"You've gotta be mighty careful with that." Daniel smiled. "If you keep trimming one leg after another, before you know it, you've got yourself a footstool."

Abe blushed a little, and Daniel clapped him on the shoulder. "I'm not saying you'll do that, boy. I'm saying I did that the first time I built a chair. You've been smart enough to quit before that happened."

Abe smiled.

Grace wondered if Daniel knew how much his approval meant to the boys. She wondered if he knew they would work themselves to death trying to please him.

Daniel pulled up the wood stump he'd dragged into the house from the cave.

He looked at his boys. "Gather around and we'll have a chair-making lesson. We've gotta make enough chairs for all of us, so we'll be plumb good at it before long."

The boys all dropped to the floor and listened with rapt attention — until Luke screamed.

Grace looked immediately at Mark, who held up a bent pin he'd found among the household treasures in the attic. Unrepentant — in fact, eager to admit what he'd done — he waggled the little pin in Luke's face.

Luke launched himself into Mark, who

tumbled backward and grabbed Luke around the neck, jabbing at him with the pin.

Daniel somehow reached into the middle of the ruckus and snagged the pin away from Mark, then ignored the boys as they rolled around on the floor.

A solid smack of a fist earned a yell of rage from Mark. He tossed Luke hard away from him, and Luke rolled into Ike. Ike would've smashed the half-built chair to bits, except Daniel swept it out of the way of the tumbling bodies and kept talking to Abe and John as if the other boys were still listening, too.

Ike jumped to his feet and took a dive straight at Mark. Mark ducked sideways, and Ike hit the floor, rolling straight for the fireplace.

Grace took a half step toward her son's certain death before Ike caught himself. Stopping inches from the flames, he charged toward Luke, roaring like the Chicago train that had taken Grace west. He shook the sturdy new house like those trains had done, too.

Daniel didn't seem to notice Ike's brush with death or the racket. He talked in his usual too-loud voice to Abe and John as they whittled away at the chair legs.

Grace raised her hands helplessly toward heaven, then turned to tidy up the kitchen and play more with her new dishes.

Sophie rocked one of her fussy sons in front of the fire while the other — Tillie thought it was Jarrod — lay fidgeting in the cradle, close enough for Sophie to nudge it with her foot and keep it rocking. "I would never get by without you, Tillie."

Sophie was strong, and Tillie knew she'd be going full speed if necessary. But Tillie's presence allowed her generous hostess to rest, and Tillie felt as if she earned the roof over her head.

Serving Sophie and Clay and their children was similar to being a slave in the work Tillie did. But there was no comparison. Just Sophie's constant thank-yous made a world of difference. But there was more to it. The freedom of knowing she stayed by choice rather than by force was heady to the point Tillie felt almost as if she could sprout wings and fly if she wanted.

"God sent you to us, as sure as can be. I thank Him for you with nearly every breath I take."

Tillie sliced through the last eye-stinging onion for tonight's supper as she opened her mouth to tell Sophie, "I thank God for you, too." But Tillie couldn't say the words. It wasn't true. She hadn't talked to God since Master Virgil had told her the truth about the War Between the States. If God was up there, He was cruel. If He wasn't up there, then what was the point of praying? Either way, Tillie didn't have the breath to waste on such a God. But talking to God was an old habit. One she'd learned at her mother's knee. Now in this pleasant house, Tillie had to fight the urge to return to her old ways.

Tillie added the last of the savory onions to the stew meat that had been simmering to perfect tenderness all afternoon. Then she stooped over the fireplace to settle the pot of beef stew onto the hook. The ranch house door swung open, and all the girls crowded in, home from school. They rushed to peek at the babies and giggled. "Hi, Ma. Hi, Tillie." Their chorus of greetings was as nice to her as to their ma. Such sweet girls.

Tillie loved being part of this happy family. Suddenly her eyes stung with the realization that her separation from God created a separation from all believers, however kind they were. That wasn't of the McClellens' making but of hers, because they talked of God often and with much sincerity. Tillie couldn't join in.

Sally had left the door ajar, and when Tillie went to close it, she caught a glimpse of Adam shaking the reins with a soft slap of leather on the broad horses' backs as he headed the buckboard toward the barn. Tillie knew Adam had gone for the girls; he did it often. She still marveled at the way the McClellens trusted Adam and her with the children. Mas — Tillie caught herself — *Virgil* had taught her no slave would be given a moment's trust. And thoughts of Virgil and the word *master,* brought thoughts of the nasty teacher they'd hired in Mosqueros.

She looked the girls over. They seemed fine, but Tillie knew better. No one, slave or free, was fine who had to live under a brutal taskmaster. She needed to talk to them again, but it was so hectic lately that she hadn't had a chance.

Tillie stirred the thick broth, the smell making her mouth water. She'd been short on food for a long time after her escape, and before that, what Virgil had given her had been skimpy and often spoiled.

Bread was baking in the oven, its smell enough to weaken Tillie's knees even after a long stretch of having enough to eat. A cobbler Tillie had contrived with dried apples and brown sugar sat warming on the cast-iron top, sweet juices oozing up through the fluffy biscuit top. The bread needed a full hour to bake, but it would be fresh and still hot from the oven when Clay came in for supper.

The whole house was overflowing with love and good food and the sweet laughter of happy, healthy little children. But were they happy? Tillie's smile faded to a worried frown as she wondered.

Tillie went to pick up Jarrod before his fussing got out of hand, but Mandy beat her to him. Beth wheedled Sophie until she got little Cliff. Laura picked that moment to come out of her bedroom, rubbing the sleep from her eyes, and Sally went to help the little girl slip on her shoes.

After a very busy day, Tillie suddenly had time on her hands, and she considered beginning the cutting for a new set of clothes for the babies.

Adam swung the door open before she could act on the idea. "You need water or more wood, Sophie?" he asked.

"No, Clay brought everything in earlier. We're fine."

After making a proper fuss over the twins, Adam tickled Sally and Laura until they screamed and ran wildly around the room.

"Thanks for getting them all wound up," Sophie said dryly.

"My pleasure, ma'am." Adam grinned, his white teeth flashing in his dark face.

"I'm glad I've got someone to make that trip to town. They wouldn't be in school if it was up to me."

The girls all froze, the smiles drying off their faces.

Sally said with casualness Tillie could tell was false, "Ma, we'd be glad to stay home if it makes things easier for you."

Sophie just smiled.

Tillie knew Sophie suspected Sally just didn't like school, as so many children didn't. But it was more. Tillie had to bite her lip to keep from saying something.

Mandy gave her a nervous look as if afraid Tillie would betray their trust.

"I was glad to make the trip. I needed to get some supplies. I'll be starting work on my cabin in another couple of weeks." He turned to Tillie. "I need to ride out and pace off the cabin so I can get a few things ordered. It'd take an hour or more."

"I really need to help —"

"That's a great idea." Sophie spoke over the top of Tillie. "You've been working day and night since the twins came. It's cold out, but the wind is low and the trail is sheltered. I think you should go."

Tillie had lived here long enough to

recognize that look in Sophie's eyes. When the woman made up her mind about something, there was no stopping her. Tillie didn't even bother to try. She found herself bundled in a heavy cloak, fur bonnet, and gloves and thrust out the door.

"That is one strong-willed woman," Tillie muttered as the door shut firmly behind her.

Adam grinned. "I guess that describes my Sophie pretty well."

Tillie glanced at him, startled. The close relationship between Adam and the McClellens amazed her.

Adam walked beside her to the barn and had two horses saddled before Tillie could offer to help. She'd done some work with the animals for Virgil and could hold her own slapping leather on a horse.

They rode out of the yard in the direction of Adam's claim, the sharp cold making talk difficult. Their breath froze white in the air. The soft plodding of the horses' hooves was the only sound save the singing of the breeze overhead.

When they reached the shelter of the canyon, Adam guided his horse toward a sunny southeastern slope and swung down. "I'm putting the house right here."

Tillie slipped to the ground and Adam tied the horses to a low shrub.

"A perfect spot, out of the wind, with good sunlight all day long." Tillie nodded as she looked at the grassy valley sweeping for a mile before the canyon walls sprung up, rugged and majestic. The sky was white. Wind brushed across the waving grass like the hand of God. A sharp cry far overhead drew Tillie's gaze. A bald eagle soared the length of the valley, free and strong and beautiful. "This must make you so proud, Adam. To own this, to have a place of your own."

Adam nodded. "It's a dream come true. I owned a herd before but lost it to rustlers. It was in Indian Territory, and I could never call the land my own. Now I'm ready to settle down, and being this close to family makes it the next thing to heaven."

"Family?" Tillie looked away from the panorama. "What family?"

Adam smiled, his white teeth making his skin seem darker, the strong lines of his face sculpted as if carved from shining black marble. "I mean Sophie and her young'uns. Clay, too, come to that. I consider Sophie my next thing to a daughter. I worked for her pa when she was growing up. Then when her first husband headed toward Texas, I came along to see that everything was taken care of in order."

"First husband?"

Adam nodded. "She was married to Clay's twin brother, Cliff. Cliff is the girls' father."

"I've never imagined Clay wasn't the girls' father. They all seem to love each other so much."

"Yep, it's worked out mighty well. Cliff was long on dreams but short on backbone, to my way of thinking, and I knew before she married him, Sophie'd need help."

"But how does that make her your daughter?"

Adam pulled his Stetson off his head and ran a hand into his tight curls. "She was always underfoot in the stables as a child. I found her tagging me almost as soon as she could walk. She was an only child, and her pa couldn't deny her a thing, so she ran like a tomboy from the first. He liked having her around when most men would have shooed her off to the house to keep her skirts clean. Her pa trusted me to take care of her, too, and it was a good thing, because it took us both to keep up with her. Between us, she learned horses and cattle and she worked the fields as much as we'd let her. I taught her carpentry, hunting, and tanning hides. You should see that woman shoot. It's a humbling thing to know she's bested me in nearly everything I taught her."

Adam curled both hands around the brim of his hat and looked away from the land to Tillie, his kindness shining from his dark eyes. "I do think of her as a daughter. God has given her into my care, and I'm thankful for finding land that will keep me near her."

"You credit God with giving you a white woman as a daughter? And yet He left me imprisoned in Virgil's house for years." Tillie shook her head. She had to clear her throat to speak the heresy that she'd accepted in her heart. It sounded horrible, but Tillie refused to live with the lie. "There is no God, Adam."

Adam's smile returned so brightly it reflected the sky. "Oh yes, there is, Till."

Adam's reaction startled her. She'd expected shock or maybe an argument.

"I believed all that once, but no more. Let's pace off your house and head home."

She took one step before Adam's hand descended on her forearm and pivoted her gently but firmly.

"I know there's a God because He spoke to me."

Tillie opened her mouth to brush aside Adam's nonsense, but there was something alive and vital in his expression.

"He came to me and called me here,

338

home, when Sophie needed me."

Tillie shook her head.

Adam pulled Tillie closer. "It happened. As real as I'm standing here in front of you. I knew Sophie needed help and I headed out. No one can ever tell me there's not a God, because I *know*. Do you hear me? I heard His voice. I had my own miracle."

Tillie wanted to challenge him, but his voice filled with a conviction that seemed to break the chains that had bound her soul ever since she'd found out the depths of Virgil's evil.

"Really?"

Adam nodded, and his hand relaxed on her arm. "There's a God, Till, and He loves you."

"He forgot me."

"He never forgets His children."

"He left me in chains."

"Virgil left you in chains, not God. God was with you the whole time, keeping your soul safe."

"No."

"We're from a people that have known chains for centuries, and yet I've seen a powerful faith in slaves, captured or free. Our people have always been too wise in the ways of hardship to believe God exists to make sure the world treats us fair. Instead, He comes to us in the midst of great misery and ministers to our souls. Don't tell me He waits until we're free any more than He waits until we're happy or healthy. God comes all the way to you, wherever you are, and all He asks is for you to accept Him."

"What about what I ask, Adam? What if I ask more of God than just to be in my soul? What if my prayers are ignored and my abuse is ignored? Why do I want a God like that?"

Adam was silent for too long, looking off in the distance. Tillie saw contemplation in his eyes. She'd spoken the truth to him, and now he'd have to admit that her truth was the correct one. But God had spoken to Adam. Was it possible? Tillie felt the wonder of it.

Finally, his eyes focused on her, and that shining smile returned. "What kind of world have we got if you don't have God? Your suffering on this earth is for nothing. Your living is for nothing. You live, you die, they throw dirt over you — is that all life is? God put a yearning in everyone's soul, crying out for more. You feel it — I know you do."

The eagle screamed again. The beauty of creation surrounded her. She did yearn for God. She'd been heartbroken — no, soul-broken — ever since she'd given Him up.

"He really spoke to you?"

Adam nodded. "Not just me, either. If it was just me, we could call it my own desire to see Sophie again. But he spoke to Buff and Luther, too."

Tillie had met the gruff old mountain men who worked with Clay. They seemed to be unlikely men to receive a miracle. "Really?"

Adam nodded. "This life is hard enough without giving up our only unshakable source of comfort."

Comfort. Odd he should use that word. How many times in the darkness of Virgil's cellar had she thought she could bear the loneliness no longer and a Comforter had come to her in the night, giving her the strength to face another day?

God's own Holy Spirit. She'd forgotten about that in her rage over Virgil's injustice. "I want to believe, Adam."

Again that easy smile. There was no doubt in Adam. Not one tiny shred. He lifted his hand from her arm and nodded at the piece of flatland where they stood.

"I'll tell you the whole story while we pace off the house. How Sophie spoke a prayer to God and He carried it on the wings of the wind to my ears, hundreds of miles away."

Tillie sighed from the wonder of such a thing. "I'd like to hear it."

Adam turned her toward his plot by resting his hand on her back. "Which side should we put the kitchen on? The east or west?"

She felt his strength, and though no man had touched her in kindness before, she didn't flinch away. In fact, she leaned a bit closer. And it seemed very logical that he'd ask where she wanted the kitchen.

"Ma, come quick!"

John's voice. This was it. She'd been terrified of it since the beginning. One of them had managed to break a leg or otherwise permanently damage himself with the doctor out of reach.

Grace flew toward the door, tearing off the oversized apron she'd found among Margaret's things. "What happened?" She ran out into her front yard.

"We've got the first new calf of spring, Ma."

The triplets fussed around the new calf and the cow, thankfully one they milked, because the rest of the herd didn't like the boys hanging around them.

Grace marveled at the competent way the five-year-olds handled mama and baby.

There was plenty the little boys could do. Daniel wouldn't let them near an ax, which Grace approved of. But all three had wickedly sharp pocketknives and were talented whittlers.

Later Daniel set them to making spindles for the backs of the chairs and even let Mark, who had a knack for fine work, turn his hand to carving fancy curls and whatnots on the wood he'd use atop the spindles.

"There has to be something I can do." Grace plopped herself onto the floor in front of the fireplace, her legs curled up under a bluish dress dotted with yellow flowers.

"These legs need to be braced." John scooted next to her, holding a chair seat with the legs attached. "Here, I'll show you how to tighten these strips of bark. It keeps the legs from spreading."

Grace loved working right alongside them. They had three chairs done by bedtime.

"Time for bed, boys."

The groans of protest were so predictable Grace couldn't hold back a grin. She looked up and caught Daniel's eye. He looked disgruntled at the whining. She smiled and one corner of his lip curled up.

"No sense getting upset about it, Grace. Boys just naturally don't wanta go to bed."

"Nor girls, either, as I recall."

Mark jumped up from the floor with fire in his eyes. "I forgot my pocketknife in the barn." He dashed out the door.

"Mark, wait," Daniel called.

"I'll help him hunt," Abe hollered.

"Boys, you get back here." Grace's voice nearly echoed in the empty cabin.

As quick as a flash of lightning, all the boys disappeared from the cabin.

Daniel shook his head.

"What are they up to?"

Daniel shrugged. "Maybe Mark's really looking for his knife. Maybe they've got something else up their sleeves. Don't worry about it. They've run these hills since we moved in last summer."

Grace got up from the floor.

She saw Daniel watching her.

"You sat on that floor as long as the boys. You're as limber as a child, Grace." Daniel gathered up wood shavings to throw in the fire.

She stared after the complaining boys. "I am most definitely *not* a child. I'm seventeen now."

Daniel dropped his wood curls. *"How old?"*

The boys came dashing back in at that instant and froze at the sound of their father's voice.

Grace turned, shocked at his outburst.

"S-seventeen," she repeated.

"Seventeen? And you were a school-teacher, alone out here in the West?"

"Well, actually, I was sixteen when I got the job. But that doesn't mean I'm a child. Sixteen is old enough —"

"What were your parents thinking to let you come out here?"

"Ma don't have no parents, Pa."

"John," Grace said quickly, "don't —"

"She's an orphan." John charged on without hearing the warning in Grace's voice.

She looked at Daniel, who was glaring at her for no reason she could understand.

"Chalk up another secret for my wife. How many more do you have?"

"She didn't have no ma." John looked at his brothers, fairly bursting with pride that he'd known something no one else had.

"Just like us?" Mark asked, his eyes wide with amazement.

"I don't want to talk about —"

"And she was raised by a mean man who 'dopted her and made her make rugs while he starved her and her ten or twenty brothers and sisters."

"Ten or twenty?" Daniel looked at her.

"O-only sisters," Grace corrected. "It's not like it sounds."

"And you're only seventeen?" Daniel's eyebrows met between his eyes as they furrowed. "Did the school board know your age when they hired you?"

With a weak shrug, Grace said, "It was no secret. I don't recall them asking, exactly. Girls start teaching school young."

"Boys, go to bed."

Grace recognized the voice Daniel kept in reserve for when he wanted the boys to mind.

The boys didn't utter so much as one "I'm not sleepy." They disappeared into their separate rooms like a flash.

Daniel could almost see them pressing their ears to the doors.

He marched over to Grace, took her by the hand, and dragged her into the bedroom she'd been sleeping in alone. It was empty except for a bed on the floor that was little more than a couple of tanned cow hides sewn together and stuffed with hay, then covered by a white sheet and a blanket.

He glared over his shoulder at the boys' rooms, slammed the door, turned on her, and hissed, "What is that all about? Is what John said true?"

She backed away from him. "Daniel, it's not important."

346

"So it is true." Daniel, speaking under his breath, advanced on her. "You had a father who worked you half to death. Rugs, Grace? He means a carpet mill, doesn't he? I know what they're like. The children who work in them are treated like slaves."

"Don't make more of it than it was." Grace backed up until she bumped up against the wall and had to stop.

"What else don't I know, Grace?" Daniel wished he had a voice for Grace like the one he used on his boys. She was the most stubborn woman he'd ever met. "You've never told me why you were hiding in my wagon. You've never told me about being adopted. You've never told me your age. Are there any more secrets you'd like to get out in the open" — Daniel leaned down until his nose almost touched hers — "before I learn them from the boys?"

Daniel saw the second Grace's temper caught fire. "And just when was I supposed to tell you about this, Daniel? At the beginning when you were accusing me of —"

Daniel clamped his hand over her mouth and pressed her head firmly against the cabin wall. "Keep it down," he growled. "The boys can hear every word you say." He lifted his hand from her lips and rubbed his palm on his jeans.

Grace glanced at the door, then did her best to whisper and yell at the same time. "You know the vile things you accused me of. And then after the avalanche you were mad all the time. And you avoid me as much as you can by working all the hours God made in a day. And ever since . . ." Grace's voice lowered even more, and her cheeks flamed red.

Daniel knew exactly "ever since" what.

"You won't even speak to me. Just when was I supposed to tell you all about myself? You've never asked because you don't want to know. You just want to stay away from me, and when you can't, you want to hurt me because you regret being saddled with a wife."

Grace stuck her nose right up to his. "And now I know just what you were accusing me of. And I think . . . I think . . ." Grace's mouth wobbled. Her eyes filled with tears.

Not tears. Dear Lord, why did you make women cry? It's not fair.

"I didn't even know a man and woman could . . . could . . . do such together. And to think I'd be with a man that way who wasn't my husband . . ."

Her tears overflowed her eyes. Her throat clogged until she couldn't go on. She tried to slide sideways to get out from between him and the wall.

He stopped her.

She covered her face with both hands, and her shoulders shuddered with suppressed sobs.

"I know. Everything you say is the truth. I've never asked you anything." He fell silent, his hands drawing her close, her face buried in her hands between them. He'd do anything to make her quit sobbing. He'd do anything to keep her safe. He wondered if there was a baby as the result of their night together, but he was terrified to ask.

Grace's shoulders finally quit shaking, and she looked up. "What?"

He leaned close and whispered, "Are you carrying my child?"

Grace dropped her hands. In the darkened bedroom, moonlight streamed in through the cracks in the shuttered window. Her tears ran unchecked down her face.

"Quit crying. I can't abide a woman's tears." He tightened his grip on her shoulder.

"How could I know such a thing?" she whispered. "I wasn't even aware that . . . well, what I mean is, I've never had a mother to explain things. And . . . for a child to begin . . . I've never given it a thought."

"You'll know because your . . ." Daniel

fell silent. He had to force the words past his throat. "Y-your . . . uh . . . lady's time —" He lapsed into silence.

She gasped. "I'll not discuss such with you, sir." She tried to step away from him.

He held on doggedly, his eyes closed tight so he wouldn't have to look at her while he discussed such an embarrassing subject. "A lady's time . . . doesn't . . . come when a woman is with child. Has yours come?"

"It doesn't?"

Daniel shook his head.

"But that will take months to know."

"No, it doesn't. It only takes a month."

"Why is that?" Grace asked, her eyes wide with confusion.

Nearly in physical pain from the topic, Daniel growled, "Because it comes every month, so if it doesn't come that month, then you know."

"Mine doesn't . . . come . . . every month." Grace licked her lips as if her mouth had gone stone dry. "I mean, it never has. I had no idea it was supposed to." With a sudden flare of temper, Grace added, "Every month? That will be a nuisance."

She exasperated Daniel past his embarrassment. "You're a woman grown, Grace. You're supposed to have one per month."

"Well, I've only had a couple of them in

my whole life."

Daniel glared at her. "How old did you say you are?"

"Seventeen."

"I was married at seventeen. My wife was the same age. She told me it started when a woman was twelve. Every month. You're not doing it right."

Grace looked angry for a moment, then her mouth formed itself into a straight line and her brow wrinkled. "I'm s-sorry." Her eyes filled with tears again. She looked down at her skinny body.

"It's okay. I reckon you can't help doing it wrong." He patted her on the arm with his big clodhopper hands.

"I doubt if I'm carrying a baby. I've never been much good at any woman things. I can't cook."

"You're getting better."

"The potatoes were awful tonight."

Daniel shrugged. No truer words were ever spoken. "We could go back to cooking in the belly of the stove. Then they were only black on the outside instead of all the way through."

"I can't sew." She looked at her pretty but gigantic dress.

"We've got growing boys. You really do need to figure that one out. Maybe Sophie

McClellen could help come spring. We don't have any goods for you to sew anyway. I'll teach you how to make moccasins if you want."

"I'll probably fail at this baby-having business, too."

"It's not a failure if you're not expecting. It would be for the best."

Grace shook her head. "You've got five children. You must love them. Of course you want more of them."

"No, I don't."

Grace looked up at him, her heart in her eyes. "Why don't you want to have babies with me?"

Daniel looked at her and ached with the loneliness of married life. "Why has God allowed such a wicked temptation to exist? He has to know how dangerous it is."

"Dangerous? What do you mean?"

"It is if you have a child — especially my child. I seem to make them in batches. Margaret barely survived the twins. She felt sickly for months before and after they were born. We never should have risked another child. Never!" Daniel gulped and felt his Adam's apple bob much as Adam's must have when he swallowed that tempting fruit in the Garden of Eden.

"I was weak. I let Margaret convince me."

"Well, Daniel, God probably made people that way."

"No, it's not God." Daniel shook his head. If he could just convince her, then she'd help him resist. It would be so much easier with her help. Margaret had worked against him. "It's the devil himself that lays this temptation down before me. I figured that out as soon as the twins were born."

"Why would you think that? God created man. He wanted children to be born so the world could go on."

"If he wanted the world to go on" — Daniel caught her by the upper arms and held her so tightly his hands shook — "then why did he make Margaret die?"

Grace was silent.

Daniel's grip loosened; he knew he must be hurting her. "The Bible says, 'And thy desire shall be to thy husband.' It was part of the punishment of Eve. I've read it over a hundred times. Eve got desire for her husband and pain in childbirth. Adam got hard work and weeds in his field."

"I have no idea what you're talking about, but I would love to have your child."

"No! I don't want to lose you. I can't lose you." Then he lowered his head and captured her lips with his own.

TWENTY-FOUR

She grabbed hold of him and hung on like a buffalo burr. "You're not going anywhere."

"I have to get out of here."

Grace caught two handfuls of his golden hair in her fists and glared. "You are the most stubborn man who ever lived. This is why you've been angry at me all this time?"

Daniel couldn't stop his hands from sliding up her sides. "You're too thin. You have to eat more."

She twisted his hair. "Don't change the subject. I have always been thin. I have survived very well with no meat on my bones. Now answer me."

Daniel closed his eyes. "Yes," he admitted. "This is why."

"Well, stop it." Grace pulled his hair tighter; the pain must have gotten his attention, because his eyes popped open. "This family is going to start getting along, and that includes you and me. And every time you're rude to me, I'm going to know why, understand?"

Daniel nodded. On a sigh he said, "But what if you have a baby? What if you die? I can't stand to —"

"Daniel?" Grace yanked his hair until he quit talking.

"What?"

Grace drew his head toward her. "I'm counting that kind of talk as rude."

A woman leaned heavily on her husband, pale and thin, shaking, near collapse. She was weeping into her hands. The husband, as sad as his wife, supported her. Hannah could see that he fought his own tears.

"The doctor says we don't dare to try again, Virginia."

"I don't mind, Phillip." The sight of Virginia, her eyes red and teary, made Hannah wonder what could leave someone so devastated. "I'll be all right."

"No, I almost lost you this time. I won't do that. No babies, Virginia — no!"

Hannah's breath caught in her throat. All this grief over a child? All she knew about children was that people threw them away. Oh, to be wanted like this. Tears welled in her own eyes at the bittersweet dream.

She studied the couple, looking at how

neat and clean their clothes were, no worn seams or faded fabric. They weren't dressed like wealthy people, but their cheeks weren't hollow and their eyes, though sad, weren't sunken with hunger. She wasn't even aware of standing or moving until the man nearly bumped into her.

She preferred to look more closely at a family before she approached them, but she felt God nudging her, telling her to speak. She had time to wait until the doctor was done checking Libby's ankle; then her little sister would stay overnight. God had brought Hannah to this office at this moment.

With her voice trembling, Hannah said, "I am trying to raise three boys I found living on the street. They are good boys, smart, polite, and honest, but I can barely afford to feed them. They aren't babies, and I know people want babies. . . ."

The look in the woman's eyes, the dizzying swing from despair to hope and longing, almost broke Hannah's heart. Her chest heaved with a sob, but she kept it inside. She would live on the kindness in this woman's eyes for years.

The man looked down at his wife. "Children who have lived on the street might be difficult, Ginnie. I don't know. . . ."

"Would it hurt to meet them, Phillip?"

Hannah, with all the skills of a master beggar, manipulator, and liar, said, "If you don't want them as your children, maybe you could put them to work. They are fourteen, eight, and six. They could live in your barn, and they'd want nothing but food. They're used to the cold. The rags they wear are all they need."

Hannah didn't mention Libby. No one would want a mute child who limped. Just finding someone to take the boys would be a miracle. Yes, they would lose Trevor's three dollars a month — the only money they had — but she wouldn't ask God for more.

"They're hungry, Phillip." Virginia's hand clutched at her husband's arm until Hannah thought either her hand or his arm would break. "I want to meet them. So do you — you know it."

Phillip held his wife's gaze for a long moment; then a smile broke out. He turned to Hannah. "Yes, we do want to meet them."

She left the couple waiting near their shed, not wanting them to see how the family lived. Then Hannah went to her brothers.

Trevor sat on the floor next to the trash barrel, reading a book to Nolan and Bruce. Elation raised her spirits as she looked at the three of them.

"How is she?" Trevor closed the book. All three boys looked at her. Libby would be home tomorrow and in need of constant care.

Hannah pulled her scarf off her head, her arms almost too heavy to lift. "The doctor said she'd be okay."

Hannah looked at Trevor. She saw the answer to her question in his eyes. No letter from Grace. She slumped into the only chair they owned.

Nolan looked at her with wide, worried eyes. "I got the bread, Hannah. Mr. Daily let me have it, and I was real careful to hide from his grumpy wife."

Despite her best efforts to protect the children from grim reality, they knew how bad things were.

Hannah smiled at her brothers. Trevor had been killing himself working for a pittance at the carpet mill. Nolan, growing fast, hungry all the time, such a bright boy, hated going to school when he could be earning money. Little Bruce should have had baby fat still; instead, he was lean and far too quiet. And he had a gift for thieving that would only get more pronounced if he kept living on the street.

"I talked to someone who would love to have children." Her heart lifted as she thought of the lovely couple who had come out of a room beside Libby's.

Hannah knew her brothers. Trevor understood what she meant, and he looked wary. Nolan, smart as a whip, was wondering if they'd feed him. Bruce turned his trusting eyes on Hannah, too obedient for a six-year-old. She knew he'd do as he was told. Nolan and Bruce would go, but Trevor needed this home, too. He needed to get out of that mill and back into school. And he wouldn't want to leave her and Libby.

Hannah prayed. She knew God would have to make it all work out, and she had no doubt He would. "They're waiting in Daily's Diner to meet you. I didn't want them to see us in the shack. If they like you, they'll take you home tonight."

Trevor opened his mouth to refuse.

She nailed him with a glare. "I want you to go with them, Trevor. To make sure the boys are okay."

"What about you? What about Libby?"

"Grace's money will come. We'll be okay."

"What kind of people are these who would take three of us and leave you and Libby in the cold?"

"They don't know about Libby. I saw no point in telling them." Hannah's hand closed hard over the wobbly latch that pinned the little door closed. "I'm sixteen. Grace got a job teaching school when she was sixteen."

"You can't teach school. You haven't been to school yourself." Trevor stood, trembling with anger. "You need me. Let the boys go."

"I haven't been to school, but that doesn't mean I'm uneducated. I can read and do my numbers. I can teach. I'll find work. You kids" — she waved her hand as if she were annoyed with them — "have made it impossible for me to work. And now, with Libby getting better and three less mouths to feed, I won't have to earn that much. As soon as I can find a teaching job, I'll take it. Libby might start talking when her foot is better, and then maybe someone will adopt her, too."

Except Libby's foot was never getting better. And that probably meant she'd never speak, either. The doctor had done all he could. She didn't tell her brothers that. She'd pick her up tomorrow, give the doctor the last bit of money she had, and bring her little sister home.

"You need me, Hannah." Trevor stepped away from his brothers and glared at her.

"The boys need you more. Please, Trevor, go."

Bitter and angry, Trevor stared at her. She

360

prayed he'd relent as she fiercely controlled her tears. She had to get him out of here, out of this life. Even though his mill money was all they had, continuing to work there would destroy him.

And if he went to this meeting angry, the couple wouldn't want him. Just the chance that they could want a fourteen-year-old was slim.

"Trevor, do this for me. This couple seems very nice, but I'll feel better if you're there to make sure nothing like Parrish happens to Nolan and Bruce. Don't think of it as being adopted. Think of it as the two of us splitting the family in two so we can take better care of them. You see to the boys; I'll care for Libby."

Trevor hadn't been one of Parrish's children. Parrish only wanted girls. But he'd heard all about the hard work, cruelty, and hunger.

After a long second, Trevor said, "Promise you'll find me if you need anything. I'll get a message to you so you'll know where we are."

Hannah's exhausted eyes dropped closed with relief. Now if only the couple would take them. Now if only Grace would send money one more time. It had been too long. Grace had never been a day late before.

Hannah knew her sister was in trouble, but she didn't speak of it. Hannah held her breath, waiting, praying. She'd have said anything to get Trevor to grab this chance.

"Promise me, Hannah."

She would never disrupt their lives. She would never see her little brothers again. She prayed for forgiveness and said, "I promise."

The couple grabbed onto the boys as if they needed them to survive. They bought them supper, including Hannah. She waved her brothers off with a smile and a full belly then returned to her empty shed, her empty cupboard, and her empty life. Adding Libby to it tomorrow would only emphasize the emptiness.

The boys had left everything behind — and that wasn't much. But Hannah had three tattered blankets to roll up in. She lay by her barrel and cried until her heart was as empty as her life.

Her house was full of furniture.

Her boys were full of laughter and food.

Her heart was full of love.

Grace kept coming back to it. For the first time in her life, she was truly, fully, joyously happy.

She had no idea about the baby, but from

what Daniel said, with her body being abnormal, she doubted she could have a child.

She wanted one. It was amazing how fiercely she wanted one. She pictured a tiny baby — a girl, she wished fervently, especially when the boys were rampaging through the house, slamming doors open and leaving them that way. Only one, not a set all coming at once.

But God had already given her so much, she didn't dare ask for more. If she asked for anything, it was for Hannah. There would be no money coming from Grace. How were they managing?

She thought of her promise to be brave. God's faithfulness to her deserved her best efforts at being faithful to him.

"It is of the Lord's mercies that we are not consumed, because his compassions fail not. They are new every morning: great is thy faithfulness."

Be faithful to Hannah and the children. Grace smiled as she prayed it. God was so much more faithful to His children than His children ever were to Him. Grace clung to that promise and attended to her new family.

"Great is thy faithfulness." The verse echoed in her head as she saw the life she had liter-

ally fallen into. It could only be God's will that she be here with Daniel and the boys. How could God have found her in that awful house with Parrish? How could He have led her to this place and, through the work of her fear and Parrish's cruel obsession with her, driven her into Daniel's home? How had God arranged for Parson Roscoe to drop by and insist on a marriage? Even the snowfall that had kept Parrish out and kept Grace from escaping in those first unhappy days were part of the pattern God had set for her life.

Oh God, thank You. Help me give back to You with my own faithfulness. She thought it when she woke. The words sang in her heart throughout the day. She remembered it while she talked with the boys and her husband. She fell asleep in Daniel's arms with that prayer on her lips. God would care for all His children.

Great is Thy faithfulness, Lord!

Whack! "We're going to go over this again, Miss McClellen."

Whack! Parrish lifted the ruler and held it ready over Sally's trembling hand. The raised welts on her palm gave him vicious satisfaction. He glanced up and saw the rage and fear on her sisters' faces. They didn't like it, but they wouldn't do anything.

He knew how children were. They didn't tell their parents about punishment at school. Parents sided with the teacher and doled out a second punishment at home. The ruler sang as it whizzed through the air and landed on soft flesh. By nightfall, the welts would go down, and palms didn't show bruising. Even if a bruise or two showed, a few lashes with a ruler were acceptable punishment.

Whack! If Parrish wielded his ruler with more force, more often than might be called for, who was to know? The other children studied, their heads kept carefully bowed. He had them well trained. Mandy and Beth did their best not to glance up, but he saw them sneak a peek once in a while. He'd make them regret that.

Whack! He sometimes let the ruler fall almost until he drew blood, especially with the girls. He would work out his anger on those little hands and imagine Grace and what the future held in store for her.

He heard Sally's stifled sobs and felt a thrill of savage pleasure. That was four. He usually gave five, but Sally McClellen was unusually stubborn. One more.

Whack! She would know better than to jump to the defense of her slow-witted kindergarten classmate. A boy. He much preferred punishing girls. One more.

Whack! He had to force himself to stop. The sound of wood striking flesh made his mouth water, and he wanted to go on all day. He saw a line of blood welling on the side of Sally's hand. He reined himself in before he marked her any more. It wouldn't do for her father to get upset. Clay Mc-Clellen had the kind of eyes Parrish didn't want looking at him.

"Go back to your desk, you stupid child. I'll be glad to give you your little classmate's punishment anytime you want."

Trembling and bleeding, Sally went quietly to her desk. She flinched every time he called on her. He made her stay in for morning recess and sit at her desk through dinner. She folded in on herself when she was in the schoolroom alone with him. He thought finally she was learning.

"We've got to do something about him," Beth hissed as she and Mandy shared their lunch pail.

Mandy looked at the schoolroom. Her eyes burned. Beth knew that look. Mandy wasn't one to sit back when the family needed protection, no more than Ma.

"We can't tell anyone," Mandy whispered

366

back. "Master Parrish says Pa would stick up for the teacher. He says we'll get a thrashing at home worse than the one at school."

"We told Tillie, and nothing bad happened." Beth chewed on her sandwich. It tasted like sawdust. "She said she'd figure out a way to help us. And Pa might not stick up for Master Parrish, either. He might see how mean Master Parrish is and beat him up and fire him and everything."

Mandy stared at the building as if she could see through the walls if she tried hard enough.

"I don't like Sally being in there alone with Master Parrish. He's cruel, and he likes making her cry. You can see he likes hurting her." Beth looked nervously at the school. Even from across the yard, she worried that somehow Master Parrish would know they were bad. He liked lashing Sally the most, but he didn't spare the rod for the other students.

"I wish the Reeves boys were here."

Mandy gasped. "Why would you want those awful Reeveses around?"

"Because no one can control them. They'd figure out a way to make Master Parrish's life miserable, maybe even get him fired like they did to poor Miss Calhoun." Beth figured out that the Reeves boys might be pure trouble on ten running feet. But after all, they were only boys. Since when did a bunch of boys hold a candle to a girl when it came to plotting? It was time to take action.

"True enough. They'd never put up with him."

Beth needed her sister to agree. Mandy was the organized one. She'd have to help. She decided making Mandy even more upset might be just the right thing to do. "Sally wasn't bad today. She just tried to explain about Clovis being young. She didn't do anything wrong."

"Nope, she didn't." Mandy kept eating, but she swallowed as if the sandwich was stuck in her throat.

"She was bleeding." Beth added that just in case her big sister wasn't 100 percent mad clear to the bone.

"I saw." Mandy turned away from the school.

Beth snatched the biggest apple out of the tin pail.

Mandy didn't fight her for it, so she knew Mandy was serious about setting Sally free from the man who seemed to delight in picking on her.

"He wasn't like this at first. He's getting

worse as the year goes on. And he seems to especially like to pick on Sally." Beth had felt the lash of those six whacks with his ruler. They all had. Six-year-old Sally, the littlest girl in school, seemed to earn the brunt of his temper, and Beth couldn't help believing it was because she was so small and defenseless.

Mandy looked away from the building. "Ma and Pa might not agree that we need protecting from Master Parrish, but I'm not going to sit quiet while he hurts my sister."

Beth nodded in complete agreement.

"I say we take care of it ourselves."

"But how?" Beth asked, thinking of the power of a teacher.

Mandy looked around the school yard. All the other children lived in town in Mosqueros. They had gone home for lunch while the McClellen girls lingered over their tasteless food.

Mandy leaned close to Beth and whispered, "I've got a plan. But we might need help."

Beth felt her heart beating with excitement. Mandy was almost as good at setting a trap as Ma. "Tillie hates that he makes us call him Master. She'll help."

"She will for a fact." Mandy smiled a mean smile.

Beth crunched into her apple, and it almost tasted sweet — like revenge.

"The weather is almost springlike, but that gap is still packed to the top with snow. What if it stays forever, Pa? What if we have to just live in here by ourselves for the rest of our lives?" Mark tugged on Daniel's pants as they trekked through the woods.

Daniel had a surprise for the family and decided to let Mark in on it. Mark was still openly hostile to Grace, and Daniel blamed himself for it. He needed to unteach the lessons the boy had learned at his side.

"There wasn't any snow in it when we bought the place in June. So it figures it melts sometimes. And anyway, that snow we got was a freak blizzard. I don't reckon we'll ever get snowed in here so rock solid again." He laid his hand on Mark's shoulder. "It hasn't been so bad, being stuck together all winter. We got the house built and all that furniture. If we'd been running to town for schooling and such all winter, we'd'a never gotten half as much done."

"But now Ma is trying to make a school for us out here. I don't wanta hafta study all the livelong day." Mark kicked at the rotting leaves and fallen branches that littered the woods.

"It comes in mighty handy to know some figuring. And reading is just plumb useful. We should count our good fortune to have a schoolteacher of our very own, right here."

Mark snorted. "If she's so good, why'd you get her fired from her job in town?"

Daniel flinched. "I think she's changed some since then." He thought of his warm, generous, playful wife. Nothing like the fussy, impatient schoolteacher she'd been. "I know she's changed."

"Well, she still comes at us with the Bible, trying to make us read it. I'm already a good reader. I don't need no more schoolin'."

Daniel tried not to smile at his five-year-old son. He remembered school. He'd spent more time fighting it than he ever had learning anything. He'd missed every day possible, and he'd quit the first second his pa had let him.

"Look up ahead. That's the surprise I was telling you about."

Mark stopped. He looked around the woods.

Weak winter sunlight filtered down through the bare branches. A light cold breeze made the treetops sway, but tall, thin saplings blocked the wind near the ground. It was a pleasant day for a walk.

"I don't see anything." Mark turned left

and right.

"Look up." Daniel lifted Mark's chin.

A grin broke out on his son's face. "A bee tree."

Daniel chuckled. "Yep. And where there's bees . . ."

Mark chimed in, "There's honey."

Daniel nodded, and he and his stubborn son shared a smile. Everyone back home would love this treat. "We're taking it. The bees will be sleeping because of the cold. They won't give us a bit of a fight."

Daniel pulled the sack off his shoulder. He'd collected every jar and crock in the house and brought them along. Mark and he would fill them all then take back what they could carry. Daniel could already taste honey on his biscuits.

Daniel and Mark were greeted like heroes. Mark even endured a hug from Grace. Daniel did more than endure one. He gave her one right back.

They ate their lunch with their biscuits smothered in honey. Daniel showed Grace how to sweeten the sourdough and add extra flour and eggs to make a cake. They all spent an afternoon in the crisp mountain air fetching more of the sticky sweet treat.

When Grace made the boys settle in for

lessons after supper, Mark went along willingly.

"Daniel, it wouldn't hurt for you to do some reading along with the boys," Grace said sternly. "You're never too old to learn."

Daniel's mouth dropped open. Then he saw Mark staring at him and quickly controlled himself. He said with mock obedience, "Yes, ma'am."

His boys snickered, and Daniel let them. In fact, he did a fine impression of them for the fun of it. He slumped over to sit in front of the fire in the rocking chair he'd built for himself to match Grace's. Grace handed him a piece of bark and a chunk of coal.

"Do the multiplication tables. Your stubborn sons think they're too hard. You need to set a good example for them. Start with the ones, and when your slate is full, let me check them. If they're all correct, you can rub them out and do more."

Daniel was stunned at her bossy voice.

Ike's giggle turned to out-and-out laughter, and the rest of the boys joined in.

Grace, her eyes shining, couldn't keep a straight face.

Daniel gave up and laughed along with them. And he did his multiplication tables swiftly. The little woman might as well know he had some book learning.

When Grace said, "Daniel, I'm impressed," his heart turned over and he kissed her.

Then she thanked him for the honey just as warmly. She thanked Mark, too.

They finished their lessons together, with Daniel reading to them out of the big Bible.

TWENTY-FIVE

Tillie heard the whispers from behind the chicken coop. This time it was no accident that she'd stumbled on the girls. She'd seen the welts Sally had tried to hide. The girls were still determined not to tell their parents, but they'd confided in her before. Maybe they would again.

When they got home from school on Friday, the girls made quick excuses to go outside, either to hide Sally's wounds or to commiserate.

Tillie watched them slip behind the little building and followed them as soon as she could, leaving two sleeping babies and Sophie with Laura on her lap.

Tillie heard Sally's little voice break. Mandy and Beth made cooing sounds of comfort. Comfort. That was what Tillie had come to give to the girls. She stood straighter as she remembered the comfort God had sent to her when she was young and afraid.

God, I'm sorry I turned from You. I am truly sorry. Thank You for Adam's miracle. It called me to my senses. Only now that I see children trapped in their own prison of fear do I remember the comfort of Your saving grace.

Tillie felt God's own arms wrap around her and protect her. Tears nearly bit at her eyes as she realized all she'd given up. The only One who would always be with her.

Forgive me.

She walked around the shed.

The three girls, sitting in a little huddle whispering, straightened and looked fearful. It cut at Tillie's heart to think she'd added fear to these little girls' lives.

"Now then, young ladies, what are we going to do to rid this town of that nasty *Master* Parrish?" She made sure to sneer his name.

Three sets of bright blue eyes hardened with determination.

Mandy said, "I told Sally to make sure you saw her hands."

Tillie realized that it had been a little too easy, especially when an observant mother like Sophie had missed it.

"Why did you do that?"

"Because we've got a plan that might need a little adult help."

Tillie had planned her escape for months. She approved of plans. "I'll be glad to help."

"Good." Mandy's eyes sharpened in a way that made Tillie glad she was on the same side as these little rascals. "Because we've got some work to do before Monday morning."

"And what happens Monday morning?"

Beth put her arm around Sally and lifted her little sister's palm so Tillie could see the cuts and welts. "Come Monday morning, we're breaking free of things like this."

A hundred less-than-Christian thoughts flooded though Tillie's mind, all centering around that awful man who'd hurt these girls. But she saw their courage and knew how smart they were.

Tillie didn't get mad. Instead, she smiled and dropped down on her knees, joining the girls' circle. "When it comes to breaking free, I'm just the woman you want."

Parrish's cruel hands reached for her. They grabbed her, and his fists landed. And then it wasn't she they were hitting; it was Grace.

Hannah jerked awake with a scream.

Parrish had Grace. Hannah knew it. Nothing less than terrible danger could have kept Grace from sending the money. But finally, after months of silence, Hannah had to give in and admit it. Grace was in trouble. Which meant she and Libby were on their own.

Libby had healed more slowly than ever this time, too laid-up for Hannah to leave her and find work, not that anyone would hire her anyway for anything but mill work, not dressed in rags like these. She'd moved the two of them to a deserted cellar because she didn't want Trevor to come hunting and see how much trouble they were in and maybe give up his new home.

Mr. Daily always remembered the bread, and there was more for her and Libby now, without the boys sharing, but that was all. For a month, except a few scraps Hannah had dug out of the garbage and a few bites she'd bought with money begged from strangers, they'd lived on nothing but bread. It took good food, meat and vegetables, to knit broken bones, and their meager fare had kept Libby from healing.

They were warmer here than the shed because of the approaching spring. But still their cellar became sharply cold at night, even with the two of them snuggled up.

The house, less than twenty steps away, had a single man living in it. He'd never noticed them. His scraps, thrown out in the alley for stray cats, had helped keep them alive.

No one showed any interest in this hole in the ground.

When Libby came down with her third cold of the winter, Hannah sat next to her, fighting back tears as she longed to give her little sister suppers of warm broth full of meat and vegetables and hearty breakfasts of oatmeal and honey.

They lay together in the pitch dark of the cellar. Hannah's nightmare had awakened Libby. Hannah could see her little sister's eyes silently worrying. They were able to see each other only because moonlight had found its way through the cracked cellar door only inches overhead.

Hannah put her arm around Libby. "I've been thinking about Grace. I'm worried about her."

Libby had never met Grace, but Hannah talked of her often. Hannah considered all that was involved in her plan; her main worry was for her silent little sister. Libby would agree to anything if it meant helping others. She'd never make a demand for herself.

Hannah brushed her chapped, calloused fingers down Libby's hollow cheeks. "Grace and I are sisters, just like you and I are sisters. We just found each other and hung on."

Libby watched her with wide eyes. Her eyes shone with love when Hannah talked to her or read her stories.

"I was six and Grace was seven. She'd already been with Parrish for three years. He adopted her out of the orphanage when she was three. That's how old I think you are right now."

Hannah held up three fingers and counted slowly, "One, two, three."

Libby touched each one of Hannah's fingers, copying the motion but not saying the words. Hannah hoped that, inside her head, Libby was learning. Soon she'd teach her to write. Then maybe Libby would find a voice through the written word.

"By the time she was four, she was picking lint off the carpet under the presser."

Hannah suspected Libby had been doing that when she'd been hurt. Children as young as three were often forced into the mills. She still wanted to cry when she thought of the shape Libby had been in when Trevor had found her.

Trevor had carried her home, dark rage in his eyes as he demanded that Hannah take her in. As if Hannah would have refused.

They'd taken her to the doctor for her broken ankle, Hannah pretending to be her mother so no questions would be asked. The ankle had to be rebroken before it would heal. Grace's first envelope of money had come the same day as the doctor's bill.

"How would you like to get to know Grace?" Hannah considered all the complications. But Hannah was out of ideas. Hunting down her big sister tempted her beyond her ability to resist.

The three-year-old brightened and sat up, looking at Hannah with eager eyes. With a sigh of relief, Hannah could tell that Libby was going to get over this cold without it going into her chest. A rugged little girl who'd lived through three operations and been thrown out onto the street with less regard than that given to a wounded animal, Libby was tough.

I wonder if maybe Libby isn't tougher than I am.

"I think we ought to go visit Grace."

The hope in Libby's expression ate at Hannah's heart. *No one should want to leave their home this much.* But Chicago hadn't been kind to either of them.

A flush tinted Libby's cheeks that made her look almost healthy.

Hannah decided then and there to act on the notion playing around in her head. They were getting out of here. "We're going really soon, and we're going on the train."

A gasp of excitement shook Libby's little body.

Hannah hugged her tightly. A train meant change. It meant getting away and starting over. To Libby, a train must sound like a dream come true. "We do have a couple of problems."

Libby's eyes narrowed, and her brow furrowed.

Hannah almost smiled at the childish determination. There was a problem. They'd overcome it. That's how children of the street survived.

Hannah almost trembled, she was so afraid of what had happened to Grace. She kept thinking that Parrish had finally found her.

Libby tugged on her dress as if to ask, "What problems?"

"Well . . . the . . . uh . . . the main problem is . . ." Hannah looked down and smiled at this sister of her heart. "We can't afford tickets." Hannah remembered Grace's plan to stow away in the baggage car. That was what she and Libby would do.

The other problem Hannah didn't speak of. What would they find when they got to Mosqueros, Texas? Hannah wanted out of the city for Libby, but she also had an overwhelming urge to go rescue her big sister. Wherever Grace was, she must be in terrible, terrible trouble.

Grace snuggled under the covers, thinking of her blissful life. A rumble of thunder had jarred her from sleep. She shifted position, disturbing Daniel, who had been holding her close in his arms.

"Rain." She gave Daniel's shoulder a good jostle. "Wake up. It's spring."

"It's the middle of March. It's not spring yet." Daniel rolled over, grumbling.

"This is Texas. Spring comes in March." Grace laughed and gave him a solid poke in the ribs with her elbow.

He sighed deeply. Then the thunder sounded again and he sat up beside her. He ran his hand over his rumpled blond hair. "Rain'll speed things along, melting us out of here." He looked sideways at her and smiled.

"Still trying to escape from this marriage, Mr. Reeves?" she sassed.

Daniel grabbed her and hugged her tight. "I reckon I give up. I am well and truly caught." He left to start the kitchen fire.

Lying in bed still, nearly humming with the pleasure of her new life, Grace watched him leave. It was more than she'd ever dreamed possible. Oh, the boys were pills, especially Mark. And Parrish might still be out there somewhere. But what could he do now? She was a married woman. Any claim of fatherhood was dissolved by her marriage. The law wouldn't stand by while she was handed over to him. And neither would Daniel.

And what about Hannah and the rest of the sisters who had escaped from Parrish? If only all her sisters could know the joy of having a family. She was suddenly glad that Parrish had chased after her. Yes, she'd been hounded nearly into the ground, but at least her sisters had been safe. And now she was, too.

She said quietly to the ceiling, "If Parrish did show up now, Daniel would protect me. Daniel loves me." He'd never said it, but Grace knew with heart-deep assurance it was true. She threw back the covers, excited to think about the coming of spring.

When her feet hit the floor, the room lifted up off the ground, spun around over her head, then turned on its side. She fell face forward, scrambling to grab the bedpost. Her hand slipped, and she crashed to the floor.

Twenty-Six

The children ran screaming across the playground, enjoying their morning recess. What little beasts they were. Parrish went to the door and rang the school bell, ending their fun with relish.

He'd dreamed about Grace again last night, about hurting her. And he'd awakened so hungry for his revenge that he needed to work it off on someone.

Parrish stood just inside the door as the children trooped into the schoolhouse. They were instantly silent. He'd trained them well. The littlest McClellen girl hung back with her sisters. She was just a bit older than Grace had been when she'd first come to him. Grace's hair had been this same white-blond color. He'd been too easy on Grace.

Sally McClellen was finding out how he should have acted. He knew just what he was going to do when he got his hands on Grace this time.

Spring was slow in coming. The weather had turned warm, but not warm enough to melt the snow in that gap. He'd heard talk around town about the Reeveses. He'd listened but had been careful not to show any interest. No one knew if that gap had ever snowed closed before. Until Daniel Reeves had moved in there, no one in the area had even realized the canyon existed.

Several times he heard men talking at church — which he faithfully attended to pick up gossip and impress parents with his piety — about scaling the sides of the canyon and checking to see if the Reeveses were faring well.

They talked, but the consensus was Daniel had beef enough and supplies to last all winter and he'd be fine. There was no need for someone to risk his neck climbing in there. Parrish learned that Daniel was a Kansas farmer with five little boys. He also knew the man hadn't been in the war, spent time in the frontier army, or been on a cattle drive, things that would have made him tough.

Luther, an old hand on the McClellens' ranch, said he might make the climb just to spend time in the mountains again. Buff, his saddle partner, snorted and said there was no such thing as a Texas mountain.

"These hills wouldn't be foothills in the Rockies," Luther agreed. Luther discussed a way across the top of the bluff, where a man could go most of the way with no trouble if he went afoot.

Parrish heard every word. He'd spent enough time scouting the area that he knew the exact place Luther meant.

Parrish was running out of patience. His dreams were coming more often. Sleep was eluding him. The children were grating on his nerves. If that fat old Luther could get in there, then so could Parrish. He could handle Daniel Reeves and his whelps, and he could haul one little woman back out with him. He slapped his ruler on his hand, hungry just thinking about what he'd do to Grace.

"Adam!" Tillie slammed through the barn door.

Adam looked up from the roan that he'd taken back from vigilantes who'd been gunning for Sophie. He straightened and smiled. He looked at her pretty face and knew he needed to talk to her, too. He gave his horse a soft slap on the rump and laid the brush aside. Swinging the stall gate closed behind him, he walked right up to Tillie. She looked excited about something, but he decided he needed to go first, before she said something that got him off the subject.

He forced himself to say what had been on his mind from the first minute he clapped eyes on her. "You are the prettiest little thing I've ever seen."

Tillie's open mouth stopped yammering as if every thought had fled from her mind.

"Yep, and you're not the same woman I found out in the hills that first night."

"I — I'm not?" she stammered.

"Nope. That woman was afraid of her own shadow."

"Did you decide that before or after I beat you up?"

Adam felt his brows slam together. "I've told you a dozen times I was trying not to hurt you. Now don't start that. You've been so busy with Sophie and those babies that we haven't even been able to go on another ride. And I need to find out more about how you want the house laid out. I'm ready to start building."

Tillie crossed her arms as if he'd just insulted her. "Why on earth would I care how you lay out your house, Adam?"

Adam wondered if women were born so scatterbrained or if it was something they learned at their mamas' knees. He figured the trait must be inborn, because his Sophie hadn't spent much time at her mama's knee, and she had that same twisting-turning way about her thinking.

"You need to like it."

Tillie's eyes narrowed. "Why?"

Another dumb question. But Adam didn't point that out. He'd learned a lot from watching Clay chase his tail around his womenfolk. He knew there was a fitting way to talk to women. At least fitting to their way of thinking, dumb as it seemed. He relaxed and smiled, though his stomach twisted in a way that made it mighty hard to keep the corners of his mouth turned up.

"Because . . ." Adam fished around in his head. He'd read some books. He'd heard talk. He knew what she wanted. He sank to one knee on the straw-covered barn floor and took her hand.

Her eyes widened until white showed all the way around, like the eyes of his roan when it had a bad scare. That wasn't what Adam wanted to see. Still, he floundered on. "Because I want you to marry me."

Her jaw dropped open. Adam was grateful it was still early spring, or bugs would have flown into her mouth.

"Since when?"

Adam's heart sank a bit, and he stood,

thinking this might go better if he was standing over her a bit. "Why, since almost forever, I guess." He held her hand tighter and pulled her close. "I've never given much thought to getting married. And since I've met you, I haven't been able to think of much else."

"Really?" Her eyes turned from scared to interested.

Adam's heart quit pounding so hard, although it still seemed as if it might knock clear out of his chest. "You're a fine woman, Tillie. I think we'd get along well together. Please, will you marry me?"

Tillie stared at him a long, long time. At last, as if her neck became weak, her head dropped down and she looked at their joined hands. "We don't know each other very well, Adam. I am so honored by your proposal, and" — she looked up, scared again, but a different kind of scared — "a woman likes to hear of love when a man asks for her hand. But I don't think we know each other well enough to call it love."

Adam nodded. "But we do know each other well enough to believe love could come with time." Adam looked at her work-calloused hands, so competent and still so soft. He smiled. "And maybe not that long a time."

Tillie smiled back. "I believe I'd like to be married to you, Adam."

Adam laughed and grabbed her around the waist. He lifted her off her feet until she looked down into his eyes, almost as though he'd knelt again. Then he lowered her until her lips met his, and she came halfway to meet him.

When the kiss ended, he settled her on her own feet again. "Maybe not that long at all, Till. And how would you like a cabin and a barn and maybe even a few children running around our ankles, like Sophie and Clay's?"

Tillie jumped as if she'd been stabbed by a hat pin. "I didn't come in here to get proposed to."

Adam's heart twisted. Was she taking it all back? Was she changing her mind? "Well then, why did you come in here?"

She grabbed Adam by the collar of his shirt with both hands and shook him.

"Master Parrish?" Sally turned wide eyes on Parrish.

He looked at the youngest McClellen. "I've told you many times to go quietly to your seat, Miss McClellen."

"But I brought you a piece of cake, Master Parrish."

Parrish knew the ways of children. He saw something in the unpleasant child's eyes that didn't sit right with him. Catching her chin, he took a moment to consider it.

No fear. That was what was missing. The McClellens had always been a strangely stiff-necked brood, harder to cow than some. But why wouldn't she be afraid after she'd defiantly broken the rules?

The brat held out a neatly-wrapped napkin. She unfolded the edges, and he saw that a slice of white cake lay on her hand. Could she really think a piece of cake would save her?

"To the front of the room, Miss McClellen."

The girl's confident eyes wavered.

The power to make her afraid rushed to Parrish's head like strong liquor. He could live on it instead of food.

Sally walked slowly to the front and stood beside his desk. Her shoulders trembled.

Parrish followed along, enjoying every slow step that brought him closer to her.

"Master Parrish?" Mandy McClellen rose from her desk, another child speaking when she was supposed to sit quietly.

Parrish would have found an excuse to punish someone, most likely Sally, but he was thrilled that the children made it so easy. "Join your sister at the front."

"Master Parrish, I want to take Sally's punishment for her." Mandy strode forward and planted herself in front of her sister.

"You'll get your own punishment. My ruler is strong enough to last through many lashes." Parrish approached the older girl. The girl stood fast between him and Sally.

"Sally's hand hasn't healed up from Friday, Master Parrish. Don't hit her again. I'll take double the lashes." Mandy held out her hand.

"You can have that indeed, but your sister will still take hers, as well." Parrish noticed Mandy's hand was steady. He wanted it to tremble. He wanted fear. He kept coming. His ruler rested on the desk behind the girls.

Beth McClellen stood from her seat. "If you won't let Mandy do it, let me. I'll take Sally's punishment." Beth joined her sisters in the front of the schoolroom. "Sally's hand is too sore. You could really hurt her, Master Parrish. You can't hit her again so soon. You punished her every day last week. That's wrong of you."

Parrish froze. The three girls faced him defiantly. Not even little Sally was shaking now. Her sisters, blocking him from her, seemed to give her courage. They were brave little girls but foolhardy. Parrish smiled. He came forward.

The littlest boy in school came forward. Clovis Moore. He was nowhere near as steady as the girls, but he stood beside Mandy, in front of Sally.

"No, Clovis, sit down," Mandy hissed at him.

"I'll take Sally's punishment, sir. I'm the reason she got such a whipping Friday. You made her bleed, Master Parrish, just because she stuck up for me. I tripped and fell. I made all that noise 'n' misrupted class. If you have to punish someone, punish me."

Clovis extended his quivering hand, palm up, ready to take Sally's lashes.

Sally's first-grade classmate Linda O'Malley stepped forward. Her cheeks were flushed as red as her hair.

"Sit down, Linda," Mandy ordered.

Linda shook her head as she bravely extended her hand. "I'm in Sally's class. If her hand is too tender and you want to punish a really little girl, then I'll take her lashes, Master Parrish. It's wrong to hurt her again when she's still sore. Sally's a good girl, sir. She don't deserve all the whacks you've been givin' her."

"Do you think I won't punish you all?" Parrish asked.

Three more children, the oldest boys in school, stepped to the front. They lengthened the line that blocked his path to Sally. Another child stood, and another. The classroom desks emptied as the children all rose and filed quietly to the front. Each one extended his or her hand and offered to be the one to take the punishment.

"It seems everyone in here is anxious to be punished today," Parrish said. He had a lot of anger. He could accommodate them all.

Parrish roughly shoved past Mandy and Beth. He loomed over Sally. "Your defenders are going to wish they hadn't stepped in. Tomorrow they'll let you take your punishment on your own." He lifted the ruler from the desk.

"Are you going to hit me because I offered you cake, sir?" Sally asked. Her blue eyes met his, her fear palpable, her courage, too.

Parrish wanted to beat that courage out of her. It was the same courage he'd always seen in Grace, and it infuriated him that he'd never broken her. Sally wouldn't be so lucky. And as soon as spring came, Grace would find herself broken, too.

"You talked. You are to remain quiet when you're in the classroom. But it doesn't matter what my reasons. You're nothing. You are an urchin who is little better than an animal. If I beat you," — Parrish glanced at the children surrounding him, all with one outstretched hand, all holding his gaze — "I will hit you because I say you deserve it, and no one will tell me different. I'm your teacher. When you are in this classroom, you will submit yourself to me in any way I say."

"My parents never hit me, Master Parrish," Sally said. "I don't think they'd like you giving me so many lashes."

"Your parents will thank me for beating some manners into you. They will take my word over yours that you are a bad, bad girl. They will probably take you and beat you more when they get you home." Parrish lifted the ruler high, planning to make this one — all of them — sorry.

"Her parents don't beat her, Parrish." The deep voice from the window turned the whole classroom around. "And they sure as shootin' aren't about to start on your say-so."

Parrish froze, the ruler suspended cruelly in the air as he looked into the eyes of the black man who had accompanied these children to church.

■ ■ ■ ■

Daniel came running into the room as she lay there, dazed. Grace looked up at him. He seemed to be standing upright with no problem.

"What happened?" He knelt beside her and eased her onto her back.

She shook her head, and the room swooped. She held her head carefully still. "I don't know. I — I guess I swooned."

Daniel's eyebrows knitted together. "Why'd you do that?"

"I was wondering the same thing."

John's head poked up beside Daniel's shoulder. "Why's Ma on the floor, Pa?"

"Should she be down there, Pa?" Luke asked. "Now that we've got a bed 'n' all, it don't seem right that you still make her sleep on the floor."

Mark stumbled into his brothers, who stumbled into their pa.

Daniel almost fell over on top of Grace.

With a sudden fit of panic, Grace pictured all four of them collapsing on her. She reached her hand up and grabbed at the deerskin mattress.

Daniel crouched lower, eased his arm behind her shoulders, and slowly raised her to her feet.

She stood beside him and grabbed her stomach. "I don't feel so good." She breathed in and out, trying to steady her rebelling stomach.

Daniel said, with a voice so faint it drew her attention, "You think you're gonna be sick?"

The boys all took a quick step back.

Grace wasn't about to admit such a personal thing. Not when she hoped to avoid doing it. "No, I'm okay."

Daniel helped her sit on the edge of the bed then knelt in front of her.

"Did'ja say she was gonna toss her cookies, Pa?" Ike asked.

"I can get a bucket in here for her, if'n you want me to," Abe offered. But he stayed in place, and none of the others offered to get the bucket. They were all here.

She wanted to be alone. If she got sick to her stomach, she didn't want them all watching. She'd throw them out if she thought for a second they'd obey her.

Six blond-haired, worried men had their blue eyes riveted on her. She could have sworn all of them, except Daniel, thrilled at the prospect of her disgracing herself completely.

"If I could just lie back down for a few

398

minutes." Grace began sinking onto her side.

Daniel jumped up and helped settle her onto the bed. "You want to throw up and you're dizzy. What else is different, Grace? Are you having any other symptoms?" Daniel hadn't blinked since she'd grabbed her stomach. He looked terrified.

"Symptoms? What are you talking about? Symptoms of some sickness?"

"No, Grace." Daniel sounded wound up as tight as a pocket watch. She could almost hear him ticking with tension. "Symptoms of carrying a baby."

"A . . . a b-baby?" Grace was stunned. "Does fainting come with that?"

"And a sour belly first thing in the morning." Daniel dropped to his knees beside the bed.

"What're we gonna do with a new batch of babies?" Mark groused.

"I remember what it was like when you guys were born. You cried all the time." Abe shoved Luke sideways; then Luke slammed into John. "They're not sleeping in me 'n' Ike's room."

"And the diapers for three babies made the house stink like an outhouse, all day, every day for years." Ike shuddered and pushed his way past Daniel to stare at

399

Grace. "Do we have to have three again, Pa? Can't we just have two like normal?"

Daniel didn't answer. He stared at her, still not blinking.

Grace hoped his eyeballs didn't dry out.

He had braced his elbows on the bed and clutched his hands together close to his chin.

Grace thought he looked for all the world like he was praying. Well, prayer wasn't a half-bad idea. Three? Two?

"Babies don't have to come in batches, d-do they, Daniel?" Grace started praying, too.

"Yep," Mark said with solemn certainty. "In this family they have to."

"So far," Luke said. "I want three again. Three's been fun, hasn't it, guys?"

John wormed his way past Ike and Daniel and plunked himself down beside Grace. "You can have one if'n you want to, Ma, but bunches are more fun. Us guys'll help you with all three of 'em. We don't mind helping out with little brothers, and they can all sleep in with me 'n' Mark 'n' Luke if'n you want. We were sleeping six to a room when we lived in the cave." John looked at Mark. "Weren't we?"

Mark asked Ike, "They really stink?"

"Well, *you* sure did." Ike gave Mark a hard

slug in the arm.

Mark fell onto the bed on Grace's feet.

She pulled her feet up out of his way and almost kneed Daniel in the nose.

Daniel didn't seem to notice that the bed was fast filling with wrestling boys.

"Daniel, say something," Grace demanded.

His face seemed to be frozen. His knuckles were white where he clutched them together like one huge fist. Daniel's voice scraped against her skin, low and hoarse and full of despair. "I was weak." He breathed in and out as if he were consciously making his chest work. He stopped staring straight forward and looked at Grace. The detached shock was gone, replaced by fury.

"You tempted me, and I was weak." Daniel lurched to his feet. Two more of the boys, who were practically hanging on their pa's back, stumbled and fell on top of Grace.

Daniel backed away from her and the bed full of boys. "I was weak, and now you're gonna die." Daniel whirled and ran out of the room.

His announcement stunned the boys into complete silence.

The door to the outside slammed.

"Adam, you're here. You came," Sally whispered.

Beth turned on her little sister, surprised but relieved. "You told Adam to come?"

Sally shook her head.

"No, Beth — I did." Tillie appeared in the window.

"But you promised not to tell." Beth was traitorously glad Tillie had broken her promise.

"I did promise, and I meant it when I said it." Tillie gripped the windowsill so tightly Beth saw her black knuckles turn white. "But after I thought about it awhile, well, I admit free and clear I broke my promise. I didn't think you girls could take him."

Mandy snorted. She pointed at the floor. Everyone looked at the spot where Parrish stood, still frozen, his mouth agape as he stared at Adam.

Mandy jerked on a cord that came up through a knothole in the floor and hung inconspicuously from a hook attached under the top of Master Parrish's desk. The floor collapsed under Parrish's feet. With a shriek, Parrish dropped out of sight with a loud crash.

Tillie stood on her tiptoes and looked through the window at the hole where Master Parrish had just stood. "Sorry, I never should've doubted you."

Mandy sniffed.

Beth giggled.

Adam and Tillie disappeared from the window. Clay McClellen came in the front door. Luther was only a couple of steps behind him. Adam and Tillie appeared seconds later.

Clay came to the front of the schoolroom and looked down at the hole in the floor.

Beth saw Parrish glaring up, rage etched on his face.

Sally leaned against Pa's leg. He rested a hand on her shoulder, and she seemed to soak in his strength.

Beth wondered why she hadn't tattled on Parrish the first time he'd punished her little sister for nothing.

"Did you dig that hole?" Pa turned to look at Mandy.

"I dug it, Pa." Beth stepped forward. If there was punishment, she'd take her share.

"I fixed the braces and rigged the trip line so we could make the floor fall in," Mandy admitted.

"I carried buckets of dirt outside and hid 'em in the woods," Sally added.

Tillie stepped up, her head bowed. "I helped them smuggle tools to town, Clay."

Adam came up beside her. "You didn't

tell me all that. You just said the girls needed help."

Tillie shrugged. "They did need help . . . this morning. Yesterday digging the hole, they were fine on their own."

"When did you do all this?" Pa lifted his cowboy hat with one gloved hand and rubbed his hair flat as if soothing his brain.

"Uh, we, uh . . . we snuck out of church yesterday morning." Mandy arched her brow as if asking how much trouble was coming her way.

"You were sitting with us. You weren't gone long enough to —"

"I left with one of the twins, 'member, Pa?" Beth said. "Right away at the start of the service. Tillie had the tools hid in the wagon so we could pry up the floorboard and dig."

"And I left with the other baby," Mandy confessed.

"I took Laura out when she started into hollering." Sally stared at her toes peeking out from under her dress.

Beth didn't blame Sally for being a bit nervous. This had always been the weak part of their plan. Missing church was a no-no. She tried to be helpful. "We watched the little ones real careful, though, whilst we dug."

"Laura even helped carry dirt a little." Then guilt clouded Sally's eyes, and she looked at the floor. Beth swallowed hard, worrying. What now? Maybe they'd all get a beating out of this yet.

Pa sighed. "What did you do, Sally?"

"I, uh, pinched Laura to make her cry to begin with, 'cause she was behaving herself right proper in church."

"Well, that was a plumb mean thing to do, girl." Luther bent down, grabbed Parrish by the back of the neck of his black suit coat, and pulled him out of the hole. Luther tossed him onto the floor like a landed catfish.

The children gathered around, enjoying watching their teacher get his comeuppance.

Pa leaned over and looked down into the hole. "You girls didn't put spikes in the bottom of that, did you?"

"Nope." Mandy sounded as though she regretted skipping the spikes.

Beth nudged her.

Clay looked at Sally and crouched in front of her. "Let me see your hand, darlin'."

Sally held her palm up. The bruising was dark, and there were several cuts in her tender flesh.

Pa gave her hand a kiss then lifted her into his strong arms as he rose and hugged her tight. He pulled back far enough to look her square in the eye. "You could have told me. I'd've listened. You're not a little girl to tell lies, and I'd've trusted you."

Sally's eyes filled with tears, and she flung her arms around her pa's neck. Beth thought Sally might squeeze the life out of him.

"Now you know better 'n to cry, Sally." Pa patted her on the back. "Remember rule number one."

Mandy tossed herself against Pa's leg.

Beth hugged him, too. Somehow he had enough arms to hug them all.

When they let go, Luther said, "Drat. I was plumb distracted by your caterwauling womenfolk, and Parrish lit out of here."

"No matter," Pa said in a mild voice that gave Beth the shivers. "I'm in the mood for hunting varmints."

There'd been a time not so long ago when there'd been only Ma and her sisters to stick up for her. Not that they needed a man, but a good one could make himself purely useful.

Pa's eyes swept over all the students. "I saw what you all did, standing up for Sally. I'm proud of every one of you. I'm sorry we didn't get Parrish taken care of sooner."

Solemn faces turned to smiles all around.

"For now, school's out until we hire a new teacher. You can all go home."

He looked at Sally, still perched in his arms. "Your ma is waiting for you in the wagon."

"How'd you get her to wait outside, Pa?" Beth asked.

"When Adam told me there was trouble, I told her I was riding to town, but I didn't say what for. She thinks we need supplies. I also left her holding both twins and Laura on her lap."

"That'd slow her down some," Beth said. "I hope she didn't hurt Master Parrish."

They all ran outside.

"Parrish must have sneaked out the window," Tillie said.

"Yep," Mandy agreed. "Because Ma would've caught on that something was wrong if she'd've seen him sneaking out, and she'd've had him."

Luther tugged on his fur cap. "You'd better see to your young'uns, Clay. Adam and I'll head after him. Send Buff out to pick up our trail. Adam 'n' Buff 'n' me'll hunt up Parrish."

Adam slung his arm around Tillie and said, "If you boys can handle one measly schoolmaster alone, Tillie and I have a few things we need to do before the wedding."

"What wedding?" Clay, Luther, and the girls all asked.

Adam grinned.

"What wedding?" Tillie asked.

Beth noticed Adam's eyes narrow as he looked at Tillie, and Beth knew what wedding. Now all he had to do was convince Tillie.

Staring at Tillie, Adam said, "I can see we definitely still have some planning to do." He snugged Tillie's waist tight and dragged her away from the schoolhouse.

Beth heard Tillie's soft laugh as they disappeared.

"The young'uns are fine with Sophie, Luth." Pa's words drew her attention back. In a voice that thrilled Beth because this was *her* pa, protecting *her* and *her sisters,* Pa said, "Reckon I want in the hunt for any man who puts his hands on my girls."

Luther asked, "How are we going to get Sophie to stay out of it?"

"That's gonna be harder than tracking down that varmint Parrish." Pa's shoulders slumped, and he walked toward the wagon.

Twenty-Seven

Grace looked at the empty doorway then reluctantly glanced at her sons John, Ike, and Mark on the bed with her. Luke and Abe stood beside her. All of them stared after their father. As if their necks were all controlled by the same muscles, they turned to look at her.

"You're gonna *die?*" John asked.

"I — I don't think so." Grace looked at her stricken son, the one who loved her first and most.

"Pa seemed pretty sure." Mark sounded as though he was prepared to face facts and not get overwrought about it.

Mark's calm acceptance — so calm it bordered on eagerness — John's teary concern, and the bed wavering as if it might collapse under the squirming weight of four people, helped settle Grace's stomach and clear her head.

She swung her feet over the side of the

bed and carefully stood. The room behaved. "Now, boys, whatever your pa said, I'm not going to die. Your mom did, but there are lots of women who have babies without dying. Why, Sophie McClellen has had a whole passel of young'uns and she's fine."

"Yeah, but . . ." Mark looked as if he was going to insist the family settle on Grace's dying.

"Enough, Mark. I'm living and that's the end of it." Grace hadn't heard that tone of voice from herself before. It was more fearsome than her teacher voice. She decided she would use it often. "Now scoot on out of here so I can get ready for the day."

The boys headed for the door. John was slow climbing off the bed, and Ike tried to pass him with a hard shove. A bare foot whizzed past Grace's face as the two of them ended up in a tangled heap on the floor, twisted up in blankets. Mark stepped on them as he climbed out. Ike yelled out in pain, loudly enough to hurt Grace's ears. He twisted his body when Mark stepped square on his back. Mark fell forward into Abe. They left the room, yelling and shoving each other.

Grace realized their antics didn't even bother her — that was just the way they moved from one place to another. She closed the door and turned to get dressed without seriously considering telling them to quiet down.

She had a worrywart husband to find. First she'd give him a big hug and tell him not to worry — she wouldn't leave him. Then, if that didn't work, she was going to hammer some sense into him.

And if she had to, she'd use a real hammer!

Parrish had learned the hard way that you needed to know where you were going and how you were getting there because you might have to leave town quickly. He always had an escape plan. He hit the ground running when he ducked out of the schoolhouse window, and he hadn't stopped yet.

"Stupid hicks are probably still there talking," he muttered gleefully. He slipped between buildings, coolly asked to rent the blacksmith's horse with no intention of returning the nag, and headed south out of town.

He rounded a curve in the trail, looked carefully around to make sure he wasn't being watched, and rode into rough country following a game trail that would take him north . . . to Grace.

"He went up the hillside, Ma," Abe yelled, pointing at the obvious tracks in the muddy ground.

Grace plunked her fists on her hips as she stood in the pouring rain. "Your pa is the most stubborn man I've ever known. Why would he go up that slippery trail this morning?"

"Reckon it's 'cause you're gonna die." Mark sounded a shade too chipper. A crack of thunder sounded as the rain soaked them to the skin.

"I'm not going to die." Grace ignored the rain to glare at Mark. "Now stop that foolish talk."

"Pa said." Mark didn't sound as if he was hoping for it. He just wasn't all that upset.

"Don't die, Ma. I love you." John threw his arms around her legs and almost knocked her over. A wave of dizziness swamped her, and she was glad the sturdy little five-year-old held her steady.

She turned and hugged him close, his sad face buried in her soaked skirt. His rain-slicked hair was cool under her hand. "Now, John, your pa's just being foolish. He's worried about me because of your ma, but lots of women have babies and live through it just fine. Your own ma did it once."

John lifted up his face and looked at her. His eyes were filled with tears.

Grace did her best to buck him up. His brothers would torment the living daylights out of him if they caught him crying.

"And how about Sophie McClellen?" Grace ran her hand down John's head and rested it on his rosy cheek.

John nodded, sniffling a little. He glanced behind him and saw all four of his brothers. He buried his face in Grace's stomach again and discreetly blew his runny nose on her dress. Grace grimaced, but she willingly sacrificed her dress to the cause of manliness.

John looked up again, looking much steadier. "You're right. And there are some kids from big families in Mosqueros. And they've all got mas."

"That's because it's real unusual for a lady to die having a baby." Grace tipped John's chin up, and after giving him a long look, she glanced at the other boys gathered around her. "It was your ma's time, boys. God is faithful to us. That's something I learned when I came here."

The thunder rumbled again, but it didn't frighten her. She only heard the rumble of spring. In it was the rumble of new life. Grace loved the sound, just as she loved Daniel and her boys and this tiny new life inside her.

She reached out a hand and caressed Abe's worried face, then Ike's. Then she turned and smiled at sassy Mark and quiet Luke. "I came here purely by accident, not planning to be your ma, and you not wanting me for the job."

"That's for sure," Mark muttered.

Grace smiled at him. "But God is faithful, Mark. God knew what He was doing. God knew you needed a ma, and more than that, He knew I needed a husband and five sons."

"You needed us?" Mark's brow furrowed.

"I needed you so much." She grabbed him and gave him a hard hug as he tried to squirm away. She let him go with a little laugh. "Having you to take care of and having you to take care of me is the finest thing that ever happened in my life. The Bible says, 'It is of the Lord's mercies that we are not consumed, because his compassions fail not. They are new every morning: great is thy faithfulness.' "

"God is faithful to us?" Abe asked. "I thought it was the other way around. I thought we were supposed to be faithful to God."

Grace smiled and pulled John toward the house. All the other boys followed. She stepped inside, out of the rain. "We *are* supposed to be faithful to God. We are supposed to trust Him to take care of us, trust that Jesus died so we won't have to."

"We do have to die, Ma," Ike said. "Everybody dies."

"No, they don't. They live their lives out on this earth, and then they go to heaven and live with God. Jesus died in our place."

"So you don't think our ma is really dead?" Mark asked.

"I know she isn't. She was a good woman who put her faith in God. He's got her right now in a safe, happy place. And He was so faithful to you that, knowing you wouldn't pick me for a ma and knowing I'd never have picked you for my sons, He stuck us together. He even sent the parson to do the marriage ceremony. And He snowed us in together so we had the whole winter alone to get to know each other."

"God did all that?" Luke sounded awestruck.

Grace nodded and gave Luke a quick kiss on the head. He hunched his shoulders as if the gesture of affection bothered him, but he stayed and took the kiss. He even grinned shyly at her.

"God is faithful. His loving-kindness never ceases. His compassion never fails. Great is God's faithfulness. He knows how to take care of us long before we do. And He is sending us this baby. So we have to trust that God is being faithful to us in this, too. He knows what He's doing."

Mark shrugged. "God oughta know what He's doing."

Abe nodded. Ike joined in. John hugged Grace one more time then backed up and knocked into Luke, who stumbled sideways and fell against Abe, who shoved him away.

Grace caught hold of Luke before all five boys ended up tumbling to the floor. She hugged him, and he relaxed enough to hug her back.

Grace asked, "So who is left in this family who doesn't know this baby is a gift from God?"

All five boys looked between each other; then they looked at Grace and said all at once, "Pa."

Grace smiled. "Your pa needs to learn a lesson about being faithful to God, boys. Let's go find him and drag him back down here and convince him God is faithful."

The boys all turned.

"Hold it," Grace ordered. "You get coats on and boots and we split up so we can cover the most area. We saw which way he went, but his tracks will disappear once he gets off the trail."

The boys scrambled into their coats with a maximum of noise.

Grace pulled on Abe's old buckskin jacket. "Ike, you take John and go up and to the north toward the sapling stand. Abe, you and Luke go straight up the hill. Mark, we'll go south toward the cave. He's just up there worrying. He's not hiding. We'll find him in a few minutes."

They smiled, eager for a chance to run out in the spring rain. They turned and went outside on a pa hunt.

TWENTY-EIGHT

Parrish spent the whole morning pushing his nag as fast as he could. He cut a switch from a low-hanging branch and whipped the beast until it trotted steadily. Parrish bounced in the saddle, taking the beating of a lifetime. As his backside took a pounding, he grew more and more irritated with Grace. He'd been mad when he'd gotten out of bed this morning. The need to slake his temper had been building steadily. If he could have knocked the sass out of that littlest McClellen girl, it would have taken the edge off, but that pleasure had been denied him, and now he burned.

"It's high time we had this out, girl," he yelled at the dripping sky. "You sent me to prison, and now you're gonna pay."

His horse snorted and looked over its shoulder at Parrish. They climbed steadily, following the trail Parrish had scouted a dozen times through the winter. They neared the steepest part, where that hillbilly Luther had said a man afoot could make it. Parrish sneered. This horse would take him all the way over this canyon wall and like it.

The horse balked at a particularly steep stretch of the trail. Parrish whipped the horse soundly. Fighting the bit, the horse charged at the slippery rocks. Parrish could see footholds large enough for a horse, even though the trail disappeared and the canyon wall swooped steeply enough that he could have touched the mountainside with his left hand while his right foot dangled over thin air.

The horse plunged up a step, then another. It slipped in the drizzling rain, regained its footing, and lurched forward again.

"You stupid brute. Get up there. Get up!" His whip lashed with all the strength in his arm. A rock dislodged under the horse's hoof, and the horse reared up and back, sliding and rolling on its haunches. Parrish saw the horse coming over backward. He grabbed the steep edge of the cliff. The horse slid out from under him. The coarse grass and shifting rock Parrish grabbed caved under his weight, and he fell after the horse. Parrish landed on a narrow ledge in the soft mud. He saw the horse fall a few feet farther, then hit a level spot and stagger to its feet. The horse looked up the hill at Parrish. With a whinny that sounded like mocking laughter, the horse turned tail and ran down the slope it had just been forced to climb.

Parrish sat in the mud, screaming his rage as the animal raced away down the trail, heading for Mosqueros. Aching joints punishing him, Parrish staggered to his feet. His fury boiled over. He shook his fist at the dripping rain, howling with fury, then remembered whose fault this really was. He turned to look up the hill and, a burning need to punish riding him, continued on his mission to find Grace. He couldn't get her out of here now, not on foot.

"So I won't try to take you with me. I'll settle with you here, girl. I'll pay you back for doing me wrong. And I'll make it hurt until you know what I suffered those months I spent in jail. Then I'll get out of this miserable state of Texas."

"Look, there's Ike, way over on that rise," Grace said to Mark.

Mark looked over and saw Ike and John waving at them. "Find him yet?" Mark's voice echoed across the canyon.

"No!" came the shout back.

They waved at each other and kept searching.

"Where do you think he's got his self off to, Ma?" Mark asked.

Grace looked down at her most difficult son. "I'm not too worried about him, Mark. He's all upset because he thinks I'm going to die."

Mark shrugged and glanced sideways at her. "Reckon you're gonna, if Pa says. He knows everything."

"Well, he doesn't know this. Why, I can think of lots of women who have had children and not died."

"Never three at onest though, Ma. That's what'll probably finish you off."

Grace stopped and took hold of Mark's shoulders and turned him to face her. "You don't have to sound so happy about it." She glared at him.

One corner of his mouth curled up as he smirked at her. He was worried about his foolish pa, who'd just gone for a walk and would be fine. But he wasn't upset in the least about her dying.

He pulled against Grace's grip, but she held on. "Mark, is this how it's always going to be with us?"

"Whaddaya mean, how's it gonna be?" Mark's face was far too blank and innocent.

"Whatever else you are, Mark," Grace said, "you're not stupid. Well, guess what? Neither am I. I can tell you don't like me. I want us to get along."

Mark stared at her, his eyes cool, his expression faintly amused. It was an expression Grace could imagine hardening into real trouble as the years went by. But for now, this little scamp was only five. She could handle a five-year-old. She hoped.

She pulled him over to a fallen tree and had him sit down. The rustle of branches and the rain, now just a faint sprinkle, were the only sounds as she sat beside him and prayed for wisdom. *Lord, how do I make a child love me?* She meditated on it.

No still, small voice gave her an easy answer. And then she remembered.

"When John and I were trapped in that avalanche, we were really scared."

Mark's expression softened a bit as he seemed to think about the danger his brother had been in.

"It made me realize that I hadn't been faithful to God the way I should be."

"Now, Ma," — Mark patted her on the hand — "I'm sure you're not all that bad. I'm sure God'll let you into heaven after you die having my next three brothers."

Grace forced her eyes to remain straight

forward even though she wanted to roll them in exasperation. "You're not listening to me, young man," she said sharply.

Mark's eyes grew cool again. She'd never had any luck reaching him with stern words or threats. Confound it, why couldn't this child be just the least bit afraid of her?

"It made me realize that I had to start living bravely for God." That caught his attention. Bravery evidently appealed to him.

"How do you live bravely for God?" Mark asked, scooting just a hair closer to her on the tree trunk.

"When I was a child, I was really tough. I faced down bigger kids and even some grown-ups who wanted to hurt me. But then I got away from my —" Grace never had been able to call him her father. "From the man who adopted me."

"You were an orphan, like us? I remember John saying that."

"Except you aren't an orphan. You always had your pa, but you know what I mean." Grace nodded. "Then, once I got away from the man who adopted me, he chased after me. I spotted him in a town where I ran to. He was supposed to go to jail, but he must have wiggled out of it somehow. I saw him on the street before he saw me and sneaked away that very night, hiding out on the train."

Mark's eyes grew wide. "That sounds really brave." He sounded impressed.

"Well, it was brave of me in some ways. But the thing is, from then on, I started running." Grace turned Mark, her hands resting on his shoulders. "I learned to always be on the lookout. I watched behind me all the time. I saw him once in a while, too. I thought I'd gotten away for good in Mosqueros. It was so far from Chicago."

"And then he got here, right?" Mark's eyes narrowed.

Grace thought the boy looked as though he might be willing to fight Parrish for her. She didn't know if it was because he liked her at least a little or because he just wanted an excuse to fight, but still, it was something.

"Yes, he got here, and I hid from him in your pa's wagon, and the parson caught me with the lot of you, and it's improper for a man and woman to stay together without being married."

Mark piped up, "So the parson made you get hitched."

Grace nodded. "And that's okay, because I love being here with you. I love you boys and I love this canyon and I love your pa."

Mark said in amazement, "You love us boys?"

"Yep," Grace said, smiling.

"Not including me, right?" Mark looked a little guilty. "I haven't been too nice. I don't expect you to love me."

"Well, you *have* been a handful, young man. But you're smart and brave. You love your brothers, and you've got a good, honest heart." Grace lifted one hand and rested it on Mark's cheek. "How could I not love you?"

Mark was tough and stubborn, but he was, after all, five. Grace saw the longing in his heart for a mother to love him. She knew that longing because she had lived with it all her life.

She said gently, "We've talked about the Ten Commandments when your father reads the Bible to us at night, haven't we?"

Mark nodded. He let her hand remain where it was. He even leaned into it a little.

"Well, Jesus said, a long time after Moses brought the Ten Commandments down from the mountain, that He had two new commandments. He said if you followed these commandments, then you would always follow all the others. Do you remember what they are? We've read those verses."

Mark said, " 'Thou shalt love the Lord

thy God with all thy heart, and with all thy soul, and with all thy mind.' "

Grace said, "Right, that's the first. Then Jesus said, 'And the second is like unto it —' "

" 'Thou shalt love thy neighbour as thyself.' " Mark sat quietly. His forehead furrowed as he thought about the new commandments.

"That's it. Love. God says, 'Love Me, and love each other.' It's simple. And so I love you. I love you because God tells me to."

"You didn't love me when I was your student and you were getting me thrown out of school."

"Yes, I did. I wanted your pa to understand how unruly you were in school. I'd tried to talk to you, but you still wouldn't mind. I'd tried to talk to your pa, and nothing changed. You boys were making it so the other students couldn't study." Grace left her hand on Mark's cheek. With the other, she waggled her finger right under his nose.

"Loving you doesn't mean you get to be naughty. I hoped by going to such lengths with your pa, he'd see reason and insist you boys behave. If I didn't love you, I wouldn't have cared how you acted. I wouldn't have cared if any of my pupils learned or not."

Mark reached up and caught Grace's

scolding finger. He lowered it away from his face. She wondered if he was going to start fussing at her again, as he always had in school.

Then the unhappy look on his face lightened, and he began to glow from within. "You love me?"

Grace nodded once, firmly.

Mark held tight to her hand and whispered, "I love you, too, Ma." Then his very young blue eyes filled with tears. "I don't want you to die." His voice broke on the last word. He flung himself into her arms and squeezed the breath out of her and cried.

"I'm not going to die, son." Grace caressed his blond hair and murmured nonsense to him until he'd worked himself through his upset.

He finally lifted his head and dashed his hand across his tear-streaked face. He looked around carefully. "Um . . . you won't tell the others I cried, will you?"

"It'll be our secret," Grace said. "And, Mark . . ."

"What, Ma?" Her name had never sounded so good.

"We'll find your worrywart pa and convince him I'm okay, and then this family can get back to normal."

Mark nodded. "Yep, we're finally going to be a real family."

Grace gave him a sound kiss on the cheek and straightened away from him. "Everything is going to be just fine."

Just then a hard arm grabbed Mark and pulled him backward off the log.

Twenty-Nine

Grace screamed as that filthy arm wrapped around Mark's little neck. She didn't think. Desperate to protect him, she lunged for Mark.

A brutal hand slapped her aside. She fell on her side to the ground and whirled around on her hands and knees, braced to attack again.

Then she saw his face.

Parrish.

"Get up, little Graceless." Parrish lifted Mark by his neck.

Mark grabbed Parrish's strangling arm with both of his little hands, squirming and trying to shout.

Parrish cut off the noise.

Mark kicked him.

Parrish shook Mark viciously. "Stop fighting me, you little —"

"Let him go." Grace shook off the paralyzing terror that Parrish had trained into her so well. She scrambled to her feet and advanced toward this beast who had hurt so many children for so long.

Parrish's arm tightened, and Mark coughed and yanked desperately against the vise around his neck. He began to fight less frantically, and Grace saw his eyes begin to glaze.

"Let him go. I'll do anything you want. You came here for me."

Parrish smiled. Fear like a cold Texas wind chilled Grace's backbone. He loosened his grip slightly. Mark, still conscious, sagged against Parrish's arm and dragged air into his lungs.

"Come over here, Graceless. When I have you, the boy can go."

Grace felt the bite of tears. She looked at Mark and didn't hesitate for a moment. She rounded the tree trunk she and Mark had been sitting on. A deep, coarse laugh erupted from Parrish as Grace came within his grasp. Parrish threw Mark aside. Mark rolled on the ground and hit the fallen tree hard.

Grace turned to help her son. Parrish grabbed her arm and jerked her upright.

Mark moaned, turning over sluggishly on his back. Blood streaked down his forehead from a nasty gash. Mark faltered as he tried to sit up, and then he collapsed, completely still.

Parrish dragged Grace toward the top of the canyon wall.

"No, I've got to help him. You hurt him, you —"

Parrish spun her around to face him. He slapped her across the face. She'd have fallen if his grip hadn't been so tight. He raised his hand again. "The only reason to go back for that boy is to make sure he's dead. Shall we do that, Graceless? You want me to go back?"

A wasteland of cruelty and sadistic pleasure glowed in Parrish's eyes. He'd do it. He'd kill Mark and enjoy every minute of it. His huge, hard hand cut into her right arm until she wanted to cry out from the pain. He'd like that.

She refused to give him the satisfaction now, just as she had in the last years she'd been with him. Her back bore testament to how long and hard Parrish had lashed her with his belt, trying to break her spirit.

His grip tightened. A step above her on the steep hillside, he towered over her. "Your choice, darling daughter. We go quietly, or we stay and see to the boy."

Grace looked back. She took one long last look at her son. The boy who said he loved her. She'd repaid that love by bringing Parrish down on this family. She never should have tried to face Parrish all those years ago. She never should have fought him. It had led to this.

Feeling like a coward after her high-minded talk of being brave, she turned away from Mark. "Let's go. I'm ready for my punishment."

Parrish jerked on her arm until it felt as though it would be torn off. That pain was nothing compared to the pain of seeing Mark lying behind them, hurt and bleeding.

"You knew the cost of going against me." Parrish's fingers dug deeper, and her arm began to go numb. "Yet you did it. You thought you could fight me." Parrish laughed again.

Grace had heard this laugh a thousand times as he used his belt on her or the other children. But there was an edge to it now. Something shrill and furious echoed behind the laughter. She looked at him as he dragged her at a rapid pace up the slope through the thick woods.

He had always been clean cut, polished, even fastidious. Now he was filthy. His face coated with dirt, his suit torn but also worn paper thin. Parrish had changed. He'd been a sadist before, enjoying the pain of others, but he'd gone beyond that.

He looked down at her, and it cried out from his red-rimmed eyes. He was mad. She'd fallen into the clutches of a raving madman, and the only way to save Mark was to stay and let Parrish have his revenge.

Parrish twisted her arm as he dragged her upward. Farther every step from the only happiness she had ever known.

She'd left Daniel on an unhappy note. That was how he'd remember her. John loved her completely, and this would break his heart. It occurred to her that Daniel had been right all along.

She was going to die.

The minute they disappeared into the trees, Mark jumped to his feet. He looked after them, thinking hard but not long. He rubbed a handful of blood off his forehead.

"Blood!" Thrilled at the nastiness of the injury and how much bragging he could do, he wiped the blood on the front of his shirt where it'd be sure to show. He plotted just where that awful man would take his ma and the lay of the land. Then he turned and ran in the opposite direction.

He needed his brothers.

Parrish gasped for breath by the time they

reached the halfway point up the canyon. The wall began to get steeper. The trees fell away. Grass grew, but the land was too full of stone for anything larger to thrive.

His grip never relaxed, but Grace didn't try to fight him regardless. The boys were in danger as long as Parrish was close. That kept her moving. No matter what happened to her, she had to get Parrish away from this canyon for the sake of her sons.

Sweat stained the ragged black suit Parrish wore. He inched his way up, looking for footholds in the canyon wall. Grace looked upward. Daniel had said if they needed to go to town he could get out this way. But it was rugged and slow. Parrish stumbled on the rocky ground. He didn't let her go, so she fell with him. She landed hard, flat on her belly on the hillside, right beside the vile man.

That's when she thought of her baby. She suddenly realized that it wasn't only her sons who needed protection. She had a baby that deserved better than dying before it had lived.

"Great is thy faithfulness."

The words came to her, whispered on the wind. Her prayer for courage. She'd thought going with Parrish to protect Mark was the right thing to do, and it had been at that moment when Mark was so vulnerable. But what about now? Where was her courage? Parrish was an old man, exhausted and not in his right mind.

Grace thought of her boys wrestling in their bedrooms, knocking each other off their new beds, playing King of the Mountain. Well, they were on a mountain right now. She lifted her knees up to her chest and kicked Parrish in the belly.

"Aaahh!" Parrish's fingers clung to her arm, but her dress ripped with a hiss and the sleeve tore and jerked the buttons loose in the back; the dress was pulled halfway off her shoulder as he slid backward. He held on to Grace and pulled her with him. They tumbled a few yards before Grace came up fighting. She caught a handful of mud in her hand and threw it into Parrish's ugly, snarling face. He swallowed it and began choking.

"You lousy little . . ." He lunged for her. "I'll teach you some respect if it's the last thing I do."

Grace jumped aside, reached out her foot, and tripped him, just as Mark always did to John. Parrish caught her skirt as he fell past her, and she fell again, head over heels, down a long stretch of the canyon-side, into the grove of trees.

She landed with a dull thump against a loblolly pine. The blow knocked the wind out of her, but she ignored her pain and staggered to her feet, fighting for each breath. She saw a tree branch and remembered the boys' sword fights. She snatched it up, the sleeve of her dress hanging from her wrist, and swung with all her might.

Parrish, charging, ran right into it. The branch smacked him in the belly with a hollow thud. It stopped him cold. He sucked in air on an inverted scream, dropped to his knees, and stared stupidly at her. Grace lifted the branch again. She owed him another one for the time he'd thrashed her and her five little sisters for reading after dark. *Whack.*

She owed him for the times he'd made her sit on the floor and fed her thin oatmeal, while he sat at his fine table eating roast beef. *Whack.*

She owed him for the little girl he'd whipped so hard she was never normal again, and as soon as he saw she was permanently damaged in the head, he sent her back to the orphanage. *Whack.*

She owed him for the blow she'd taken just now, which might have hurt her unborn baby. *Whack.*

And she owed him for the blood on

Mark's head. Her son might be dead even now. She lifted her arms high for this last solid blow. Then she had to go to Mark.

Mud splattered into Parrish's face. Then a hail of mud balls pelted him.

A shrill scream from overhead whirled Grace around.

Mark swung down out of the tree, hanging from a vine. He plowed, feet first, into Parrish's chest, knocking him on his back onto the ground.

Abe and Ike charged out of the woods, roaring like Johnny Reb charging into battle, armed with sticks and stones.

Luke and John were right on their heels, screaming like banshees. Mark, out of control on his vine, swung back and slammed into all of them, knocking them down like dominoes.

He fell off the rope, bounced a few times, then turned, along with his brothers, and charged at Parrish, who sprawled flat, too addled to notice all the little feet kicking him.

Grace dashed forward to get the boys to stop.

Then . . . she didn't.

She pulled her dress back onto her shoulders, looking at her dangling sleeve and thinking she had no idea how she would sew it back on. With a shrug, she left it there and dusted her filthy hands. After an unsuitable length of time, she said, "All right. That's enough."

The boys must have worn themselves out, because they stopped almost immediately and turned to her, grinning.

"You really pounded him, Ma," Ike said. He dropped a heavy hackberry branch and ran over and threw his arms around her, nearly knocking her farther down the hill.

Abe slammed into her from the other side, thus balancing her again.

The rest of the boys swarmed her.

"Wow, Ma, we saw you beating that man up. I never knew you were tough like that." Mark looked up at her, his eyes shining with admiration.

Grace thought of all the times she'd tried to get this little scamp to respect her when she was teaching school. Apparently all she'd needed to do was get in a fistfight on Mosqueros's Main Street and he'd have behaved.

Parrish groaned from where he lay on the ground.

"Who is he, Ma?" Ike asked.

"Yes, Grace. Who in the world is that poor man you and my boys have beaten into the dirt?" Daniel stepped out of the woods.

"Where did you come from?" Grace tried to think back, a thousand years ago, to this morning. Daniel had declared her as good as dead and walked off in a snit. The big dummy.

"The woods." Daniel shrugged, looking between Parrish and her as if he might be the slightest bit afraid his turn came next.

She planted her hands on her hips. "Have you by any chance noticed what is going on in your canyon, Mr. Reeves?"

She spoke in the voice she'd always used when she was the schoolmarm and he was the father of unruly students.

"I heard the screaming."

"Pa," Mark said, "you should've seen Ma whacking this guy in the head. It was really something."

John ran up and slammed into Daniel's leg. Daniel stood still, solid as a tree.

Grace wondered where he'd gotten such good balance. Practice no doubt.

"Pa, I've decided Ma's not gonna die having that there baby." John jabbed his thumb at Grace.

"John, it's rude to point." Grace noticed Parrish trying to get to his hands and knees. She walked over and whacked him once with her branch, still to hand. He fell back face-first in the mud.

"Speaking of rude, it might be rude to beat that man with a stick, Grace."

John tugged on Daniel's leg until Grace was relieved her husband had equipped himself with a good, tight belt.

"What is it, John?" Daniel asked, still looking at Parrish and Grace and the stick.

"I don't know about our other ma, but I think this one's pretty tough. I reckon she can kick out babies galore and not let it bother her none."

Daniel asked hopefully, "You think?"

Grace asked nervously, "Galore?"

"You gonna tell me who that man is, Grace, honey?"

Grace stuck her nose straight up in the air. "Are you going to quit scaring us all to death with your talk about babies killing their mother?"

Daniel tilted his head as though he was thinking. "I'll try and buck up."

"That's my father." Grace jabbed her thumb at Parrish. She saw herself point and tucked her thumb into her fist and tried to look innocent.

All six of her menfolk turned to look at the man Grace had just walloped.

"Uh . . . you weren't close, I'm guessing," Daniel pushed his hat back and scratched his head.

"I ran away from home, and on my way out of town, I told the police he was a thief and turned over his account books that proved it."

"He tried to strangle me, Pa," Mark said, obviously thrilled to have had a brush with death.

"He what?" Daniel's brow furrowed in anger.

"And I played possum while he drugged Ma away. Then I went for help."

"It's *dragged,* Mark," Grace corrected. Just because they'd had a life-and-death struggle was no reason to let their grammar slip.

Daniel pointed at Parrish. "He drugged you?"

She flinched when Daniel pointed but held her tongue.

"Mark showed us where he hightailed it with Ma. He was kidnapping her, toting her off the 6R right over the canyon wall," Abe added.

"And we've gotten plumb used to having her for a ma and we don't wanta break in a new one," Ike added.

"They are mighty hard to train," Mark said with a sigh. "We've got this'n just how we like her."

"We don't just like her, Mark," — Luke

whacked Mark in the shoulder — "we love her."

"You love me, Luke?" This was the first time Luke had said such a thing.

Mark shoved Luke back. Luke stumbled into Abe.

"That man hit you, Mark?" Daniel stepped toward his son.

"Get off'a me, sissy-baby." Abe knocked Luke backward, where he stepped on Mark's toe, who jumped sideways with flailing arms and swatted John right in the face. John slugged him, but because his eyes were closed from the blow he'd just taken, he missed Mark and punched Ike.

Ike grabbed John around the chest and lifted him in the air.

"Will you boys cut it out?"

They all froze and turned to Grace. John's feet dangled in the air. Mark, holding his foot, howling with pain, was cut off in mid-scream.

She smiled. "Thank you. Please don't make me shout again."

They nodded fearfully.

"Yes, that man hit Mark." Grace studied her temporarily subdued children. She turned to Daniel. "He didn't drug me." She glanced at Mark. "That's poor grammar, son. He *dragged* me."

"He dragged you?" Daniel's voice rose as if his patience was falling by the wayside.

"He came here looking for me. He found me in Mosqueros last —" Grace was blank for a moment. It seemed as though she'd lived here always with these men she loved and with whom she had a perfect, tranquil life — except for the screaming and punching.

"January," Daniel supplied immediately. "The twelfth. It was a Friday. We got home at about six in the evening."

Grace glared at him. Apparently he remembered to the minute.

"What?"

She continued. "He's been trailing me for the last two years. He must have gotten out of jail in Chicago somehow. And he isn't a man to let a young girl do him harm without getting revenge."

Daniel looked at Parrish, moving slightly, groaning occasionally, lying on his belly. "He did a bad job of getting revenge this time."

"After he tookened Ma," — Mark jumped into the space between Daniel and Grace — "I went and found the guys. And we set up a trap for him. We was gonna corner him and I swing-ed down outta that tree." Mark pointed up but was too busy telling the story to make it clear.

Abe stepped between Mark and Daniel, adding to the number of people between Grace and her confused and sweet and stubborn-as-an-ox husband. It would always be like this.

"Ma saved herself." Abe jumped up, swinging an imaginary club in the air.

He clonked Mark on the head with his arm. Grace caught Mark by the shoulder before he could retaliate.

Ike jumped in between Abe and Daniel. "We had to hurry or she'd've polished off clobbering him before we got here."

Daniel looked over the long line of children at Grace. His eyes suddenly narrowed and focused on her. He rounded the boys and had her by the shoulders. "What happened to your face?"

Grace lifted her hand and realized her right cheek was swollen. "Mark's bleeding. He had it way worse than me."

She saw the effort it took Daniel to tear his eyes away from her and glance at Mark. It was purely encouraging.

He looked down at Mark, who had done his best to keep himself coated in blood.

Daniel let go of Grace and crouched down in front of Mark. "Are you all right?"

Mark shrugged and stared at the ground

and kicked at a clod of dirt. "Aw, shucks, Pa. It ain't nothing."

"It *isn't* nothing, Mark," Grace corrected by reflex, tugging on her wrecked dress to keep herself decently covered. "I mean, it isn't *anything.*" Grace shook her head. "It is *too* something."

"Are you folks doing okay here?"

All of them whirled around at the new voice.

THIRTY

Clay McClellen walked down the last stretch of the steep slope. Three men were right behind him, one of them the sheriff. All of them were armed and determined and looking right at Parrish.

Grace could feel Clay taking in Mark's bleeding face, her bruised face and shredded dress, and Parrish's inert form.

Parrish groaned loudly and pushed himself to his hands and knees, wobbling all the while.

"You folks have some trouble with this feller, too?" Clay jabbed his index finger at Parrish.

Grace had to clench her jaw to keep from telling him it wasn't polite to point.

Daniel stepped forward, showing he was head of the family.

Grace harrumphed. "About time you took charge, Daniel." She realized that Daniel had indeed seemed to become more in charge as she'd come to know how the Reeves men worked.

Daniel heard her and glanced back. Then he turned to Clay.

Parrish stumbled to his feet.

"Hang on to him this time, will ya, Luth?" Clay asked.

A man Grace remembered from church, wearing fur and leather and a full beard, stepped over and grabbed Parrish by the shoulder. Another man, looking much the same, stood on the other side of the unsteady prisoner. He went by the name Buff, and he resembled a buffalo somewhat.

Daniel turned back to Clay. "This varmint knocked Mark out and tried to kidnap my wife. I want him arrested."

"I'm not going to be arrested." Parrish fumbled in his pocket.

Grace gasped.

"Watch him, Luth," Clay said. "He might have a gun."

Luther grabbed Parrish's hand and pulled it up. It contained a piece of paper.

"I'm hunting her." Parrish burned her with his eyes, but Grace noticed he didn't point. At that moment she discarded a lot of what she considered proper manners. She had no desire to live by rules that appealed to the likes of Parrish.

Luther took the paper out of Parrish's hand and unfolded it. He studied it for a moment then looked up at Grace. He turned the paper so everyone could see it. "You know anything about this, Miss Calhoun?"

A wanted poster. With her picture on it. Her picture, saying she was wanted for stealing money in Chicago. The silence was deafening. Grace felt the group study her likeness on that poster. She'd never seen it before. She looked up at the sheriff. His eyes, cool and detached, seemed to measure her for a jail cell.

She looked over at Clay McClellen. His expression didn't show much at the best of times. She had only to imagine what he was thinking.

Clay's other friends were just as remote. She looked at Parrish, greedy for her to be turned over to him. It had happened in Chicago the first time she'd tried to run away.

Parrish had found her, and she'd fought him. She'd been too small, eleven years old, to fight very hard. He'd been lashing her soundly with his belt on a cold, snowy street, when a policeman had come by. She'd run to him for protection.

Parrish had told the policeman he was her

father and she was getting the beating she deserved.

The policeman had told her, straight into her bruised and bleeding face, to go home quietly and behave herself from now on.

Grace had gone home and taken her beating. There had been many more through the years.

She waited now for the same thing to happen. When she'd married Daniel, she'd hoped a husband's rights overrode a father's. But she hadn't known about being wanted by the law. Parrish expected his word to be taken over hers. Finally, nearly choking with fear, she looked to the one person here whom she expected to support her, even though the law would most likely side with Parrish.

Daniel.

His expression was as cold as ice. His eyes cut through her like a frozen blade. He was going to side against her. Her lips trembled. She closed her eyes against the tears and the terror of what lay ahead when she was again in Parrish's power.

The sound of paper crumpling brought her head up. Sheriff Everett had grabbed the paper, wadded the wanted poster into a ball, and tossed it down the hillside. "You no-account varmint, what kind of skunk tries to shake the blame for his own wrong-doing by accusing a sweet little woman like Grace Calhoun of being a thief?"

"Grace Reeves," Daniel reminded the sheriff.

"Grace could no more rob someone than she could fly." Clay McClellen marched straight up to Parrish. "What kind of fools do you take us for? She taught our children. She lived among us for months. We know her, and we know you."

Clay grabbed Parrish by his shirtfront in a way that made Grace wonder for the first time why they were here. Following Parrish, of course. It was no coincidence that they'd all come at once.

"You're just the kind of man who'd hide behind a woman's skirts." Clay gave Parrish a good shake then shoved him backward. Only Luther and Buff held him up.

"Low-down coyote." Buff shook his head. He said with contempt, "It's 'bout what I'd'a expected from such as you, Parrish. You hit little girls."

"He hit little girls?" Grace gasped. "When did he do that?" Grace balled up her fist and took a step toward Parrish. "He used to make up excuses to hit me and my sisters."

Daniel grabbed her by the arm and held her back.

"You got sisters, Ma?" Mark asked. "Does that mean we got us some aunts and uncles somewheres?"

Daniel pulled Grace up against him so he braced her from behind. Just as he pulled her close, her dressed sagged off one shoulder again.

"Grace, what happened to your back?" Daniel's voice was barely audible, as if he were speaking around a huge lump in his throat.

Grace shoved at her dress and tried to turn away from him, but if she did, all the other men here would see the marks, not to mention entirely too much of her skin.

She tried to whisper, but she knew every man there heard every word. "Parrish had a taste for working his children over with a belt. There are marks on me that will never heal, Daniel."

He pulled her against him, as if he could protect her back from ever being injured again. With both arms around her waist, he said, "My wife is the most honest, upright woman I've ever known. Hanging is too good for anyone who says such things against the mother of my six children. And anyone who puts marks like this on his child needs to be locked away for good."

Grace's heart swelled with love as she

leaned back against Daniel's strength. Looking over her shoulder, she saw Daniel's eyes burning with the cold fury she'd seen before. But now she knew it was all aimed at Parrish.

She folded her arms so she could hold his hands tight against her and realized she'd only begun to know the faithfulness of God. He'd brought her to this time and place for His purpose, and she'd do her best to be worthy.

"You stole a horse before you left town, Parrish," Sheriff Everett said.

"Can our aunts and uncles come to visit, Ma?" Abe asked.

"Only aunts, Abe," Grace said. "And I don't know. I've kind of lost touch with them." She wondered about Hannah and the little girls. Maybe Hannah could come. She'd write the second she could get a letter to town.

Clay McClellen scratched the side of his head. "Six children?"

"And horse thievin' is a hangin' offense in the West, Parrish." Luther looked at the group of children.

Grace could see Parrish's lips moving as he counted.

"Yeah," the sheriff said, "but the horse bucked him off and it was heading toward home when we passed it. Don't rightly know if we can hang him on that."

"He needs hanging. I say we go ahead and call him a horse thief," Luther said.

"Anyway, it don't matter about our horse — he's done a sight more 'n horse thievin'." Sheriff Everett pulled some papers out of the pocket of his white shirt. He unfolded them, and Grace saw more wanted posters. "I've got posters here hunting for Parrish all over the West. You stole and cheated your way here, then lied your way into a job."

"Why didn't you notice them when he was working at the school?" Buff grumbled.

The sheriff looked sheepish. "It don't look that much like him. And whoever thinks the schoolmaster is a swindler?"

"You hurt our children." Clay's voice was as cold as the grave. "You threatened Miss Calhoun."

"Mrs. Reeves," Daniel said.

"Now you're going back to Mosqueros to face Texas justice," Clay said with satisfaction.

"That's if we can keep Sophie away from him until it's time for a hanging," Luther pointed out.

"She'll mind me." Clay said it with utmost confidence, but Grace thought his eyes wavered a bit.

Luther caught Parrish by the left arm. "We've got a long hike outta this canyon."

Buff caught him by the right. " 'N a long, hard ride home."

"Parrish!" Grace shouted. Buff and Luther paused and turned so her father faced her. "You've spent your life hurting children. You, the father to so many, don't know a thing about fatherhood. God is the perfect Father, Mr. Parrish. I commend you into His hands and hope you'll give Him a chance to make the rest of your life a better one."

Parrish glared at her as if she'd slapped him.

The two men dragged Parrish, limping and bleeding, up the hill.

"I'll be over as soon as the pass is clear with Sophie and the girls for a visit," Clay said. "It oughta be passable in another month or two." Clay reached out his hand and shook Daniel's firmly. "And congratulations about the baby."

"Thanks kindly, Clay." Daniel smiled.

A burn climbed up Grace's cheeks at such a personal thing being discussed in front of these men. The embarrassment, combined with the fear, Parrish's hard hand, and Daniel's kind words, caused tears to fill her eyes.

Clay took one look at her watery eyes and ran.

The sheriff trudged after the others.

Grace wiped her eyes and turned to her family.

"He was your pa?" Ike asked.

Grace nodded.

"He was a mighty poor one," John said. He came up and threw his arms around Grace's legs, nearly knocking her over.

Daniel held on and kept her on her feet. "Amen to that."

Luke came up and threw himself against Grace's and Daniel's legs. He hit a little too hard, and they staggered sideways down the hill.

"Watch out, stupid." John turned and tried to club Luke with the back of his closed fist. Luke ducked and John hit Ike instead.

"Hey, you little runt." Ike charged John.

Daniel tightened his grip on Grace and, with a fast swoop, spun her out of the way of the collision.

Grace's stomach was left behind. She breathed quickly to control her nausea and stave off humiliation.

Ike slammed into John and Luke. They fell, sliding downhill. Shouting and threatening each other, they slid into Abe, who went down amid the flailing arms and kicking feet.

Mark started laughing uproariously. He bent over and grabbed a clod of muddy earth and heaved it onto Abe's head. Abe shouted and jumped to his feet. Mark ran screaming toward the cabin.

"Daniel," — Grace poked him in the stomach to get him to stop laughing — "make them stop. Someone's going to get hurt."

The shrieks were deafening.

"Oh, let 'em play, Gracie. It keeps 'em quiet."

All five boys whooped like wild Indians. A scream that sounded like real pain made Grace jump. Daniel held on and firmly turned her around to face him.

She saw the love in his eyes and forgot all about the madhouse in the woods behind her. "I'm not going to die, Daniel. I'm a strong woman. Having babies is going to agree with me. I know it."

Daniel's eyes closed; then, after a moment, he opened them. "God has been faithful to us, to bring us together."

Grace realized he'd been praying when his eyes were closed. "It's a pure miracle is what it is. To think Parrish made me hide in your wagon, and it all led to this."

Daniel pulled her close. "I don't think of it as a miracle, I don't reckon. I think of it as how everything was meant to be. God worked all the twists and turns. He was watching out for us, caring for us, without us even knowing."

"He was faithful," Grace said thoughtfully. "And remembering God's faithfulness was what gave me the courage to fight Parrish. I knew that if God was with me, Parrish couldn't stand against me."

"And God *is* with you, Grace. He wanted you to come here and make our family whole again. He's not going to take you from me now."

Grace laid her hand on Daniel's chest. "And even if He does —"

Daniel's arms tightened on her waist. "Don't say that, Gracie. I love you. It would kill me to lose you."

Grace said firmly, "Even if He does, it will be His will, His time. He will still be faithful to us and we will be faithful to Him in return, whatever this life holds."

Daniel shook off the sadness of her words and nodded. He lowered his head. Grace closed her eyes and stood on her tiptoes, reaching for him.

A crash from behind them sounded as though the boys had brought a tree down on their heads.

"We'd better go see," Grace said.

"I can tell by the screaming it's nothing serious." Daniel pulled her back and kissed her.

The boys kept screaming, but now Grace was happy for it because it kept them busy while she kissed her husband fervently.

He was right.

The screaming did keep them "quiet."

ABOUT THE AUTHOR

Mary Connealy is the author of the Lassoed in Texas series including *Petticoat Ranch* and the soon-to-be-released *Gingham Mountain*. She also has coming soon: *Of Mice . . . and Murder,* book #1 of a three-book series with Heartsong Presents Mysteries, and *Buffalo Gal,* book #1 of a three-book series for Heartsong Presents. Her novel "Golden Days" is part of the *Alaska Brides* anthology. You can find out more about Mary's upcoming books at www.maryconnealy.com.

She lives on a Nebraska farm with her husband, Ivan, and has four grown daughters: Joslyn (and her husband Matt), Wendy, Shelly (and her husband Aaron), and Katy.